Aegyir Rises

Guardians of The Realm: Book 1

All characters in this book are fictitious. Any resemblance to actual persons, living or dead, is purely coincidental.

ISBN: 978-1-9162306-2-0

Aegyir Rises

Guardians of The Realm: Book 1

Amanda Fleet

The Guardians of The Realm Series

Aegyir Rises
Aeron Returns
War
Invasion
Chaos

To Sly and Nero, who accompanied me for some of this journey, but who weren't able to see its completion. And to Max, who's still beside me.

Prologue

My name was Reagan Bennett.
I had a fabulous life.
I lost everything. *Everything*.
Three weeks. That's all it took.
This is my story.

1

Finn grimaced from the effort of standing firm while my fists slammed into the pads in a satisfying one-two, one-two. "Oocha! Okay. What's happened?"

"I saw Helen today." I threw another combo.

Finn's cornflower blue eyes settled on me, his gaze wary. "Uh huh? And?"

I pummelled the pads he held with punch after punch until my arms sagged like wet string.

"Stephen's getting released." Helen's stepson and the man I'd put in prison.

"Feck. Already?"

His eyes widened but the news wasn't news to me. I'd been counting the days of Stephen's incarceration since he was found guilty of grievous bodily harm. On me. He'd also caused the death of my best friend, Sarah, though he'd never been tried for that. I knew as well as Stephen did when his sentence would end.

My arms exhausted, I indicated to Finn I was moving on to roundhouse kicks and he shifted the pads.

"When did you see her?" His brow creased and the remnants of his Irish accent emerged. He was closer to Dublin than Cumbria right now.

"This afternoon. She came over."

Finn sucked his teeth. He knew how rare a visit from my adopted mother was. We hadn't parted on good terms.

Actually, we'd barely even started on good terms.

"John with her?"

"No." I wiped a sweat-slick lock of black hair out of my eyes.

My next kick made Finn stagger and he shifted his balance. John was Stephen's dad, Helen's second husband; no relative of mine. Not even adopted. Thank God.

"Okay, you call it." I stepped back and let my arms drop to my sides.

Finn called and I followed until he knew I was running on vapours.

"Okay. Home," he said. "Did you make anything or are we picking up takeaway?"

"I cooked."

"Excellent!" He dropped a kiss on the top of my head and hugged my sweaty body. "Meet you in the cafe?"

"Sure."

We were at the gym where we both worked – a modern building with fantastic facilities. Downstairs was split into a cafe open to everyone and the weights rooms which were for members only. Finn was a personal trainer there; I worked part-time on reception. Some of the advantages of working-out here were the free hot water and excellent showers.

I found Finn waiting in the cafe on the ground floor, fiddling with his phone, blond spiky hair darkened by his shower, his work uniform of sweatshirt and jogging pants replaced by jeans, t-shirt and biker jacket. Both motorbike-helmets sat on the table.

"Take it steady going home? My blood sugar's in my boots." I picked up my helmet. Blood red. As opposed to Finn's more conventional jet black.

"I can tell. You're that fetching shade of pale olive you go when you need food." He held his arm out and I tucked underneath it as we crossed the brightly lit cafe towards the plate glass doors. "Come on. Home."

Finn's pride and joy was parked at the back of the gym. He'd saved up for years to get it. It wasn't the most powerful bike available by a long chalk, but it could shift if you wanted it to, and Finn had hankered after a motorbike since I'd met him. He'd bought it in barely working condition but stripped it down and rebuilt it one summer, with help from Paul, my adopted dad.

My stomach clenched with bittersweet memories. That was the year Sarah had died. That Stephen had assaulted me. I jammed my helmet on and slid on to the bike, tucking my arms around Finn's middle, trying to blank the memories. Finn flipped the stand up and revved the engine, and I thought about our tiny cottage. Would the door withstand a good kicking any better than I had?

Back at the cottage, Finn tidied away my helmet and jacket while I headed for the kitchen.

"Shall we get a dog?" he said, joining me.

He took a carton of milk out of the fridge and drank straight from it, peering at me over the top as I heated up dinner. Distraction techniques so I wouldn't think about Stephen?

"Don't give me that look," he said. "I'm gonna finish it and anyway, you and I share more than spit on a regular basis."

County Dublin was still in the ascendancy. His 'I' was shifting even further towards 'oi' and his 'th' beginning to lose the h and gain a d. He finished the milk and then crumpled the carton and tossed it in the recycling crate next to the bin. "So, shall we get a dog?"

I stirred dinner, scraping the bottom of the pan to stop the sauce from catching. "What kind of dog?"

"I dunno. A dog kind of dog!"

Where was this coming from?

I sprinkled some salt into the pot. "A puppy? A rescue dog?"

He leaned his hips against the worktop, his posture softening. "A rescue dog."

Yeah, Finn didn't do cute. Which was just as well since I had a broken nose, a chipped tooth and a couple of bent ribs. He was also big on rescuing. Usually people, but he wouldn't be able to leave a dog shelter without needing to give a new start to any mutt that seemed unlikely to be re-homed. He'd be disappointed not to be allowed to rescue them all.

"So?" he said.

"Let me think about it. We're meant to be saving so we can get a bigger place. With heating."

Finn winked, then picked up two bottles of beer and waved one at me. I nodded, and he flipped the cap off and handed it over.

"You still okay to do the self-defence class with me on Thursday?" He clinked his bottle against mine.

"Yeah. Perfect timing to brush up on how to kick the living shit out of someone."

"That's not really what we teach." A grin poked a crease into his cheek. "But yeah, it would be good to keep your skills up."

The self-defence classes were something Finn had persuaded his boss, Billy, to run for free once a month. I helped, trying to show the women who came to the classes that it didn't matter if you were smaller and lighter than your attacker, you could still defend yourself. I'd do a better job of that if I wasn't six feet tall of course.

Finn pulled me against him. "You okay about Stephen?"

"Mm. I'm hoping someone knifes the fucker before he's out."

An image of Sarah's shattered body at the bottom of the escarpment filled my brain. Knifing would be too quick for him.

"Okay. Settle, petal."

He kissed the nape of my neck, snapping me out of my daydreams of a slow death for the man who'd beaten the shit out of me. Just once. But one time too many.

"Oh! I finished those calligraphy pieces today," I said. "They're in my portfolio."

"Yeah? Can I see?"

"Are your hands clean? Because if you get grubby paw-prints on them, I will charge you."

Not that that would help the finances. I was hoping to make cards from prints of them to sell online, so we could replace the toaster before it electrocuted us.

He moved back and held clean-looking hands out for me to inspect. I still didn't trust him with my best work of the week. I handed him the spoon, retrieved the folio and opened it on the battered melamine-topped table, to reveal heart-shapes filled with love poems written in intricate calligraphy.

I'd qualified from college in graphic design, but jobs in the area were thin on the ground. I guess Helen had been right about *something*. Paul had believed in me enough to support me through college. Well, him and Finn. Paul had moved down south not long after he and Helen divorced and perhaps I should have gone to live with him when he offered. Things could have been so different. But then I wouldn't be with Finn, so I was better off where I was. Broken bones and all.

Finn leaned over to see the portfolio but kept his body clear. "They're amazing. As always."

"Thank you. They're for the toaster-fund."

The "getting a place with central heating fund" was yet

to gain more than a few pounds.

I tidied them back into the portfolio and returned it to the lounge. Finn was dishing up when I re-joined him.

I squeezed into the chair at the back of the small square table that lurked in the corner of the kitchen. Since Finn and I clocked in at six foot four, and six foot, it took a special kind of choreography for us to work round each other in the tiny space, but it was all we could afford. I'd insisted on us having a table in here because I hated eating in the lounge from a plate on my lap, but if we both sat at the table, our knees bashed each other's.

Finn put a plate in front of me and slid into the seat opposite. He ate a forkful of dinner, nodded enthusiastically, and added about quarter of a bottle of hot chilli sauce to it. I rolled my eyes.

"What?" he said, his mouth full. "It's great." He chewed and frowned. "You really okay about Stephen?" Old memories conjured shadows in his eyes.

"Do I have a choice? He's served his sentence."

He stabbed his fork into a piece of chicken. "He comes near you and I can't promise I'll keep my cool."

"If he comes near me again, I'll beat the fucker up myself."

He flinched. "Okay. You're definitely kick-boxing with me tomorrow. Burn off some of that fire." He glanced across to the fridge where a series of magnetic letters held up his work schedule. "When am I on late? Will you come to the gym those nights?"

"I'll be fine. He wouldn't be stupid enough to come here again."

Finn's breath hissed out of his nose and he drank a long gulp of beer. "I'm gonna call John and tell him that if his son comes within half a mile of this place, I'll kill him."

I rested my hand over his. "You're going to do no such

thing, because John will record you and then if you and Stephen *do* come to blows, he'll use it to crucify you. He hasn't forgotten how you hit your dad."

"Yeah, well. He hit Mum."

I let it drop. He'd watched his dad beat his mum when he was a kid, then protected her when he was bigger. At seventeen and almost the size he was now, he'd hit back. He'd assumed his mum would leave his dad after that, but she'd stayed. Finn's father had thrown him out and Finn hadn't set foot across the threshold of their house in seven years. His father claimed he didn't have any children.

"You called her today?" I said.

Finn nodded. "She's fine. Well, she says she's fine. You able to go over this week?"

"I can pop in on Tuesday. Anyway, I cooked, so you're doing the dishes." I stacked the empty plates, hoping to shift him away from fretting over his mum.

I wandered through to the lounge and curled in the corner of the threadbare sofa, unsettled. Our cottage might not be much, but in the years since the attack, it had become my sanctuary – the place where I could shut out the world and be me. The idea that Stephen would be out in a matter of days... I didn't for a moment believe he was a reformed character.

I ground the heels of my hands into my eyes.

Don't let him come here. Please *don't let him come here again.*

Finn sauntered through, switching the telly on as he sat down.

"Mind if I watch the footie?" He cocked a brow at me.

"What would you do if I said yes?"

He caught my eye, smiling, but said nothing. I needed distraction, and footie wasn't going to do it. Finn was though. I slid my leg over Finn's so that I sat on his lap facing him and undid a button on my top.

“I have an offer for you.” I popped another button.

“Uh huh?” He scanned down my cleavage and back up. The noise levels rose in the match, and his attention flicked to the telly before locking back on me.

“Mm. And you look at the match again while I’m telling you and the offer’s off.”

“Okay. Sorry.”

He knew damn fine what the offer was. Behind me, a roar indicated a scored goal, and I could see him itching to look.

“The offer is…” I trailed a finger over his chest. “Unlimited sex tonight… or… you get to watch the footie and have no sex for a month.”

His hands settled around my backside. “No chance of watching the footie and then having slightly more limited sex tonight?”

“Nope. The deal is the one I’ve just outlined. And is only valid for ten seconds.”

He held my gaze, looking as if he was weighing up the options, but he did this every time. On cue, after about nine seconds had passed, he clicked the telly off. “You did say *unlimited*, didn’t you?”

2

I needed to draw. Nightmares had wrecked half of my night and Finn wasn't around to distract me this morning. I'd see him later once he'd finished work and I could punch seven bells out something. Until then, it was me and my thoughts. Not a great combo when I was this wound up.

I flipped through one of my sketchbooks. Most of them had drawing upon drawing of Finn in various states of undress – after all, he was a mighty fine specimen, and I'd always loved drawing the human form more than anything else. A couple of sketchbooks had doodles and designs for logos or other sketches that might get me my hoped-for job in graphic design, but the book I had in my hands was my 'Realm' sketchbook.

My dreams had been populated by the same place for as long as I could remember, but it wasn't anywhere real. It could almost be a film-set for something set in medieval times. Without exception, everyone wore leather and wool – leather trousers, leather boots, wool shirts and leather jackets, but there was never anything modern in the dreams. No phones, no TVs, no plastic... Oh, and everyone carried a sword and had a dagger tucked into their belt as if at any moment they would be called to battle. I didn't know what the name of the place was – in my dreams it was only ever referred to as the Realm.

I closed my eyes and let my brain drift. The dreams

were so detailed and realistic, at times they felt closer to memories. In the latest one, I'd been walking through a courtyard surrounded by gorgeous flowerbeds – a kaleidoscope of flowers in full bloom billowing out from behind neatly clipped low hedges. It had been so real, I could smell the heady perfume that suffused the air. Even now I could imagine the scent of the roses.

I sketched the corner of the courtyard where pinkish-grey flagstones matched stone walls with fruit trees trained neatly over their surface. In my last dream, it had been late summer there and the boughs of the trees sagged with ripe apples and pears.

I often dreamed of this courtyard. It teemed with people in tight groups, always seeming to be gossiping and scheming, their heads close, their eyes darting as they whispered behind hands to one another. As soon as anyone passed, they'd be tight smiles and courteous bows, then they'd be straight back to the whispers and the side-eyes. More often than not, a tall, dark and *very* handsome man walked with me, my hand tucked into the crook of his arm. Faran. My husband. Who *adored* me. We seemed to be pretty important there. Wherever we went, people bowed respectfully. I was punching *well* above my weight with him. I would never swap my life with Finn for anyone though, drop-dead gorgeous or not. And anyway, Finn wasn't exactly a gargoyle.

It hadn't needed a child-psychologist to explain why I dreamed of a place where I was loved after I'd been left on a hospital doorstep at a day old, then handed from pillar to post umpteen times before Helen and Paul had finally adopted me. I wasn't a lovable child. So Helen had told me in our many fights.

I finished my drawing of the courtyard and turned to a fresh page to draw Faran. Like me, he had leaf-green eyes and thick, dark hair, bordering on black. Unlike me, he had high, sharp cheekbones and full lips with a sharp Cupid's bow to them. Interestingly, in my dreams my hair was always long rather the short crop I'd had forever, and I had no tattoos or piercings. Did some corner of my brain crave convention, after all? Or did I just have less to rebel against there?

Drawing my mythical Realm soothed me almost as much as drawing Finn did. The scritch-scratch of my pencil on the paper, the blending of colours, the focus… my brain couldn't be anywhere else. At times like that, it was good to be inside my own head and to escape from Real Life.

I finished my picture of Faran and a smile tickled my lips. He *was* a handsome bugger. I flipped the cover shut and tidied everything away, a peaceful feeling settling on my shoulders. I grabbed a quick bite of lunch, then set off to meet Finn at work.

Our cottage lay on the very outskirts of the town – once you were past our lane, you hit the countryside. We were the last of three old farm labourer houses, clustered together on a side-road. At the end of the side road, next to our place, fields led up to an escarpment. The gym lay on the other side of town, about twenty minutes away.

Grey clouds covered the sky and I shrugged my leather jacket closer around me and jammed my hands in the pockets to keep warm. A residential area lay between our cottage and the centre of town and I peered into the gardens as I walked, smiling at the near-identical squares of neatly mown lawns surrounded by a strip of border. A dampness coated the air and I smelled leaf-mould and mushrooms as I passed the one garden that had been converted into a vegetable plot. Maybe one day, Finn and I would have a place like this.

As I turned on to the main shopping area, my attention

was pulled away from trying to imagine life as a suburban housewife with 2.2 children. A young lad, maybe seventeen or eighteen, was hassling a woman in her forties. Nothing serious – just catcalling and suggestive hand gestures – but it was enough to flip a switch in me.

"Hey! Fuck off!" I sprinted towards them, ready to weigh in.

It wasn't necessary. The lad took one look at me charging towards him and legged it, ducking and weaving past the few shoppers on the street, before shooting across the road, making a car brake sharply and honk loudly. I turned to the woman, who rapidly took five steps away from me.

"You okay?" I said, catching my breath and reaching out to touch her shoulder in a gesture of comfort and solidarity.

She clamped her bag against her chest, eyes wide. "Leave me alone!"

"I'm not—" I held my hands up, palms out. "I was just checking you're okay."

"Go away! Leave me alone! I'm calling the police!" She yanked her phone out of her coat pocket, her knuckles white, shielding her handbag from me.

Did she think I was about to *rob* her?

I backed away, hands still raised. "Forget it. Just forget it!"

I sucked a deep breath in, injustice burning my core. I'd been trying to *help* her. The woman caught a sob in her throat and hurried away from me towards an older woman who'd loomed into view. Margaret Thatcher handbag; sensible flat shoes under a tweed skirt. Yeah, *she* wasn't going to ring any alarm bells. She slid her arm around the younger woman's shoulders.

"You okay, pet?" she said, casting me a filthy look over her shoulder and leading the younger woman away from me.

I didn't hear the reply, but I understood the body language alright. I closed my eyes, biting my lip, and turned towards the road leading to the gym. My scowl hadn't lifted by the time I met Finn in the staff-room.

"What's up?" he said, frowning as he got up from the comfy seats.

I told him. When I finished, he scruffed my hair up affectionately. "You did the right thing."

"Except she was more scared of *me* than the yob who was giving her grief! Why is it that whenever I try to help someone, it all goes tits up?"

Finn's gaze travelled over me, pausing on the studs in my ears and nose before he quirked a brow up.

"Yeah, okay. Maybe the sight of me running full pelt towards her wasn't *entirely* reassuring," I said. I *was* in my full war-paint and clad in black leather.

"You think you might possibly be on a hair-trigger this week? I mean, you didn't need to *run* at them."

I glowered at him, making him laugh.

"Come on then. Let's go work this out of your system. Your heart's in the right place." He winked at me. "Though you might need to finesse the execution a bit."

Story of my life.

3

An hour later and I'd blocked Finn's mock attacks and pretend-poked his eyes out for the umpteenth time. Always one to believe women should be able to defend themselves, he'd been teaching me self-defence since we first met, when I was fourteen and he was fifteen. The bullies at school got a rude awakening that year.

A manoeuvre later, I caught him off guard, smacking him in the midriff and making him cough and clutch himself.

"Oof! Enough. I get to box now. Come and hold the bag." He swiped his palm across his middle, smiling at me.

"Sorry."

I held the bag steady for him, wondering who he was imagining punching the lights out of. He settled into a steady rhythm, so focused that I wasn't sure he was still on earth. Slowly, he drifted back to the here and now, finishing his workout with a volley of punches before stepping back, breathing hard. I hoped to God he didn't end up hitting Stephen like this. I couldn't bear to lose Finn, and John would make sure he'd be put away for a *long* time if Finn even sneezed too violently in Stephen's vicinity.

I arched a brow at him and he gave me a sheepish grin, slick with sweat.

"I promise, I'll keep my cool if I see him," he said, untaping his hands.

I nodded curtly. I wasn't sure I would.

***

"Pub on The Hill for lunch?" suggested Finn when he joined me in the gym cafe, showered and changed.

"Perfect."

I jammed my fingers into the back pocket of his jeans and he looped his arm over my shoulders, kissing the top of my head. Outside, I squeezed in behind him on the bike and wrapped my arms around his waist. He kicked the stand up and we roared off, leaving dust swirling in our wake as we headed out of town and up to the pub.

The Pub on The Hill was an old favourite of mine and Finn's. It did good food and real ales and there was usually a table near a fire to be had at this time of the year if you timed it right. We found seats next to a wood-burning stove, tucked the helmets under the table and shed our jackets in the warmth. I'd seen Finn scan the pumps with interest as we came in.

"You want me to drive back?" I said, half hoping he didn't. "They've got two guest ales on I think."

Finn wouldn't even drink the froth off a pint if he was driving. "Mind?"

I groaned internally but shook my head.

The cosiness of the pub, the good food and being able to have a laugh with the man I loved, allowed the knots of tension to melt away.

"You know me too well," I said as we finished the main course and ordered more drinks. He cocked an eyebrow at me. "Coming here. Thank you. It's what I needed."

"I only came for the beer," he said, winking. "Knew you'd drive back."

I leaned back in my seat, breathing in the scent of wood smoke. "Why do you want to get a dog? Has your mum put you up to it? Practice for potential grandkids?"

He laughed loudly. "Much as she would *love* us to be providing her with grandkids, no, she didn't suggest we get a dog."

Finn's mum wasn't the only one who would love us to have kids; Finn did too. He'd make a fantastic father. I'd make a terrible mother.

He picked his glass up. "Anyway, she'd want me to be a good Catholic boy and marry you before we had kids."

"She doesn't seem to mind you being a terrible Catholic boy and living in sin for years."

Finn's eyes met mine over the top of his beer. "Are you wanting me to make an honest woman of you?"

"No. Relax."

He wasn't stressed.

His attention wound out to the bar and he stared for a few minutes, only looking back when the waitress brought dessert menus.

"Share one? Or are you up to a whole one to yourself?" Finn asked, scrutinising the card.

"I'll just have a bit of yours if you're having one."

He nodded and his gaze drifted back over my shoulder.

"Is she *very* pretty?" I asked, my voice full of hard edges.

He turned back to me, puzzled. "Who?"

"Whoever it is that you can't take your eyes off. At the bar."

He winced. "No one."

"You are such a shit liar."

I swivelled in my seat to scan the bar. John and Helen stood nursing drinks, Helen's too-tight jeans squashing her curves into a muffin-top, John's rigid posture under his fleece top telling me he knew we were there. I slewed back round before they could make eye contact.

"Sorry. I didn't know whether to tell you or not." Finn

bunched his lips in apology.

"If they come over, we're leaving."

"No, we're not. I haven't finished my pint. And we were gonna share a pudding."

On cue, the waitress returned, brows raised, pencil poised.

"Er, yeah. Can we get a Death by Chocolate and two spoons please?"

Finn handed the menus back and slid his hand into mine. "Helen's on her way over." His grip on my hand tightened, his face telling me to stay put.

"Reagan. Finn," she said, standing next to the table.

Her eyes picked over the piercing in my nose and the line of studs in my ear. I regretted not putting my war-paint on after training. Her focus shifted to Finn and her lip curled slightly.

"Did you want something? Other than to spoil our day?" The tension ground into my shoulders.

Helen took a couple of deep breaths, her scraped-back fake-auburn hair pulling her face tight. "Reagan, I thought you should know that Stephen will be out on Thursday. He'll come and stay with me and John."

"Thursday?" I said. "You're *kidding* me!" The anniversary of Sarah taking her own life. "Christ, Sarah's parents will be gutted."

She swallowed, twisting her wedding ring round. "Yes. Well. I didn't make the decision."

"You made the decision to hire that scumbag lawyer to defend Stephen. If he'd had even a *shred* of humanity, he wouldn't have questioned her like that. Sarah had been through more than enough, yet you sat back and watched as he asked her questions about her sex life and made out she was a slut. How would *you* have felt, having to answer questions like that in front of a roomful of strangers?"

"Stephen was entitled to a defence," she said, thin-lipped, her make-up settling into the lines around her mouth.

"No, he wasn't, because he was guilty and should have pleaded that."

My voice rose and Finn pressed on my hand, trying to calm me. Faces began turning in our direction.

"Your step-son took explicit pictures of her, without her permission, then shared them online when they broke up," I said. "He humiliated her. And instead of doing the decent thing and persuading him to plead guilty, you hired that sleazy *bastard* and put her through more hell."

Helen planted her hands on her hips, glaring. "Maybe you should remember who persuaded her to take it to court."

I shot to my feet. "Get out of my *fucking* sight, Helen. I will *never* forgive you or John for supporting Stephen. Never. You might as well have thrown her off the escarpment yourselves."

She opened her mouth but Finn rose before she could speak, standing in her personal space and drawing himself up to his full six foot four.

"I think you should probably go now, Mrs Gray."

I smiled internally. Finn only ever called her by her proper name when he was seriously pissed off, emphasising that she and I no longer shared a surname. I'd kept Paul's surname – Bennett – when Helen remarried, one more thing we'd argued about. Helen retreated back to the bar. John scowled in our direction and I had to work hard not to stick two fingers up at him.

We both sat again and Finn rubbed my knuckles. "You okay?"

"Just peachy. Are they leaving?"

He peered over my shoulder again. "Mm. John's downed

his drink and they're putting coats on. What work have you got this week?"

"Twenty hours. I'll keep the door locked at home."

That hadn't worked last time. Stephen had smashed it in, in a drunken rage, before beating the shit out of me for persuading Sarah to report him to the police. Finn had come back just as I was losing consciousness. Only the fact that I'd needed an ambulance had stopped him from killing Stephen on the spot.

I took a deep breath and exhaled hard, trying to blow away the memories.

"The papers are going nuts about the fracking." I tilted my head towards a table where copies of the local rag sat piled up, full of doom-laden headlines about how the region would be desecrated. "You think the oil company will ride it out?"

"Dunno. I hope not."

We'd already had to take a circuitous route to the pub to avoid a bunch of placard-waving angry protesters. At the outset, the company had made it all sound so innocuous; so beneficial. There would be jobs and opportunities. No one mentioned the downsides. No one said that the new jobs and new opportunities wouldn't actually go to the locals. Maybe the tide would turn in the protesters' favour but it was too late to stop the fracking. The main process had already started.

You'd never be able to put a Green label on Finn and make it stick, but he adored the countryside and being outdoors and despised the thought of even a tiny portion of it being spoiled.

He leaned back in his seat, licking the froth of beer from his lip. "I hope they find nothing down there and it will all have been a monumental waste of time and money." He tweaked my fingers, brightening suddenly. "Hey. Pudding's arrived."

I smiled, despite myself. If only all of life's problems could be solved by chocolate.

***

By the time we left the pub it was dark and pouring with rain – my least favourite road conditions. Finn gave me a sympathetic look as we stepped out, but there were no other options except for me to drive so I fired up the bike, feeling him slide in behind me and wrap his arms around my middle. I drove back only doing about half the speed we'd done getting to the pub but he wouldn't care.

Back at the house, Finn put the bike away in the shed opposite the cottage while I scooted into the dry. He joined me in the kitchen, stripping off his wet jacket and hanging it over the back of a chair. Mine was already dripping on the cracked lino.

I checked the time. My shifts at the gym meant I was free most Sundays and I normally Skyped with Paul every couple of weeks.

"I'm going to get changed. Can you listen out in case Paul calls?"

"Sure."

I hurried upstairs to get out of my wet clothes. As I was coming back downstairs, Finn said, "He's out this week."

I ducked into the lounge and Finn smiled up at me. "She's here now. Back in a bit Paul. I'm soaked."

He handed the laptop over and I settled myself into the corner of the worn sofa. "Hey, Paul. How are you?"

"Oh, I'm fine, Reagan. Finn said that Stephen's going to stay with Helen and John." A frown settled. "Sarah's family must be horrified."

I didn't know what to say. Horrified barely covered it.

Paul was in the swish conservatory of his house down

south. From the windows behind him, it was raining as hard there as it was with us. I'd almost moved to the south when he did. When everything had been going so wrong with Helen and John and Stephen, he'd offered yet again for me to go and live with him, but by that time, Finn and I were together and so I'd stayed in the north.

Finn came back into the room, scrubbing his hair with a towel. He plonked himself on the sofa and slipped his arm around me. "How's Livi?" he asked Paul.

Paul's partner, though they hadn't married. She had a son and a daughter almost the same age as me and Finn, but I didn't really know any of them. Livi rarely joined the Skype chats and I knew it was because Paul wanted it to be time for me.

"Oh, she's fine. Off to a pal's at the moment. Divorce woes. The pal's, not Livi. Obviously."

I laughed. "Obviously. You still sure you won't get married?"

"As sure as the seven hundred other times you've asked that. And if we're on that topic... Finn, when are you going to ask me about marrying my daughter?"

Finn pinked lightly and didn't reply. Paul didn't push it. Unlike Helen, Paul loved Finn. He was a mechanical engineer – hence helping to rebuild the bike with Finn. Paul would be delighted if we got hitched.

"Did you want me to come up?" asked Paul. "When Stephen's out."

The corner of my mouth lifted. "No offence, Paul, but if Finn can't protect me, I'm not sure you can."

Finn stifled a snort behind me. Paul wasn't even as tall as me and had the build of a whippet.

"That's not what I meant. Did you want me to talk to Helen and John?"

"I wouldn't waste your petrol driving up," I said. "You

could phone her, but she won't listen."

"She wouldn't even answer. At least if I had my foot in the door, she'd have to hear me out. I don't like the idea of Stephen being so close."

A warmth crept through me. "I know. And it's really lovely of you to offer, but you'd be wasting your time."

Paul let it drop. We chatted on for a bit, catching up on each other's news before promising to call again in a fortnight. I closed down the laptop and put it on the low table in front of the sofa. Made from old wooden beer-crates, it had been a present to Finn from his best friend, Rick, and was the only piece of furniture we actually owned. Finn drew me against him, wriggling until we were stretched out together on the sofa.

"You okay?" he said, tracing circles on the small of my back.

I propped myself up to look at him. "The man who almost beat me to death is getting released from prison on the anniversary that my best friend threw herself off a cliff. If I hadn't persuaded Sarah to go to the police, Stephen wouldn't have attacked me and Sarah wouldn't have been put through so much hell that she couldn't bear to go on. No. I'm not okay."

I pressed my forehead into his neck.

"It's not your fault. You can't keep blaming yourself for any of this." He teased his fingers through my hair.

"Who *should* I blame?"

"Stephen! *You* didn't do anything! You were an amazing friend to her. If she hadn't gone to the police, she'd still have been put through hell, because Stephen had shared the files. He now has a criminal record and is on the sex offenders list."

"I should never have trusted the courts."

Finn tipped me so he could see my face. "Why? Stephen

got put away and will *never* be able to have the dazzling career John thinks he should have had."

I grunted. John had thought that the pictures had been no more than 'high jinks'. Silly teenage stuff. His darling boy could *never* be involved with blackmail or sharing explicit images. In John's mind, Sarah was to blame for letting the pictures be taken.

Except she hadn't.

Stephen had taken them without her knowledge, setting up his phone to record them while they made out, then cropping or blurring *his* face but not hers.

I wormed closer to Finn, jittery. If Stephen got drunk and came here again, would I survive a second beating?

4

Lilja and I sat on the benches by the fountains, watching the different factions group and gossip. And plot, no doubt.

"I'm getting married."

I turned to Lilja with a start. "Who? Penna?"

Her finely drawn mouth lost some of its smile and she shook her head. "Unlike you, I've not been lucky enough to marry for love as well as position. My parents have said I've to marry Signar."

Signar was a Seer, like Lilja.

"Penna would have been a better match," I said, my heart sad for her.

"Penna is a Guardian." Her voice was clipped. Only Guardians could marry Guardians.

"Sorry. I know how you feel about him."

"He would have been perfect." She ground her teeth together. "But our children would be nothing. Not Guardian, not Seer."

I chewed this over. She was right. I had been lucky. Everyone in The Realm had their roles and restrictions and you rarely got to marry who you wanted.

"I truly am sorry." I squeezed her hand. "But Signar's also a good man. Faran speaks very highly of him."

She laughed mirthlessly, flipping her light brown hair over her shoulder. "Signar is an excellent man. I'm sure we will have marvellous Seer children."

My gaze spun out over the gardens, raking the entrance to the knot-garden. I tried to imagine how it would have been for me if I'd not loved my husband before we were married. Or if Faran had been made to marry someone else. "When's the wedding?"

"Two months. Will you be my Matron of Honour?"

"Of course! I'll try to do a better job of it than my sister did for me!"

The scene before us dissolved into black and she turned to me, her expression solemn as she grasped my hands. "You know he will be free. He will seek revenge."

I searched her face, my heart racing, my mouth dry. She pressed something small into my palm.

"Blue for danger. Do not forget."

***

Peep peep peep peep peep peep peep peep.

I woke with a groan. Finn had shifted in the night and his watch was now right next to my ear, the alarm deafening me. I jabbed him in the ribs and he rolled away.

"When are we getting an alarm clock that sits on your side of the bed?" I grumbled.

He silenced his watch. "You want a coffee bringing up or are you gonna go back to sleep?"

"I'm going to go back to sleep."

"Okay. Sorry."

He kissed my forehead and there was a cold draft in the bed as he got out, followed by a soft scuffling sound as he gathered up everything he would need for work. I turned over and burrowed back under the covers.

It was late morning by the time I woke again. I hadn't meant to sleep in so long but my body obviously had other ideas and at least my sleep had been nightmare-free.

I scooped the post up from the doormat as I passed the

front door, sifting it into junk, mine and Finn's, before tossing all the junk into the recycling box. Finn's post looked like it would be junk once he opened it.

In the kitchen, I switched the kettle on, craving coffee. I leaned my back against the sink, contemplating putting thicker socks on when my gaze snagged on something. A beautiful opalescent bead threaded on to three slim leather cords lay dead centre on the table. Delicate silver filigree knotwork encased the bead and caught the light. I picked the bracelet up and turned it round in my hands, frowning. Why hadn't Finn given this to me yesterday? Maybe he'd left it as a surprise, though I'd have expected him to leave a note with it. I ducked to look under the table but nothing had fallen there. I put the bracelet back on the table. Why had he got me this? It wasn't my birthday for a few weeks and we rarely had the money for surprises. I tore open the envelope addressed to me, still pondering the gift.

My hands froze as I read over the letter inside.

***

I was in the middle of making dinner when the thunk of Finn dropping his kit-bag in the hall met my ears. He joined me in the kitchen, leaning his elbows on my shoulders and his chin on my head. "Hey."

I twisted around so that he could kiss me. "Hey. Thank you for the bracelet."

He scrunched his face up. "Delighted as I am that you think I've bought you something, I haven't. What bracelet?"

"The one you left on the table."

"Not me. Maybe it's from your hunk in the Realm."

I pressed my back against him making him step back, and reached across to the table to pick up the charm strung on leather cords I'd found that morning. The intricate patterns swirling around the bead looked alive as they caught the light.

"This isn't from you?"

He took it from me and scrutinised it. "No. But it's very you."

My stomach knotted. "So who's it from? No one's been here and it was on the table when I got up."

Alarm flashed through Finn's eyes. "Was the door still locked?"

I thought back. I couldn't remember. But if he hadn't left it for me, it couldn't have been locked.

"Maybe it's from Lena?" he said, dubiously. "It's very her, too."

Lena lived with Ösk in the first cottage in the row. We were good friends and when she came over, she usually banged the door and walked straight in if it was open. She was into Celtic knotwork and Norse mythology and when she wasn't suited and booted for her job as an accountant, wore long tie-dye skirts and leather cuffs decorated with runes or knots. Maybe it *was* from her, though I'd have thought she'd have left a note with it if she'd come over before I was up.

"Yeah. Maybe it's from her. I'll ask her."

Finn settled his arms around me, scanning the kitchen. "Okay, well, you like a bracelet that I wish I *had* got you. But what's happened?"

"Nothing's happened. Why?"

He tilted his head to one side. "Is there a pile of clean, dry, *ironed* clothes on the bed?"

Rumbled. Christ, this man knew me too well. "Mm."

"And have you really washed the windows inside and out? And tidied? And hoovered?"

"Mm..."

"Okay, so I'll ask you again. What's happened? You're not the one in this relationship with the tidy genes. You only do housework to take your mind off something worse. Feck. Is Stephen out early? Has he been here?"

I held the letter I'd received out to show him. "No! I got an interview."

A slow smile sneaked across his face. "For your dream job?"

My heart fluttered at the thought. Finn spun me around, hooting and hollering, almost clattering me into the table as he did so.

"Hey! It's only an interview. I haven't actually got the job yet!"

He put me down but kept his arms locked around me. I bit my lips. "I have so many holes in my portfolio."

"So fill them. What were you faffing about doing housework and ironing for when you could have been doing that?"

Which was worse? To have the gaps, or to fill them and it not be good enough?

"When's the interview?" he said, leaning past me to stir the dinner that I'd forgotten was on the stove.

"A week today."

His eyes bored into me. "Why aren't you happy? You've wanted a job like this since you left college. What's wrong?"

I rested my head against his shoulder. I wasn't sure he'd understand. I didn't think he'd ever wanted something so badly that breathing became difficult.

"It's too important. I'm going to screw it up. And not all of us have a fairy godfather."

"Watch it, or I'll tell Billy you called him a fairy."

Billy. Mine and Finn's boss. Good at spotting potential. Or at least good at spotting Finn and helping him after Finn's father had disowned him. After he'd been thrown out of the family home, Finn had worked for Billy tidying up the gym and being a general dogsbody, while he sofa-surfed around his friends.

"God, Finn, I *really* want this job."

He made a chuffing sound but said nothing for a moment. Perhaps he did understand.

"Can I help? You need me to model for you?"

I laughed. "Oh, if there's one thing my portfolio is *full* off, it's drawings of you. No, they've sent a brief and want me to take a set of designs based on it to the interview. But thank you."

"You know Billy'll give you great references for the work you did on the gym logo and everything."

"Yeah. I think it might be that work that got me the interview."

When I was fresh out of college and desperately trying to get a job in graphic design, Billy commissioned me to redesign all the artwork for the gym for him. He also gave me a job on reception, despite all the war-paint and piercings and total lack of experience, so maybe he is my fairy godfather too.

"Fancy a night run tonight?"

Finn's solution to most problems – run it out of your system; run to celebrate; run to think. He'd been converting me to the cause since we met, all those years ago when I was the new kid at school and he was my only friend.

Running in the dark with Finn was gloriously liberating. Perhaps because it was also borderline terrifying. The dark was where the monsters lived. At least Stephen wasn't due out for three days. Finn tickled my back, obviously wondering why I was hesitating.

"Yes, if you know where my head-torch is and if it works, and only if it's a shortish one," I said, aware that he'd been working out all day one way or another and half expecting a sarcastic comment.

"Yeah, I know where your torch is and some spare

batteries. Three miles do you?"

"Mm." I caught his expression. "Oh shit. I forgot to define how fast."

"Yeah, one day you'll learn."

I grimaced. Three miles to Finn was merely a short stroll which meant that the run would involve steep verticals. Then again, if I'd said easy pace, we'd have been running half the night.

He squeezed me hard, snapping my brain back to the room. "You'll be fine. You won't screw it up. You were destined for that job."

I hoped he was right.

***

My calves burned but Finn wasn't going to slow one jot so if I didn't keep up with him, I'd be on my own. When the hill finally levelled off and he stopped to wait for me, I leaned on my knees, hauling in my breath, my eyes fixed on the pool of light from my head-torch. Even when my breathing steadied, I didn't straighten. Finn walked back to me, tipping his head so that the light from his torch joined mine. "You okay?"

"Yeah."

"Liar."

"I'm fine. Just don't leave me behind. It's too dark."

His palm caressed my back. "Sorry. He's not free yet and anyway, I won't let him near you. You need to start moving again before you get chilled. Come on."

He ran his hand over my shoulder blades and down my arm to grab my hand, dragging me back into a gentle jog along the edge of the escarpment, next to the fence. Finn's attention was divided fairly evenly between the path, me, and the landscape below, where the fracking company was exploring. I was glad it was too dark for Finn to see the mess they were making. He was edgy enough over Stephen without getting bent out of shape about that too.

We turned and picked our way back down the hillside, into a light breeze. However much I hated running uphill, I hated running downhill even more. Finn had footing like a mountain goat and I called out to him not to leave me.

"Rea, for the hundredth time, the best way to deal with scree is just to run with it. Accept your feet are gonna go from under you and keep going."

I skittered and slithered my way down, crashing into him when I reached the bottom and making him laugh.

"Alright?" he said, blinding me briefly before dipping his head.

I scowled. "Fine."

The thin path re-emerged after the scree slope, hugging the edge of the hill and following the line of a rocky outcrop. In the long summer evenings we would share a couple of beers and drink in the view from an area where the grass at the side of the path widened out. The rock face sprang up like a wall, rising vertically for several metres, its grey surface mottled with ancient lichen. If you turned left at the top instead of coming down the scree slope, you could see for miles but it was always whipped by the wind. Leaning against the rock face, it was sheltered and the view was more than good enough.

We ran alongside the rock face until we drew level with a large boulder that dominated the ground. As we approached it, my scalp prickled and cold slithered down my back.

"Do not let him in!"

I blinked. The voice was familiar and I hunted through my brain, trying to locate whose it was.

Lilja's?

My feet ground to a halt. Finn ran on for a few strides

before coming back to me.

"Rea? What's up?"

I couldn't shake the feeling and closed my eyes, my hand reaching out for the rock face. As soon as I touched it, my brain filled with the sight and smell of blood. Swords whirled and slashed, wielded by men and women clad in leather. My eyes pinged open again. "The Realm."

"What?" Finn peered at me.

My mouth opened and closed and my breathing snagged in my throat. "The Realm. It's here."

I stepped back, snatching my hand away from the rock. The fear and anger and frustration that I'd felt only moments earlier were gone. As was any image of the Realm from my dreams.

"Ignore me," I said. "I just felt a bit weird. Come on. Let's go home. I'm getting cold."

I started jogging away from the rock face. The further I got from it, the less the hairs stood up on the back of my neck. I glanced back a couple of times, but there was nothing there.

"Race you back?" I said. There was no way I would win, but I needed to put distance between me and this place.

Finn grinned at me. "If you insist."

He set off like a hare, but soon fell back, and stayed no more than five paces ahead. He still won, but he was never out of sight.

Back at the cottage we both stretched out, before stripping in the kitchen and throwing our kit into the washing machine. Finn's eyes drilled me.

"Not a good time to do a night run after all? I thought it would help you decompress about the interview."

"It was great. It did stop me stressing about the interview. I guess I'm still stressing about Stephen though."

"Share the shower?"

"Yeah if you're still in it when I come up. I'll get this lot on."

The shower wasn't really big enough to share – it was a simple handset over the bath with a curtain that had a tendency to stick to your body. We shared the bath more than the shower and that was a snug fit. By the time I joined him in the bathroom, he was brushing his teeth, the room warm with steam. I showered quickly, brushed mine and joined him in bed.

He leaned over and clicked the switch behind the headboard to put the night light on. It didn't always help to chase away the nightmares, but at least it wasn't pitch dark when I woke from them. A soft pinkish glow filled the space on my side of the bed, the light catching the edge of the bead at my wrist. I fingered it, tracing the filigree.

"Blue for danger. Remember."

I gasped, searching the room for who had just spoken, but there was no one there other than me and Finn. I touched the bead again.

This wasn't from Finn, and deep down I didn't think it was from Lena, either. So who *had* left it on the table for me?

5

The bridge of my nose squelched into my face and blood poured from my nostrils. I tried to dodge the next blow but Stephen grabbed me by the hair and smashed my head into the edge of the table, chipping my tooth and splitting my lip. I crumpled on to the floor, spitting blood and he kicked me, flipping me over as if I were a doll. My breathing shuddered to a halt, pain burning in my chest and no air moving. The front door opened and roaring filled my ears.

I sat up, gasping for air. I always woke at the same point in the nightmare – just as Stephen had broken my ribs, leaving me with a chest that wouldn't inflate. The point where, five years ago, Finn had returned to find Stephen trying to kill me in a drunken rage after the police had interviewed him. Finn's cottage – *this* cottage – had been my home and refuge, but Stephen had smashed the door down.

I drew my knees up and wrapped my arms around them, glancing down at Finn's inert form. A frown had chased across his face when I sat up but he seemed deeply asleep again now. I reached down and rested my hand on his shoulder.

"Finn?"

Nothing. I shook him lightly.

"Finn?"

Still nothing. Perhaps I should leave him to sleep.

Except that I knew I wouldn't get back off unless he'd reassured me. I shook his shoulder more violently and was rewarded with him opening his eyes and peering at me blearily.

"Stephen dream?"

I bunted into his shoulder. I could still smell the blood in my nose and feel the fear that I would never breathe properly again. Finn shifted until he was lying on his back with me across his chest, one hand against the small of my back, the other stroking my hair. "You're safe."

"I know."

But how long for? In two days, he would be out, with scores to settle.

***

In the morning, I got up when Finn did, dismayed to see the shadows under his eyes from a disturbed night. After he went to work, I re-read the brief for the interview. It was to design new branding for a clothing company who drew their inspiration from the 1940s and 50s. Part of the brief was a sheet of images of the kind of clothes they made and I studied it. I would never in a month of Sundays wear anything like them, none of them being black and most of them being dresses. I sketched out some preliminary ideas, but inspiration felt low.

By mid-morning, I was standing outside Alison Cullen's house, waiting for her to answer the door, hoping there would be no fresh bruises on her face. I glanced around the garden, admiring the neat borders and pretty spring flowers. Rory and Alison lived in the same semi-detached house in a modern estate where Finn had grown up. For a short while, Finn and I had been near neighbours. At the far end of the cul-de-sac was the house Helen and I had moved into after Paul had left. We hadn't lived there long and I had no special attachment to it. I'd been in this street far more times after we'd moved into John's house than before, coming to see Finn before he'd been thrown out.

The door opened and Alison stood in the entrance, drying her hands on a tea-towel. "Hi, Rea. In you come!"

Finn's mum was rake-thin, with more worry-lines around her eyes than she should have at her age. At least neither eye was blacked today. Her grey-blonde hair was clipped back, suiting her elfin face and she had the same bright blue eyes that Finn had. She reminded me of a bird about to take flight: always restless, always slightly fluttery. Slim-fit jeans were topped off with a fleece top and her feet were clad in a ludicrously thick pair of socks.

I grinned at her as she ushered me through the pristine hall. "Can I smell cake?"

"Chocolate. Baked especially for you."

"Ooh. Thank you!"

I followed her to the kitchen at the back of the house. It faced south-east and the low spring sun flooded the room, making the primrose-yellow walls glow. Two mugs already sat next to the kettle and she waved the jar of coffee at me.

"Yes, please."

"I haven't had chance to ice the cake yet. Do you mind?" said Alison over her shoulder.

"Of course I don't mind. Don't be daft. It looks fabulous."

"Take some back to Finn for me?"

"Sure."

I wondered how she would explain so many missing slices to Rory. I knew he knew that I came over, although he probably wasn't happy about it.

"How's Finn?" asked Alison, standing on tiptoe to put the coffee jar back in the cupboard.

"He's great. He said to say hi, that he loves you and to find out when your work schedule and his next mesh, so you can grab a coffee with him."

Alison was as likely to cross our threshold as Finn was to come here. They met when their shifts matched up and they could 'accidentally' see each other in town and go for coffee together. Alison worked as a cleaner. Most of her work was at a set of offices where she cleaned early in the morning before the staff came in, but she also cleaned domestically for a few people. She and Finn managed to catch up with each other about every three weeks and I knew the times were more vital than air to both of them.

"I'll give you my dates for the next couple of weeks," she said, pouring boiling water into the mugs. "Then he can text me and let me know which day he's free."

"Sure."

That would be a text to the phone Finn had bought her. The one Rory still didn't know about in all likelihood. The one with mine and Finn's numbers pre-programmed into it, along with a support line for victims of domestic abuse.

Alison cut the cake deftly into eight. She popped two slices into a plastic box and handed it to me. I tucked the box in my bag. Two more slices went on to plates which she gave to me with a nod to take through.

The Cullens' house was bright and airy, the walls pale and the carpets a dark taupe. The centre of the lounge held an old-fashioned three-piece suite and a smoke-glass coffee table. I think the decor was almost as old as me, but it was scrupulously clean and tidy.

"And how are you?" asked Alison, as we sat down.

I traced my finger around the chintzy pattern on the sofa. "Er. Mixed."

She waited and my gaze flitted around the room while I wondered how to start. My focus snagged on a wedding invite propped on the mantelpiece and skipped on.

"Rea?"

Alison was as much of a mum to me as she was to Finn. She'd always wanted a daughter, I'd always wanted a mother who'd listen to me, so we were well-matched.

"I have an interview for that job I really want." Start with the easy one.

"The graphic design one? Excellent! When?"

"Monday."

"But that's what you wanted, so why are you so stressed?"

"God, you sound like Finn!" I twitched my shoulders. "I'm scared I'll screw it up somehow."

"What will be, will be. If you're meant to have it, you'll have it."

My tongue bit down on the question I wanted to ask her – was she meant to be married to a bully of a husband who beat her? Instead I took a bite of cake, and groaned with appreciation. "Excellent as ever!"

She scrutinised me. "Why are you really stressed? Is it just about the job?"

"Partly. I mean, I'm ridiculously nervous about the interview. The job would be perfect for me. It's in design; it's full-time. Finn and I might even manage to move somewhere with central heating. Or a spare room."

I trailed off. Even talking about it pushed my anxiety sky-high.

"Okay. What's the other part?" Alison tucked a stray hair behind her ear, leaning forward in her seat slightly, her smile inviting me to open up and tell her everything.

I hesitated. "Stephen's getting released. On Thursday."

She pressed her lips together, her eyes wide. "Are you worried he'll come over again?"

"Yes. No. I'm worried he'll come over and Finn'll kill him. You know as well as I do how he protective he is of the women in his life."

She bit the inside of her lip and I knew I'd pushed too hard. I glanced over to the wedding invite again, just able to see the names. A Cullen cousin. I knew Finn hadn't had an invite. I also assumed that he'd be the only Cullen on either side of the Irish Sea who wasn't invited. Still ostracised after all these years, despite being the one defending his mother rather than attacking her.

"Stephen won't come over. He'll be on probation, won't he?" Alison said, bringing me back to the room.

"That assumes a level of sense and logic that Stephen has so far failed to display."

"Did you want me to talk to Finn?"

I snorted. "Oh, he'll be perfectly sensible when you talk to him and then if Stephen does turn up, the red mist will come down. I'm sure he didn't mean to hit Rory the way he did."

"Oh, no. He did," said Alison softly.

I let my gaze settle on her. "If I got the job, maybe we could afford a bigger place and you could move in with us…"

She held a hand up. "Rea, don't you badger me as well as Finn. I couldn't move in with you. You know I couldn't."

I backed down. If she left, she couldn't stay inside permanently and Rory would batter her if she set one foot outside. "Are you and Rory going to the wedding?" I gestured towards the mantelpiece.

"Oh, yes. Rory is Patrick's godfather as well as his uncle. It should be a good day. The Cullen clan usually know how to throw a party. I take it Finn's not been invited?"

"No."

"It's a shame. Patrick and Finn were like brothers when they were little."

I sipped my coffee. What could I say? I wasn't even sure if I should tell Finn that Patrick was getting married. He'd probably want to know and to send a card and a gift, but he'd be spitting tacks that even a cousin who'd been like a brother to him wasn't going to rock the boat by inviting him.

"Patrick probably wanted Finn there," said Alison, gently, her head on one side. "It'd be Rory's brother that said no."

I said nothing. Whoever had said no, it was another instance of Finn being shut out for daring to hit back over seven years ago.

"Do you need to do anything for your interview? Prepare a talk or something?"

"No. I need to take along a portfolio of my work and any references or commendations, plus do a design based on a brief they sent. I've got a couple of personal recommendations but I need to fill a few gaps in my portfolio before I go. Funnily enough, they seem more interested in design than in pictures of Finn."

Alison laughed. "I don't think I know what a graphic designer is."

"Well, this company creates logos and branding that gets used on websites and marketing and so on. The brief is to design that kind of thing for a clothing company. It's a junior post, so I don't know how many of my designs would make it to the clients if I got the job, but it offers great experience and further training. It'd be perfect for me."

"Good money?"

"Better than I'm on but nothing spectacular. But Finn and I might be able to rent somewhere a bit warmer. Or bigger. If I get it." I finished my slice of cake, before my stomach churned with nerves too much. "What are you wearing to the wedding?"

She shrugged. "What I wore to Siobhan's. Who's going to remember?"

"Well, you know where I am if you want to go shopping

for a new dress."

"You'll be too busy with a new job."

Her eyes sparkled, reminding me as ever of her son. We chatted on for another hour or so before reluctantly, I stood up. "I'm going to have to go. I really do need to think about filling those gaps in my portfolio before next week and I'm working this afternoon. Have you got a copy of your shifts for me to give to Finn?"

Alison disappeared for a moment, returning with a sheet of paper covered in neat writing. I tucked it into my bag, careful not to crumple it up too much, and hugged Alison.

"Thank you for the coffee and cake. I'll let you know how the interview goes. Finn'll probably text you tonight."

She hugged me back hard, her tiny frame threatening to crack from the pressure, and stood back.

"Good to see you. Catch up soon."

***

I perched at my desk on reception at the gym, name badge on my chest, enough war-paint on to feel secure but not so much it would scare the customers. Most of the clients knew me anyway and there weren't usually many newcomers appearing in an afternoon. On the desk, only marginally concealed from sight, lay my sketchbook. In the long stretches between answering the phone or clients arriving, I doodled ideas for the brief I'd been sent. Even if Billy caught me doing it, he wouldn't be upset. I crossed out most of the ideas – they were too spiky or dark. Had too much edge to them. A bit like me. Finn popped by a couple of times to bring me coffees but he was fairly solidly booked for training sessions in the afternoon.

I'd just finished jotting some notes when brakes squealed outside the gym, followed by a loud thump and screams. I scooted around to the door to peer out. An elderly man had been knocked down by a car and a group mustered around him. My heart quickened. The man didn't look in great shape.

"He stepped out in front of me!" A pale man stared helplessly at the prone figure on the pavement, his car door open.

I rushed outside. "Has someone called an ambulance?" I crouched down to press my fingers against the man's neck and found a weak flutter there.

Someone at my shoulder said that they had and that the ambulance was on its way. Cold drizzle seeped into the man's lightweight coat and I grimaced. His skinny frame would chill rapidly.

"I'm going to get some towels from inside to try to keep him warm until the ambulance gets here," I said. "Does anyone have a brolly to keep him dry?"

I rushed inside, told one of the other staff what was going on and grabbed an armful of towels. When I got back outside, the driver was standing next to the car, wringing his hands, and the gaggle of pedestrians around the man on the pavement had grown. Two people held umbrellas over him. I draped the towels over him, talking to him, but there was no response and my heart lurched. I chewed my lip, my breathing uneven, not sure what else I could do to help. Blood stained the side of his head and he looked as if he'd crumpled in the middle.

The distant sound of sirens caught my attention and I looked up. Straight into the red glowing eyes of someone… some*thing* that hadn't been there a moment earlier. It seemed as surprised as me when our eyes met. Shadows writhed, making a shape. The eyes peered out from what seemed to be a cloak with a hood, but most of the form was swirling and indistinct. It pressed a long, bony finger to the place where its lips would be, as if to shush me, and bent back to the old man. Wide-eyed, I watched as the thing reached into the man's chest and retrieved a small glowing ball of yellowish light. It drew the ball of light into its cloak where the shadows extinguished it. The wraith-like figure stared at me for a second longer and then vanished.

The paramedics arrived, elbowing people out of the way, including me. Their faces turned grave as they examined the man. They were too late. The police arrived, and a flurry of activity swarmed through the gym as the police used it as a place to take witness statements. The dead man was taken away in a body bag.

A youngish policeman called me forward to give my statement and I perched on the chair, threading my fingers through each other.

"I didn't see the accident," I said. "I heard the brakes go and then a thump, but I was on the reception desk. The old man was already on the ground when I went out."

"Do you know if he was still alive then?"

I gulped, nodding. "I could feel a weak pulse in his neck. I got the towels to try to keep him warm."

He scribbled in his notebook. A large, raggy-edged plaster wrapped his thumb, grubby over the knuckle and with a disconcerting, rusty stain over the pad of the thumb. "Did you see anything else?"

My heart banged against my ribs. *Yes*. "Er, no. The paramedics arrived and we were all told to move away."

The policeman asked me a couple of other things, made brief notes, and let me return to reception.

I settled on my stool, my hands still shaking, my mind running back over everything. What the hell had that thing been? And when it took the light out of the old man, was that why he died? Had it *killed* him? My head was too full of what had happened to be able to concentrate on my design.

While it was fresh in my mind, I turned to a clean page in my sketchbook and drew what I'd seen, storyboarding it out: man hit by car; man gravely ill; strange wraith-like creature; it shushing me; the ball of light. No one else had seen it, I was certain.

Finn came over as I was finishing my sketches and contemplating going home. He leaned his forearms on the counter, peering over at me.

"This is the first chance I've had to come over. Did you see the accident?"

"Sort of. Heard it more than saw it. Saw the result, though." I swallowed hard, a sick feeling in my stomach.

"What the hell happened?"

I relayed the details to him, omitting the light-stealing wraith... for the moment.

"Was the driver drunk?" asked Finn.

"I don't think so. The police breathalysed him. I think the old guy stepped off the pavement without looking."

"That's horrible." His gaze drifted over my sketchbook and he grinned. "You been working on the brief?"

"Yeah. Show you when we get home?"

"Sure. I've got to run, anyway. Is that you finished for the day?" He leaned back to see out of the door to the gym. "It's still raining. Did you want to take the bike?"

"Thanks, but I'm okay. I'd rather walk in the rain than drive."

He nodded and pushed himself away from the counter. I gathered my things together, glad my shift was over. Interesting as working reception could be, I wanted to go home and think about what I'd seen.

***

"Hey, Rea!"

"In here," I called back from the lounge, tucking my

sketchbook down the side of the sofa.

A moment later a half-drowned Finn stuck his head around the door.

"Still raining?" I quipped.

He pounded upstairs, returning a few minutes later in dry jeans and a sweatshirt from the gym. Half of Finn's clothes were from the gym. He flopped down beside me and I swivelled to face him, tucking my feet under his broad thigh, a squashy cushion between my back and the arm of the chair.

"So, how was Mum?"

"She was fine."

He peered at me and I smiled reassuringly. No, no bruises.

"I've got her rota for you. Text her when you see a day you're both free? Oh, and I have chocolate cake too."

He was still scrutinising me. "What aren't you telling me? Did she have a shiner?"

"No. She was absolutely fine." I stopped and he arched his brows, clearly not buying it. "Your cousin Patrick's getting married. There was an invite at your mum's."

His brows switched to a scowl.

"Sorry." I slipped my arm around his middle. "I thought you'd want to know. It's at the end of next month. I can get details of the wedding list and stuff next time I see your mum if you want."

"Hm. Beer?"

"No, I'm grand thanks."

He stalked out, shoulders set. Better to leave him be. He'd come back when he was ready.

By the time he returned, sipping from a bottle, his jaw had softened and his shoulders were more relaxed, but I knew him too well to believe he was reconciled over the lack of a wedding invite.

"You were working on stuff to take to your interview?" he said as he sank down next to me, making the sofa creak.

"Mm." I handed him the folder. "I'm not feeling the love for it yet."

Finn read over the brief and leafed through what I'd been working on over the afternoon.

"They're just my initial thoughts," I said. "It got too busy when the accident happened."

"I know. Why these colours?" He held up the sheet showing the design palette of dark greens and greys.

"I was trying to capture the vintage feel. British racing green and all that. You don't seem convinced. Is that because you're not convinced or are you still pissed off about the wedding?"

"Both." He grinned. "I am still pissed off about not getting invited to Patrick's wedding but I'm also not sure about these colours. They're too gloomy. Some of these dresses are bright polka dots and stuff. I mean, yeah, the trousers fit the darker colours, but it feels too serious for the whole range they do."

"Fair point."

Finn turned the page to find the drawings I'd done following the accident. "What's this?"

Puzzled blue eyes met mine and I swallowed. "Okay. This is going to sound like I'm crazy."

"Well... You are crazy."

I punched him lightly and he dipped his head and kissed me soundly.

"So what's this for?" he asked as he moved back, pushing the sketches towards me. "Is it a storyboard or something?"

"The old man on the ground... that's the guy who was knocked down."

"Uh huh. And what's this thing?" He pointed to the

creature made of shadows.

"I don't know. I saw it. Just after I put towels on the guy to keep him warm. That thing was on the other side of the man. It saw me and shushed me – like it didn't want me to react to it – and then it reached into the guy on the ground and pulled out a ball of light."

Finn's brows had almost reached his hairline. "Yeah. You're right. You do sound crazy. Are you being serious?"

"Mm."

"So this thing takes a ball of light. Then what?"

He clearly didn't believe me. I took a deep breath. "And then it tucked the light under its cloak and vanished."

Finn chewed his lip. "Did anyone else see it?"

I shook my head. "No. I don't think so. It seemed surprised that I could see it, to be honest."

I rubbed my brow. Now I'd said it all out loud, it sounded ridiculous, but I knew what I'd seen. The fact I *had* seen it creeped me out, and sweat dampened my armpits.

He said nothing for a few breaths.

"Finn, I swear to you, that's what I saw!"

He took a swig of beer, his focus on the set of sketches.

"Okay. I believe you think you saw this. I just don't believe it's real," he said eventually.

Wrong words. Too close to things that Helen and John had said: *"We believe you* think *that Stephen is blackmailing Sarah; we just don't believe that he* is.*"*

I stood up, brushing Finn off, hearing him sigh behind me.

"Rea..." He followed me to the kitchen. "Rea..."

I faced him square on. "It's what I saw."

"Okay." He still didn't seem convinced. "So what do you think it was?"

"No idea. The way it reacted to me... it was scared of me." I was sounding crazier with every word so I stopped.

"Forget it."

Finn made to rub my shoulder but I swatted him away.

"Okay. It's what you saw," he said, his voice soft.

"Don't say it unless you mean it... Your mum told me not to wear too much make-up for the interview."

He blinked at the change of topic. "Um... She might have a point. I don't know what the company's like but maybe you should swap the nose-ring for a stud and cut back on the eye make-up? Look like you do for reception. And maybe only wear a couple of earrings? You do give the impression of 'fuck off and leave me alone' sometimes. Maybe dial it back a bit?"

He meant it kindly but I scowled at him, still burned by the earlier remark. He held his hands up in peace. "Hey, don't shoot the messenger. Just saying."

"Well don't. This is me. Why should I pretend?"

He screwed his fingernail into the corner of his eye. "Everyone pretends in an interview. Wear what you want once you have the job."

He was right, but I wasn't ready to let him know that yet.

My mind ran back over what I'd seen outside the gym. I knew why Finn was sceptical and I had no explanations for *what* it was I'd seen. But I'd definitely seen it. How would I react if Finn told me *he'd* seen something like that? I sighed. Probably exactly the way he just had.

"Oh, nearly forgot. I asked Rick and Billy if they wanted to come over tomorrow evening. Do you mind?" Finn broke through my thoughts, dragging me back to the kitchen.

A few years older than us, Rick worked in the tattoo place and had been Finn's best friend since they met. He'd decorated both mine and Finn's skin over the years. Billy, our boss, was Rick's partner. Finn had introduced them, albeit inadvertently. When Finn had gone to get his first tattoo – the Celtic knotwork that circled the top of his right arm – the two had ended up talking about fitness and training. By this time, Finn had started his course and needed a case-study to write up and offered to train Rick, which then led to Rick joining the gym and meeting Billy.

I rested my back against the chipped worktop, glad of the change in topic. "No, it'll be good to see Rick. Haven't caught up with him in ages. Is he after any designs?"

I'd given Rick numerous designs for tattoos over the years, but he normally asked in advance rather than turned up hoping for some.

"I don't know. I don't think so, I think he's only coming for beers and craic, but if you have any, he'll buy them off you. He said someone had been asking for my dragon again."

Finn's dragon tattoo stretched across half of his back, its wings spreading over his shoulder blades, its tail coiling down his spine, its body made up of Celtic knotwork, the intricate knots tangling and resolving perfectly. It was one of several tattoos that decorated his back and the tops of each arm, all in simple black with clean, crisp lines. I'd designed them all.

"No chance. I designed that for you and no one else."

Finn grinned. "That's what I told him."

"Are they needing food as well as beer?"

"No, they said they'd bring pizza."

"Grand. You ready for dinner? I'll finish up while you text your mum."

***

As I was drying the last of the dishes, dance music started up in the lounge. I went through to be met with the sight of Finn dancing like a muppet and singing along in completely the wrong key. Several wrong keys actually as he couldn't hold a tune if it only had one note in it. He beckoned me over to dance with him. I shook my head but he caught my hands, dancing with me with no relationship to the beat of the music or style, just holding my hands and waving them around, looping his arm over me and twirling me randomly.

"God Finn, you're a loon," I said, joining in as well as I could but finding it hard to anticipate what would be coming next. Jiving? Tango? Seventies bad disco? Random dancing of the kind you do with five-year-olds at a wedding? Nothing that bore any resemblance to a dance I knew, but it was hilarious fun.

The music moved on to something slow and he frowned. "I'm not sure how that fits in with 'disco shuffle', but hey."

We slow-danced before a completely cheesy track came on and Finn began boogieing as if he was demented. I was laughing too much to dance once Finn began his Saturday Night Fever routine. It morphed into his Pulp Fiction routine which could have been quite cool if he hadn't been hamming it up so much. He grabbed my hands and I gave up and joined in, abandoning any pretence of hip sophistication. We danced, if that's the right word for it, for about an hour until I was sobbing with laughter.

And then I was just sobbing.

Deep, shuddering, wailing, snot-laden sobs against his broad chest while he rubbed my back and held me close, and utterly inappropriate frothy disco music played on behind us.

"Finn, I'm sorry."

"Shh." He kissed my temple. "Let it all out."

"I was having so much fun dancing."

"It's fine."

When I was finally composed enough to draw back, his top was soaked with tears and snot.

"I'm sorry."

"What for?" he said gently.

"I got snot all over your top."

He leaned back so he could look at me. "S'alright. It'll wash." His hands locked at the small of my back. "You okay now?"

"Yeah. I don't know where all that came from."

"The fact you're stressed about the interview. That Stephen is getting released. Thinking about Sarah." He canted his head to one side. "Close?"

Spot on. He stretched his arms up and flexed his shoulders. "Come on. Bed."

"Yeah… Finn?"

"Mm?"

"Don't ever change. You're perfect."

"Apart from the grotty socks and footie addiction?" He raised a brow as if being snarky, though he looked bone-deep happy.

"Yeah. Apart from that."

6

I am coming for you.

I cried out as I woke, my breathing ragged. Finn stirred next to me, drawing me tighter to him, but didn't wake. I steadied my breathing. It was a dream. Just a dream. The pinkish glow from the night light revealed an empty room and I rubbed my hair back from my face.

I

Am

Coming

The voice was in the room. Somewhere in the room. Snarling, malevolent, rasping. And in the room.

For you

The voice was so close to my ear that the breath brushed my skin. I screamed.

"Jaysus! What? Hey, Rea, Rea... it's okay. It's only a dream. Come here," Finn soothed, pulling me back to him.

"Finn, it's in the room. It's in the room!"

"Rea, it was a dream. Shh. Shh."

"It's in the fucking room! It said it's coming for me!"

Finn reached across and switched the bedside lamp on, squinting in the brighter light. "Rea, there's nothing here. See for yourself."

I stared around the room, my heart racing. Which would be worse? Seeing something or seeing nothing? The bedside light chased the shadows from empty corners to reveal a perfectly normal room.

"It was in here," I insisted.

"What was?" said Finn, still half full of sleep.

I didn't know. I just knew it was coming for me.

"Will you check the house?" I asked.

He opened bleary blue eyes, looking at me as if I might have lost my mind. "Check the house? What for?"

"Please, Finn?"

He groaned. I caught sight of his wristwatch and guilt flooded me. Almost a quarter past three.

He pushed his hair back and rubbed his face, sighing heavily. "You won't go back to sleep unless I do, will you? Want to come with me? Or stay here?"

I hadn't even considered that. If I went with him and it was there, it could get me. If I stayed here and it was hiding, it would get me as soon as Finn was gone.

"Come with you." I figured that if there *was* something out there, Finn would murder it rather than let it get me.

We padded around the house, switching on every light. By the time we were in the lounge, I felt completely stupid. Finn put the lights out and I tailed him back into bed.

"Sorry," I whispered.

"It was just a dream," he murmured. "Go back to sleep."

I rested my cheek against him and listened to his breathing as it slowed and settled. His grip on me loosened marginally and I knew he was fast asleep again. I started on some relaxation exercises, focusing on my breathing, trying to match my breaths to Finn's.

As I was finally dropping off, a voice whispered in my ear.

I. Am. Coming. For. You.

And then it laughed.

***

I never got back to sleep. The slightest sound in the house made my heart pound and my eyes spring open. I'd swear the voice in the night had been in the room, right next to me, despite everything. What the hell was coming for me? That creature with the old man? Except that thing – whatever it was – had been scared of me. Stephen?

I finally crawled out of bed long after Finn had gone to work. In the kitchen, I laughed at the fridge magnets, neatly arranged into two messages – one telling me Finn loved me, the other a selection of rude words. While the kettle boiled, I rearranged them, smirking. It had become a competition between us as to who could leave the filthiest string of words for the other. Finn usually won.

I scrolled through the messages on my phone. Lena had got back to me: *Nope. I didn't leave you a bracelet. You around for coffee this week?* I texted her back to say coffee would be great and put my phone back in my pocket, my skin prickling. If Finn hadn't left the bracelet and Lena hadn't, who *had*? And how the hell had they got into the house? There was no way Finn would have left the door unlocked. I stirred my coffee, trying to shrug off the unease that had made itself at home between my shoulder blades, but it wouldn't budge.

"Come on. There's no one here. Get your arse in gear and get ready for Monday!"

My voice bounced off the walls. The solitude of the house didn't comfort me. I checked the back door was locked. It was. So was the front door.

I blew out a jittery breath, grabbed my coffee and took it through to the lounge. There, I settled down to try to work on the brief for the interview, playing with the colours. I sighed as I stared at the new version, pretty sure I'd now overcompensated for my darkness and made it too light and frothy. I tore the page out of the book and crumpled it up. Dejected, I texted my old tutor from college – Maggie – to see if I could go over and throw some ideas around with her. We'd stayed in good contact since I left college. A sensible, dependable woman, she'd not only be great to help me wrestle the brief into some semblance of order, but she might just calm my shattered nerves. She replied almost immediately, suggesting we meet that afternoon.

By lunchtime, I was clean out of inspiration and the floor around me was littered with screwed up paper. It was bright and sunny out – perfect to take the bike out for a spin once I'd been to see Maggie. Except Finn had it. I called him.

"Hi, Rea. Everything okay?"

"Fine. Sorry to call you at work. Can I come and get the bike after I've been to college? I've been drawing all morning and I want to blast some air through my lungs. I'll come back and pick you up when I finish."

"Sure. I'll be done by half five. That give you enough time? I can always pump iron if not."

"Plenty. I'll call you after I leave college."

***

By half three, I was out on the open road. Maggie had been enthusiastic over my designs, allowing me to feel a tiny bit more confident about the interview, and now the fresh air was clearing my head and lungs, blowing away images of wraiths and the memory of insidious, creepy voices.

I turned away from the town and on to a quiet road that had few bends and even fewer speed cameras, accelerating hard up the hill behind the quarry, adrenaline fizzing through me. The rain from earlier in the week had gone and my heart soared as I opened up the throttle and let rip. The most fantastic view over the valley burst into sight, right at the top of the hill. I turned the bike in to a lay-by and peeled my helmet off, drinking in the scenery. The lights from the fracking site twinkled benignly and I wrinkled my nose. I would rather they weren't there. The main process was due to start any day, if it hadn't already and this glorious view could be ruined forever if there was as much gas down there as they hoped. I rested my weight back, feeling the tug of the bike as it shifted beneath me, and the crisp spring air chilled my nose as I sucked in deep lungfuls.

Fields hazed with the almost luminous green of winter barley criss-crossed the valley below me and sheep dotted the hillside. Lambing wasn't far off. Down in the south of the country it would already have begun but the hill-sheep needed the worst of the frosts and cold to be over before bringing fragile new life into the world. It was a Spartan existence with few barns for mollycoddling lambs in up here.

The bright sun held the promise of warmth. When the clocks changed in a couple of weeks, the evenings would stretch out, inviting me and Finn to sit outside in the shelter of the cottage, sipping beers into the sunsets. Yeah, life could be good sometimes.

From the fracking site came a low boom, and the earth shuddered and settled as if it had coughed. I scowled. Whatever they found down there, it wouldn't be worth it. I stretched my back and gazed at the rural scenery, hoping that the tremor would be enough to shut the plant down for a while. Or permanently.

A tractor chugged across a field, a flock of birds trailing it, searching for food. A dark shadow crawled over the valley and I squinted upwards, trying to work out which clouds were creating it. The sky was almost clear and I turned back to the valley, frowning. The shadow had passed the tractor and was inching inexorably over the fields towards me. As I peered at it, I realised it wasn't a shadow. It was mist. Black mist. It hugged the ground, undulating its way up the side of the hill, reminding me of the way mercury moved. Mist normally filled space but this was a tight ball, only a few metres in diameter, its boundaries sharp.

Ice trickled through my veins and I chided myself. I was being irrational. It must be the shadow of a cloud.

The hairs on the back of my neck stood up, and sweat slicked my palms as the black mist kept on coming, but I was transfixed, my heart racing as the light in front of me blinked out inexorably. As soon as the blackness touched me, it rocked me backwards. My head filled with the sound and fury of a pitched battle; my ears filled with screams. Whether my eyes were open or closed, all I could see were clashing swords, spurts of blood, people lying slain on the ground. The stench of blood and death filled my nostrils.

"I invite you in."

Had *I* said that?

I reeled. A cadaverous face contorted with anger loomed before me, leathery skin stretched over the skull, red eyes burning. *"I accept."*

Every fibre of my being screamed with rage and injustice. I wanted revenge. I *demanded* revenge. I would cause death, the like of which neither realm had seen before.

"Together we can overthrow Eredan and rule together." The demon grinned at me.

More bodies. More blood. Then smoke.

I sank back on the bike, crumpling like a rag doll, stunned. I peered cautiously at the hillside. The black mist had passed and I squirmed around in my seat to see where it was, but it had vanished. Puffing my cheeks out, I stared at the valley. All I could see was what had been there before – rural tranquillity. The sensation of malevolence and resentment ebbed away, letting me breathe freely again, and I dragged in deep, cool lungfuls, trying to cleanse the last traces of fury from my body.

The height of the sun made me check my watch.

"Shit!"

Finn would be expecting me any minute and I was at least quarter of an hour away. I yanked my phone out and called him.

"Hi, Finn. Sorry, I'm going to be a bit late picking you up."

"You okay? You had an accident?"

I snorted. Finn rode the bike far faster than I did but he was always sure it would be me who would crash it.

"No, I'm fine. Time ran away with me, that's all. See you soon."

I could have sworn the visions that had overwhelmed me had lasted mere moments but, somehow, I'd lost more than half an hour. I tugged my helmet back on and rode down the hill to the gym, trying to work out what the hell had happened.

And why I recognised the monstrous face.

***

"What time are Rick and Billy coming over?" I asked when we got home.

"Soonish. They said they'd call on their way and find out what pizzas we wanted."

Finn took my helmet and disappeared off to tidy it away, leaving me thinking about what had happened while I was out on the bike. It had felt more than real. It had felt like I was *remembering* what I'd seen.

It was the Realm. With a lot of blood. But I wasn't remembering any of it from a dream, I was sure of that.

Finn's phone beeped as he re-joined me in the kitchen.

"Hi, Rick." He chatted for a moment then looked across

to me. "What pizza are you wanting? And don't you dare have anything with anchovies on it."

"Ha. I might, just for that. Er, pepperoni? With extra green peppers since Rick's buying."

Finn relayed our order to Rick and slid his phone back into his pocket. "Can I see your updated designs before they get here?"

"Sure."

In the lounge, Finn sat next to me, flipping through the sheets I'd been working on earlier. "I like these colours better. What did Maggie say?"

"She liked those colours better too."

He passed all the sheets back to me and picked up my other sketchbook. "Ah. Your dreams. And another drawing of your hunk." He pulled a face as he turned a page.

"I know. Even in my dreams I have gorgeous boyfriends!"

"Good save."

He looked over all of the pictures, closed the pad and rested his head against the back of the sofa. Shadows pooled under his eyes.

"I'm sorry about last night," I murmured. "You're exhausted."

He cracked one eye open to peer at me. "It's okay. Who did you think was coming to get you? Stephen?"

"Not this time. I don't know who. Or what. Something evil. It honestly felt like it was in the room with us."

"Like the thing you thought you saw with the guy who was hit by the car?"

I hesitated. "Mm. Very like the thing I saw at the gym. Except whatever it was last night wanted to kill me."

He closed his eye again. "They're just dreams, Rea. Dreams can't hurt you."

I wasn't so sure.

"I had a really weird experience when I took the bike out," I blurted out.

His head shot up, his eyes wide, and I rushed to reassure him. "No. I didn't have an accident or anything. I stopped in the lay-by above the valley and this black mist came over me."

"Black mist? What, the cloud-base dropped?"

"No. A ball of black mist. I thought at first it was the shadow of a cloud, except the sky was almost clear and the clouds weren't moving. Anyway, as it passed over me, I had these intense visions of a battle and I felt completely peculiar. Like I hated everyone and that I'd been seriously mistreated and wanted vengeance. Then the shadow moved on and it all stopped."

Finn's face told me how mad he thought I'd just sounded. "Uh huh? I think you might be over-tired. You've been sleeping so badly since you found out about Stephen."

I paused, about to argue, then rested my forehead against him. I couldn't deny I was exhausted. "Yeah. Probably. It was just really odd."

So was finding a bracelet in the house. And so was seeing a creature take a ball of light from a dying man.

***

A bang on the door heralded the arrival of Rick and Billy. They walked straight in, not waiting for either of us to answer the door, Rick's meaty arms full of pizza boxes. He was a shade shorter than Finn but more than a shade wider and it wasn't only muscle filling his frame. Wild dreadlocks were loosely tamed by a bandana and several days' stubble darkened his chin. From the top of his t-shirt, dark curls of chest-hair sneaked free. Were it not for an almost cherubic snub-nose, he would look like the last man on earth you would want to meet in a dark alley. But his eyes always sparkled with humour and he was one of the kindest and most generous men I knew after Finn.

Billy plonked a crate of beers on the table next to the pizza boxes. Ex-army, he struggled to look like a civilian with his ramrod posture and barrel-chest.

"Rea's got some good news to share," said Finn, serving up slices of pizza on to plates.

"Are you pregnant?" said Rick, making me and Finn burst out laughing.

"Er, *no*. I have an interview for the graphic designer job. Monday."

"Oh. Well that's great news too." Rick grinned, leaning over to hug me.

"Mm. Time enough for kids in another decade," I said, shooting a look at Finn. He'd rather we started now.

"Don't leave it too late." Billy handed a plate to Finn. "Who knows what's around the corner."

"Don't blame *me* for waiting." Finn served pizza on to the plate and passed it back.

"Will you all stop ganging up on me? Thank you. Beer?"

All three men nodded. I cracked open three cans and slid them on to the table. Once Finn had finished distributing pizzas, Rick moved the remaining slices into one box and tidied the others away. It would be a tight competition between Finn and Rick as to who was the neater.

Billy and Rick had always struck me as an odd couple. It'd taken a long time for them to move from being good friends to anything more and although they'd now been together for a couple of years or so, they both steadfastly refused to move in together.

"Oh, I forgot to tell you," said Finn as we carried plates and beers through to the lounge. "Fiona asked me if she could hire me privately."

Fiona was one of the women at the gym who currently had Finn as their personal trainer. He was the only member of staff with a waiting list.

"Christ, that's the fourth this year! What did you say?" Billy settled down on the lumpy sofa next to Rick. I tucked my legs under me on the armchair, and Finn sat on the floor in front of me. We only had three seats, and even they filled the room, with their wide, unfashionable, padded arms.

"I told her no, of course," said Finn.

Billy paused, his gaze resting on his protégé. "You've more than paid me back. I wouldn't mind if you made a bit more money for yourself taking on private clients."

Finn swallowed down a mouthful of pizza. "Well, apart from the fact I wouldn't be that disloyal, I'd also have to get private insurance and everything."

Billy smiled. He'd have Finn's loyalty forever.

"Well, if you wanted to, you know I wouldn't object. You'd probably make more than you do with me!"

Finn sipped his beer. This was an old argument. "Billy, you believed in me when everyone else thought I was a stroppy teenager. No, I'd rather work for you, debt or not."

A year after Finn had started working at the gym, Billy made a deal with him: if he helped Finn to get qualified as a personal trainer, Finn had to work for him in the gym until the debt was paid off. Finn had practically bitten his hand off at the chance. That was six years ago.

Billy chewed a mouthful of pizza, his eyes humorous. "Well, you *were* a stroppy teenager. With a lot of attitude and a temper like a tinderbox. But, you know, you reminded me of what I was like at your age. The army discipline sorted me out. All you needed was guidance."

By guidance, he meant the punishing drills he'd put Finn through. He'd made Finn box, lift weights, run bleep-tests... anything that would teach Finn how to control his frustration and temper.

The topic of conversation shifted to footie, with Finn and Rick bickering about their teams' chances in the league. Billy and I concentrated on eating the pizzas, neither of us having a huge enthusiasm for the delights of twenty-two men kicking a ball around.

The pizzas finished, Rick turned to me. "I know I haven't actually asked, but have you got any new designs for me? Especially something that looks like Finn's dragon without actually being Finn's dragon?"

"No. No new designs for you and I'm not giving you anything that even half resembles his dragon. That one's exclusively his. Anyway, no one else would wear it as well as he does."

Finn grinned. "You'd better put an order in. After Monday she'll be a professional graphic designer."

I pretended to cuff his ear. "Cut it out."

"Is that what you're stressing about?" said Rick.

Finn's breath hissed in his nose and I wondered what he'd already said to Rick.

"Stephen's released tomorrow," said Finn quietly.

"Already?" Alarm flashed all over Billy's face. From Rick's expression, this wasn't news. I wondered when he and Finn had talked.

"Yeah. Already."

"Where's he going to stay when he comes out?" Billy asked.

Again, I had the feeling that Rick already knew. I sipped my beer, heart racing. "John and Helen's. The prodigal son no doubt."

Rick shot a look at Finn that I couldn't quite work out. "He's served his time. Maybe he should be allowed to move on with his life."

"Fine. He can move on out of Cumbria," Finn spat back

at Rick.

Billy was also shooting daggers at Rick who put his hands up, pleading forgiveness. "I'm only saying! Maybe he's a reformed character?"

"Or maybe he's exactly the same," I snapped. "I guess we'll see soon enough. If he batters down the door and tries to kill me again, we can all take that as a 'no'."

Silence clotted around us and Finn reached up to catch my hand, his thumb circling my knuckles. Rick picked up my sketchbook, waving it at me, obviously desperate to change the topic. "Can I see what you've been doing?"

"Sure."

He'd picked up the Realm sketchbook and he and Billy leafed through it.

"Are these book illustrations?" asked Billy.

"No. Though maybe one day I can call on them for that! No, I have recurring dreams of this place."

"Ooh. He's a bit of a god," said Rick, turning the pad towards me and Finn. "Finn, are you happy about her dreaming about him?"

"Oh, it's worse than that. In my dreams, I'm married to him."

"Finn! Get a ring on her before she ever comes across this chap!" said Rick, laughing across at us.

A weird feeling rippled through me as if it *was* possible for me to meet him. I tried to shake it off.

"Oh, he's just a figment of my overactive imagination. And anyway, Finn is my dream man."

"Pass me a bucket," said Billy, sounding sterner than the dimple in his cheek implied.

Rick closed my sketchbook and tidied it away for me, asking if he and Billy could also see my designs for the interview. I went over them with them, interested to get Billy's views as a business owner. Their views on the colour palette matched Finn's and Maggie's and I begrudgingly accepted defeat.

As the conversation shifted to whether Billy should extend the gym opening hours, I caught an undercurrent between Rick and Finn. In all the years they'd known each other, they'd barely argued, but there was a distinct prickliness there tonight. Had Rick pushed it, saying Stephen had served his sentence? Surely he'd know how badly Finn would react to that. Rick had been the one Finn had leaned on while I was in hospital recovering from the assault, and the one Finn had talked to when Sarah had died and I'd fallen apart. Maybe Rick genuinely believed that once you'd served your time, you should be given a chance. Neither Finn nor I were ever going to believe that about Stephen though, and Rick should know that.

I shuffled in my seat, no happier with Rick than Finn was. He'd *seen* the state of me. He *knew* what Stephen had done. To me. To *Sarah*. Was Rick really okay about him walking the streets of our town again?

At half past nine, Finn was getting restless. I leaned forwards and stacked the plates together on the table, looking pointedly at the clock. If neither Rick nor Billy took the hint, I would yawn loudly and stretch. It always worked.

There was no need for such theatrics tonight though as Rick grinned at us. "Have we outstayed our welcome?"

"No, no. It's fine," said Finn hurriedly.

"Well," I said, pretending to stifle a yawn. "I've possibly had enough excitement for today and Finn's on early tomorrow. And we've eaten all the pizzas and drunk all the beer, so…"

"We get the message," said Rick, shaking his head and rolling his eyes.

Finn said nothing but his posture softened. The other two gathered themselves and there was a flurry of goodbyes. Rick hugged both of us; Billy slapped Finn on the shoulder and nodded at me and finally we were left alone. Finn leaned my back against his torso.

"Thank you. You know I hate having to ask Billy to go."

"He'd understand. You'd only need to remind him you're on early!"

"I know, but..."

I turned in his arms and kissed him.

"Mmm." Finn rested his forearms on my shoulders, a mischievous expression in his eyes. "No chance of any more excitement tonight?"

"I didn't say *that.* Come on then. Bed."

I could worry about my strange visions tomorrow.

7

Thursday. My first port of call would be the florist. Every year since Sarah's death, I'd left flowers on her grave and at the escarpment to mark her birthday and the day she'd died. I also needed to do some work on my designs, ready for Monday. I'd hoped to be able to see Maggie again, but she was busy all day. Since I didn't want to be alone in the house when Stephen was released any more than Finn wanted me to be, I decided to camp out at the library after lunch.

As I popped some bread in the toaster, a book on the kitchen table caught my eye. It was leather-bound and seemed old, its cover held closed with a leather thong that encircled it twice. My heart thumped. It hadn't been there last night. First a charm-bracelet, now a book. How the hell were these things arriving through locked doors? And who on earth was leaving them?

I stared at it, my skin prickling with sweat. I reached behind me and tried the back door. Locked. Edging around the table as if the book might attack me, I went to the front door. Also locked.

Back in the kitchen, I scraped my hand over my face, my breathing jagged, and flipped the cover of the book open. Inside, runic writing covered the page and I leaned closer, trying to see if it was handwritten or printed. It looked printed. The pages crinkled as I turned them. The whole book seemed both old and new, reminding me of a facsimile of a medieval manuscript. Detailed, hand-painted illustrations decorated the pages and I marvelled at them.

My breath suddenly stalled in my chest.

They were of the Realm.

What the...?

I snatched my hand away as if burned. Where the hell had this come from? Only close friends had ever seen my pictures and none of them could draw. The only person I knew who could have drawn them as well as this was Maggie, but although I'd mentioned my dreams to her, she'd never seen my sketches. My hand trembled as I reached for the book again. I opened it at the beginning, turning the pages slowly. The first picture in the book was of the wraith-like figure I'd seen with the old man and my mouth desiccated. I scanned the runic writing but I couldn't make head nor tail of it. Several pages further on were two pictures that drove cold into my belly. One was of the guy I was married to in my dreams. A perfect rendition of him.

The other picture was of me.

I stepped back, dizzy. What the hell *was* this? How had pictures of my recurring dreams ended up in a book? How had a picture of *me* ended up in the book?

I looked again, trying to control my breathing. Maybe it wasn't me. The woman had long hair, no piercings, no heavy eye make-up.

I swallowed, my heart pounding. It was me.

What was this all about? Who had left it here? And what on earth did it say?

My phone beeped. Finn.

"Hey, Rea. Where did you decide to go today?"

My eyes were still on the book. "Um. Well, I'm going to leave flowers for Sarah this morning. Meet you for lunch afterwards?"

"Sure. You okay? You sound weird."

"I'm fine. Just upset about Sarah."

"I know. Text me if *anything* happens, and come to the gym?"

"I will. Promise. I love you."

"I love you too."

I rang off and pulled up Google on my phone, searching for runic alphabets. None of the results matched the writing in the book. The closest was an old runic alphabet used in northern Europe many centuries ago, but even that wasn't a great match. I squinted at the small screen of my phone and wondered about booting up the laptop. I sighed, rubbing my jaw. I needed to visit Sarah. Maybe I'd find something in the library this afternoon that could help me work out what the writing said.

***

The graveyard was quiet. Dew still clung to the grass between the graves and the gravel path crunched under my feet. From a nearby tree, a bird sang its heart out, and on the far side of the cemetery, a couple of rabbits lolloped together.

When I reached Sarah's headstone, there were already fresh flowers from her family. I wondered if they still blamed me for what happened. I certainly did. She was my only friend other than Finn, and I'd let her down so badly.

I arranged my flowers in a spare vase and placed it next to the stone, before crouching to talk to her for a while. I came here pretty often to tell her all the news and gossip, but I only went to the escarpment twice a year.

As I dried my eyes, a middle-aged woman spoke softly to me from the adjacent plot. "Don't weep. Her spirit lives on and will last forever. Just as your spirit will. The body may go, but the spirit will find a new one."

I wiped my nose. "I don't believe in reincarnation."

"Just because you don't believe it, it doesn't make it untrue."

She smiled kindly as she tucked salt-and-pepper hair behind her ear, and turned away. I wished I did believe in reincarnation – it might make Sarah's loss more bearable. The thought that my beautiful, funny, amazing friend lived on in someone new might compensate for the knowledge that if I hadn't pushed her to go to the police, she might still be here. But I didn't believe it, and my heart was splintered at her loss.

It was a stiff hike up to the escarpment. Once I reached the top, I gazed out for a moment at the green fields and scattered woods, before placing the flowers at the spot Sarah must have jumped from. I steeled myself to look down to the rocks where she'd landed, my mind spooling back to finding her there. I was the one who'd found the note in her room, saying she couldn't go on. I knew where she'd go. If only I'd got up here faster, I could have stopped her.

I perched on a rock and wrapped my arms around my knees, hugging them tight to my body. "Sarah, I'm sorry. I'm so sorry. I miss you so much!"

I stayed there until the cold wormed its way into my bones and I had to leave. After one final glance towards the rocks, I eased myself up and stamped some warmth back into my frozen feet, before making my way back towards the town to meet Finn for lunch.

***

The check-out desk divided the ground floor of the library into two areas – adult fiction to the left and reference to the right. It was busy there that afternoon and it took me a few minutes to find a table, but eventually I found one in the reference section, next to a computer terminal.

I itched to work out what the hell the strange book was, but I had enough sense to do a significant chunk of work on my design for Monday first.

After about an hour, I pushed my design aside and laid the weird book on the table, next to a battered notebook. I chewed my biro. Maybe if I could find out what the book said, I would work out how it had arrived on my kitchen table. Through locked doors.

I wiped clammy hands on my thighs and took a deep breath. I opened the book, staring dry-mouthed at the incomprehensible symbols, and twirled the pen in my fingers. Was *any* language still written in runes? I was pretty sure that any online translation page wasn't going to be any help if the writing was old, even if I could find a way to input the text.

The library allowed you to use the computers for free if you had a library card, so I logged in and repeated my earlier search for runic alphabets, spending more time looking at the results. Nothing matched all of the runes used in the book and I rubbed my eyes. This was hopeless.

I shook myself and sat up straight. It must say *something*, right? I pulled up the alphabet that most closely matched the book and found the page where there was an approximate pronunciation guide. Looking at the book, I jotted down the sounds for as many of the first line of runes as I could.

Nothing. Well, nothing useful. Some of the runes in the book didn't appear in the online guide, and sounding out those that did, made it sound like Klingon.

I gnawed the end of the pen, staring at the runes. In my brain, guttural phrases chased each other around.

And then made sense.

I blinked. The runes suddenly seemed familiar and first

of all words, then whole phrases sounded in my head. I dragged a hand through my hair. The words were alien and if you'd asked me to read them out, I wouldn't have been able to, but I understood the meaning. I swallowed. How could this make sense?

Something tickled at the back of my brain – not quite a memory; not really a dream. I *knew* this script. As I scanned the lines, the stories rang loud and clear in my head. They described an ancient mythology with things called Elders and Guides and spirits.

The Guides

Beings have three parts: character, vitality, form. The form is the body; the character and vitality come from the spirit. At conception, a bond forms between the body and the spirit and the spirit gives the body vitality and character. Without the spirit, the body cannot live. At death, the body is too weak to hold the spirit and the bond between the spirit and the body breaks. The spirit leaves willingly, eager to move to a new body. The Elders told us that it is the desire of the spirit to find a body which will not fade with age and it flits from host to host, ever searching for an immortal form.

To assist the spirits, the Elders created the Guides. The Guides eased the transition from life to death. They accepted the spirit from the dying body and transferred it to its new host. When a Guide accepted a spirit, all of the spirit's vitality was held back and the Guide received none. When a new body was found, all of the vitality flowed from the Guide to the new body, giving it life and character. For millennia, the Guides performed their roles without fault, waiting patiently to accept the spirit from the dying before carrying it safely to the next body. The Guides were ethereal. No one Outside could see them, only Guardians. At most, Outsiders could perceive them as mist.

The Elders did not know what would happen if a Guide took a spirit before the body was at the point of death.

Aegyir was a Guide and for millennia he waited with the dying, accepting the spirit as the body expired and taking it to a new host. One day he went to accept the spirit of a dying man who was one of identical twins. Aegyir sat with the wrong brother and grew impatient. The body seemed strong, yet Aegyir had been sent to guide its spirit. He placed his hand over the man's heart, expecting to receive the spirit and the man to die but instead, the spirit resisted Aegyir. In his impatience, Aegyir reached into the man and ripped out his spirit.

When Aegyir took the spirit from the man, its vitality was still flowing into the man's body. The vitality needed to be bound but the bond with the man had been severed before it was ready. Hence, a bond formed with Aegyir and all of the spirit's vitality flowed into Aegyir. Aegyir was transformed from an ethereal being with no substance, into a solid form. Without vitality, the man died.

The spirit was split. The part of the spirit that gave character could find no space in Aegyir's body and was cast into Chaos. The part of the spirit that gave vitality became bound to Aegyir, giving him strength and power.

The Elders demanded that Aegyir assist the spirit to a new host body but Aegyir, revelling in his new strength, refused to obey the Elders.

The first war between The Guardians and The Guides had started.

Towards the beginning of the story, an illustration of a shadowy figure – a Guide – filled the lower half of a page. It crouched over a person, its face largely shielded by a hood and its body concealed within a cloak. Red eyes glowed from beneath the hood and long, bony fingers stretched out over the chest of the prone person. A ball of light emerged from the chest. It was exactly what I'd seen outside the gym, two days ago.

At the end of the story, an illustration of the Guide called Aegyir attacking the man he killed covered a whole page. In this image, the light wasn't in a ball, but stretched out as if made of elastic. At the man's body, tendrils of the light seemed to be being pulled free of his body. At Aegyir's end, tendrils flowed into his shadowy form. I stared at Aegyir's face.

I am coming for you.

My heart thumped and I glanced around the library. A couple of curious faces met my gaze, but nothing even half resembling either a wraith-like Guide or the monster Aegyir. I don't know what I was expecting to see, but the picture of Aegyir was exactly the same as the thing I'd seen when the black mist enveloped me. I turned back to the book and re-read the story.

Only Guardians could see these things; Outsiders couldn't. I had no idea what a Guardian or an Outsider were, but *I* could see these things. Or, at least, I had on Tuesday when the old man died. I still couldn't work out how the hell I could read this book, or why someone had left it in my kitchen.

I studied the pictures. They were hand-painted, but I still thought the text was printed. Whoever had drawn them was very talented. Although they mirrored my drawings of the Realm, they were clearly done by someone else – not me. It was like looking at a fake of my drawings – same pictures, but different execution.

My head was splitting and I checked my watch. I only had a few minutes before I had to meet Finn for a quick snack ahead of the self-defence class. I gathered the book and my notes together and packed them away. As I did so, a faint glow at my wrist caught my attention. A strange blue light emanated from the charm, making the patterns in the silver appear to writhe as if they were alive. I tilted my wrist, examining the bead. I'd never seen it glowing like this before.

Blue for danger.

My head shot up and my gaze locked with that of a woman opposite me who was glaring at me. Unnerved, I finished packing my things away and tugged my sleeve over my wrist, even though being stared at wasn't unusual. As I left, I passed the desk she'd been sitting at but it was now empty.

I pulled my jacket around me and hurried across town to the gym. A light drizzle gave the pavements a tangy odour – part dog-piss, part damp dirt. I dodged umbrellas and turned my collar up, trying to gain a bit of shelter by walking close to the shops. Every now and then, a climate-destroying blast of hot air from the open doors of cheap clothes shops hit me. I kept my eyes peeled for ex-convicts.

When I arrived at work, Finn was sitting at one of the cafe tables, his eyes fixed on the door.

He jumped up as I dashed in. "You're late."

I rolled my eyes. "All of two minutes! Sorry!"

He hugged me, holding on tight.

"It's okay. I haven't seen him," I said.

"Good." He steered me towards the food service area, his shoulders softening.

While we ate, Finn ran over the running order of the self-defence class.

"You sure you're okay to do it?" he asked. "I can get one of the women here to do it instead."

I smiled. "I'm fine. You never spook me and the class will be good for me."

"Did you work on your design at the library all afternoon?"

I hesitated. Finn had already said that I sounded crazy over the Guide I'd seen outside the gym. How was he going to take the news that a strange book had turned up at the house, with pictures of the Realm, the Guide, and me in it?

"Rea?"

"Er. Most of the afternoon. But I also found a weird book and I was looking at that. I'll show you at home."

"A weird book?"

I wasn't sure what to say. Finn squinted at me.

"Is the course fully booked?" I said, trying to deflect him.

"No. Almost. Three spaces."

"Okay."

Finn peered at me for a moment longer but I pointedly kept on eating my food. I could tell him when we got home.

***

The self-defence course went well. We covered a variety of manoeuvres and all of the women practised both with me and then with Finn. The course over, Finn grabbed the bike helmets from his locker and we headed out. As we passed the reception desk, someone spoke to Finn and he paused to reply. I carried on, expecting Finn to join me as soon as he'd finished chatting.

As I left the building, a bloke stepped into my personal space, filling it.

"Look who it is... Cuckoo!"

It took me too long to recognise the man. It was several years since I'd seen him and he was carrying a couple more stones of weight – some fat, a lot of muscle. Stephen. Fear bunched my guts and battered my heart against my ribs. He was just outside the door, flanked by two of his friends from school-days. They smiled nastily as I scanned their size. I might, *might* have been able to take on Stephen on his own, but not these two as well. I hunted around desperately for Finn, realising he wasn't next to me, but he was still inside, joking around with the girl on the front desk.

"Not so brave without your pet bodyguard, huh?" said

Stephen.

His two friends moved so that I was surrounded, the wall of the gym behind me. Where the hell was Finn? My eyes sought him in the doorway of the gym, but there was still no sign of him, only his deep laugh rumbling from inside the building.

Stephen took a long drag on his cigarette and blew the smoke in my face. "It's good to be out and about again. Free to do what I want."

He stepped closer. My heart hammered in my chest and small dots appeared in my vision. The cigarette smoke stung my nose and made my eyes water. Stephen smirked and blew a smoke ring that circled my nose before dissipating. I wondered where his clothes had come from. John? The hoodie was at least two sizes too small and his belly bulged over the waistband of his jeans.

"Didn't think Finn would leave you alone, knowing I was out. I was kinda hoping to see him," said Stephen.

"Yeah, he'll be sad to have missed you too. You do know there's a CCTV camera, right above you?" I said, standing my ground, despite my legs feeling like jelly.

Stephen glanced up at the camera. "Just having a friendly word. Nothing to stress about." He took another drag on his cigarette. "Anyway, prison wasn't so bad that it would put me off finishing what I started." He blew smoke into a long thin ribbon above me.

Finn came out of the gym, took one look in our direction and marched over, interposing himself between me and Stephen. The two pals of Stephen's might have been brave enough to help try to intimidate me, but faced with Finn they abandoned Stephen with alacrity.

"Don't you *dare* come near her," Finn spat. "You come near her again and I'll kill you!"

"Finn!" I said, holding his shoulder, hoping the red mist

wasn't about to come down.

Stephen peered over Finn's shoulder at me, all acne-scars and bad teeth. "Word of advice, *Cuckoo*. Stay out of my way."

"Yeah. Word of advice from me. Stay out of Finn's way. And mine."

Finn drew himself up to his full height, his eyes burning. "You want a fight, you fight with someone your size."

I half wished Stephen was stupid enough to try it but he wasn't.

"Finn," barked a sergeant-major voice at our side.

Billy, Finn's only decent father figure.

Finn turned back towards the gym and took a step away from Stephen, his hands clenching and unclenching at his sides. Billy moved forwards to stand between the two of them.

"Everything alright here?" he said.

"Yeah, we're fine. Stephen is just threatening me with finishing what he started."

I shouldn't have said that. Finn's face blanched and he took a step forward, jaw tight, fists bunched. Billy put his hand on Finn's shoulder, shaking his head.

"Stephen, I think you should leave. I don't take kindly to people threatening my staff."

Stephen's lip curled and he shoved back dark, greasy hair with nicotine-stained fingers. "I'm going. But you know what? I would *love* it if Finn had a go. I don't think he'd cope with prison. And a pretty boy like him? Well, I guess he'd be popular. If you know what I mean. Then again, maybe he wouldn't mind that. He does hang out with faggots." He blew smoke right into my face again. "See you around, Cuckoo."

His two pals lurked a few strides away. With their grubby sweatshirts and ripped jeans they could have been clones. They eyed Billy warily. No, you could never miss the fact that Billy had been in the army and been trained to kill people.

Stephen gathered the side-kicks to him and swaggered down the street. I puffed out a long, shaky breath and pressed my hand against Finn's chest to hold him back, feeling the anger vibrating in him. He was so protective of me and part of me loved him for it, but only part of me. The other part was scared his temper would land him in deep shit one day.

Across the road from us, a man caught my eye. He was leaning on the wall, his eyes locked on me, his face hard. He wore a mid-thigh woollen coat, buttoned over dark trousers – far too professionally dressed to be in Stephen's circle. And more interested in me than a normal rubbernecker would be.

Just as he was beginning to completely creep me out, he pushed himself away from the wall and followed Stephen and his pals down the road. I frowned. Was he someone John had asked to keep an eye on Stephen?

Once they were out of sight, I turned back to Finn and Billy.

"Finn. Keep your cool. Or go back inside and I'll hold the bag while you work it off," said Billy.

Finn scowled. "I'm cool."

"Good. Reagan, you okay?"

"I'm grand. He didn't do anything. To be honest, I think he was hoping to bait Finn. Wind him up so he lost it and he could claim self-defence."

Finn said nothing. Only he knew how close Stephen had come to achieving that.

"Okay. Go home. Stay alert. Rest assured, he's barred from the gym. Finn? Well done for keeping your cool."

***

Back home, Finn hugged me against him. “You okay?”

“Yeah. He didn’t do anything except blow smoke at me.”

“But he could have.”

There was nothing I could say. Finn couldn’t be at my side *all* the time. If Stephen wanted to hurt me, he’d find a way to hurt me.

Finn’s hands slid down my back to lock at my waist. “You want a coffee?”

No. I wanted to get hideously drunk. “Yeah. Thanks.”

He switched the kettle on and leaned his hips against the sink. “You were gonna tell me about a weird book.”

With everything that had happened, I’d almost forgotten. I rummaged in my bag and slid the book across the table towards him. His brow crumpled. “Where’d you get this?”

“It was on the kitchen table when I came down this morning. I take it from your face that you didn’t leave it there then?”

“No.”

It had been a long shot. How the hell had it just arrived? From the wide-eyed look Finn had, exactly the same thought had landed in his brain.

“Run that past me again. It was on the kitchen table?” he said.

“Yeah.”

He scraped a hand over his face, leaving it covering his mouth for a moment, before saying, “How?”

“I don’t know. And Lena said the bracelet’s not from her.”

His gaze swivelled from the book to me. “I locked the doors. I *always* lock the doors. And today of all days… I locked the fucking doors, I swear. Only Mum has a key.”

"I know. And they're not from your mum."

He massaged his jaw. "Stephen? To wind you up?"

I shook my head. "He's only out today, and the bracelet arrived on Monday. And anyway, he'd just smash the door down and trash the place. He wouldn't leave us *gifts*."

"So who? *How*?"

"I don't know."

He leaned forwards and picked the book up, turning it over in his hands and flipping through the pages. "What is it? What language is that?"

"I don't know. It's some strange mythology about these things that guide your spirit from one body to the next when you die, except one of them went rogue and killed someone too soon."

His head shot up, eyes wide. "How do you know? Did you read it? How? Are these symbols code, like A equals one, B equals two kind of thing?"

"No. It's nothing like that. I don't know how I could read it. I just could."

Finn stared at me for a moment, then leafed through the book, stopping with the page open at one of the illustrations. "This looks like the stuff you draw. Your dreams."

"I know. Keep going. Recognise anyone?"

He turned the pages, pausing when he reached my Realm husband. "What the…?"

"Go on," I said, my voice croaky. The picture of me was on the next page.

Finn saw it immediately and his eyes locked on mine. "That's you!"

"Mm. That's what I thought."

"Has someone seen your sketchbooks?" His brow crumpled. "I don't understand how your drawings are in a weird book. Or how the book got in the house."

"No, my sketchbooks are here. Only you and Rick and Billy have ever seen them." I chewed my lip. "The drawing right at the start? That's of a Guide – something that turns up when people are dying. That's what I saw on Tuesday."

Finn turned back to it, raising his brows in query. I scrambled up to fetch my sketchbook, opening it at the drawing I'd done after the elderly man had died at the gym. I turned the pad round and showed him. The pictures were almost identical.

He put the book back on the kitchen table as if he might catch something from it.

"I'm changing the fucking locks." He scrubbed his hand through his hair. "How did they get in? Whoever left this, how did they get in?"

His breathing came in brisk breaths, his face tight. He couldn't be at my side all the time, but he'd assumed I could be safe here. If someone was getting through locked doors to leave weird gifts on the table, they could get through locked doors and beat me to death.

He rested his backside against the sink, coffees forgotten, and I cuddled against him, wondering if I should say what was in my head. In for a penny...

"Do you think they're coming from the Realm?"

He leaned back, searching my face. "Oh, shit. You *genuinely* think that! Rea, the Realm is a *dream*. How can these things be coming from there?"

I fingered the embroidered logo on his top. "What if it's not a dream?"

He breathed steadily, saying nothing for a moment. "Rea, it's a dream. I don't know how these things are getting into the house, or who's breaking in, but it isn't someone from a *dream*."

I touched my forehead to his collarbone, breathing in his scent of body wash and *him*. "Yeah, I know. Ignore me.

I'm just tired."

He stroked my hair back, tucking a strand behind my ear. "I'll change the locks. Put a chain on. And you need to see the GP and get something to help you sleep." He kissed me. "Oh, Christ, sorry, I'm *starving*. What do you want for dinner?"

"I'm not hungry."

Seeing Stephen had stolen my appetite. Finn was right – Stephen *could* have hurt me outside the gym. Yeah, he'd have been caught on CCTV and that would have put him back inside, but it was slim comfort. And talking about the book and the bracelet hadn't helped.

Finn caught my eye. "Rea, you have to eat. Bolognese? I'll make it."

I eased out of his arms and perched at the table, thinking about the book while Finn made dinner. He slid a plate on to the table in front of me along with some cutlery and sat opposite. I picked over the food but my stomach churned and I felt nauseous. Eventually I pushed the plate away from me.

"Sorry. I'm not hungry."

"Rea, you need to eat."

"You have it."

Finn finished his meal in silence but didn't clear my plate as well, wrapping it in cling-film instead and putting it on the side, ready to go in the fridge.

"You might feel up to it later," he said over his shoulder though I knew I wouldn't. "Go through. I'll wash up."

I did as I was told. Finn joined me a few minutes later, wrapping me against him on the sofa. I smoothed my fingers over his face, feeling the roughness of a day's stubble on his chin.

"Thank you for not losing it tonight," I murmured.

He grunted. "Yeah. Well."

So it *had* been a close-run thing.

"Why does Stephen call you Cuckoo?"

I wriggled closer to him, closing my eyes. "Because he thought me and Helen stepped into his dead mother and sister's shoes, the way a cuckoo invades another bird's nest and pretends to be something it's not."

In some ways I could see Stephen's point. His mother and little sister had been killed in a car accident when he was thirteen, leaving just him and his father. Within a year, his father had married Helen, and I came along as part of the package. Ready-made happy families. Except we weren't happy. Or much of a family.

"I need to get hammered," I said.

"Is that a good idea?"

"No, but I don't care. Or need your permission."

"True. Beer or vodka?"

"Vodka."

He levered himself up and disappeared, coming back a moment later with a couple of glasses and an almost full bottle of vodka. I smiled.

Less than two hours later I was hideously, gloriously, near-catatonically drunk, despite Finn's numerous exhortations to slow down. When I asked him to refill my glass for the umpteenth time, he prised it from my hand.

"Nope. One of us has to think about your liver."

I rubbed my face, frowning.

"You need a pint of water." He stood up, hauling me to my feet. Thankfully he held me up while I swayed, waiting for the room to settle. "Come on. Water."

He dragged me to the kitchen, poured me a huge glass of water and dropped a large tablet in it which fizzed and chased itself around the bottom of the glass. He handed the glass to me once it had stopped.

"What have you put in it?" My words slurred messily.

"Just vitamin C. Drink it."

He held the bottle out to me to show me. I drank the water which tasted slightly of orange and handed the empty glass back. Finn smiled fondly.

"We should get you to bed. Do I need to carry you up to the bathroom or can you manage?"

"I'm too tired. I'm going to crash down here."

"You're not getting that make-up all over the sofa."

"Hmm."

I stood up and wobbled precariously. He laughed. "Feck. You really are legless, Rea."

Before I could protest, Finn plonked me over his shoulder in a fireman's carry and took me upstairs to the bathroom. He sat me on the edge of the bath, rummaged through the cabinet, handed me a bottle of make-up remover and stood over me while I scrubbed the war-paint off. He loaded up my toothbrush with paste and handed it to me, and I brushed my teeth obediently.

"Right. Go to the loo and then I'll put you to bed. I'll be outside."

A few minutes later, he deposited me on the bed. "Do you need a bucket?"

"I'll be fine." I flapped my hand at him then stopped as it made me even dizzier. "Ooh."

"Rea, is the room spinning?"

"Mmm. But if I rested my head on the floor it would stop."

"I'm getting you a bucket."

He disappeared, returning with a large bucket which he put next to the bed and another pint of water. I crawled up the mattress and he stripped me down to my undies and pulled the covers around me.

"Night night. You are *so* gonna regret this in the morning."

"Mm... Finn?"

"Yup."

"Thank you."

His face relaxed into a lopsided smile and he leaned over and kissed my forehead. "Get some sleep. And don't barf on the carpet."

8

Finn clattering around in the kitchen woke me and I scraped a hand over my face and hair, feeling like death warmed up. The light fired bullets through the backs of my eyes, searing paths into my brain and I squeezed my eyes shut. My brain flipped over fuzzy memories from the previous night and I groaned.

"Morning sleepy." Finn stood in the doorway to the bedroom, a mug of coffee clasped in his hand. "Christ, you look hungover."

I peered at him blearily. He was dressed ready for work – a pale turquoise polo shirt with the gym logo embroidered on it, over black jogging bottoms.

"How the hell do you look so good this morning? I thought I was only keeping pace with you." My voice sounded as if I'd been gargling with gravel.

He sat on the bed, grinning unapologetically. "Well for one, you drank about three times what I did and for two, you're half my weight even if you are only a few inches shorter than me."

I struggled into a sitting position, wishing that my head wasn't about to explode. "We got any Pop Tarts?" Part of me was craving sugar. Another part of me wondered if I was about to be sick.

"Sadly, yes. You keep sneaking them into the house when I'm not looking. Please don't tell me you want one."

I felt myself going green at the thought. "No, not yet. Make me a House Special?"

He put his coffee down and unwound his legs, returning a minute later with a glass of fizzing liquid. The House Special. Some vile combination of soluble vitamins, alka-seltzer and only Finn knew what else. Tasted like shit but worked a treat on hangovers. The trick was to down it in one. If you sipped it, you wouldn't make it to the end of the glass. I chugged it back and handed him the empty glass, grimacing at the taste. "Thanks. Sorry I got so wasted."

"No worries. Did it help?"

I shook my head gingerly and winced. Finn lay on the bed next to me, rolled on his side and used his bent elbow as a pillow. "Coffee? Or a cuddle?"

"Cuddle. Then a coffee. Then a Pop Tart."

"Not happening." He laughed, coiling his body around me. "Cuddle, coffee, then I'll have to get off to work."

I went to slip my arm around his waist but his top was rucked up and I ended up with my hand on his bare abdomen.

"Don't tickle me," he grouched good-naturedly.

I let my fingers brush the hairs below his navel, not quite tickling, but not quite not.

He grabbed my hand. "Okay. I'm making you a coffee if you're gonna tickle."

When he came back with the coffees, he wrapped himself around me again. "Can you face food yet?"

My stomach twitched and I swallowed hard. He laughed unsympathetically. "Yeah, thought as much. You're going green just talking about it."

He kissed me, his tongue catching the inside of my lip. I slid my hand under his t-shirt again, smiling to myself as his muscles contracted sharply. My hand was freezing. We didn't break apart for several minutes.

"Hmmmm." He rolled away, his expression soft. "I really *do* have to go to work. You're on the door this afternoon aren't you? I'm done at four. I'll go and work out until you're finished. What are you doing this morning?"

"I have a couple of things to finish up for Monday."

"Can you do that in the gym? I don't want you in the house alone. Not after last night."

"It's too noisy there this time of day. I can't concentrate enough. I'll go to the library. I need to have a last look at the designs for Monday and then I'm going to do some more on that weird book."

He held my gaze for a moment but said nothing. I knew he'd be happier if I went in to work early.

"You walking in?" I asked, nestling down in the pillows.

"Mm. Please don't tell me you want the bike because you'll still be over the limit until tonight after what you sank last night."

I shook my head as rapidly as my hangover allowed. "No, I was going to suggest we went for a run after work."

A bit of fresh air out on the country roads might do me some good – physically *and* mentally.

"You gonna be up to that?" He looked at me disparagingly.

"Another House Special and I'll be fine. No intervals. No hills."

He grinned. "Alright. No intervals. No hills."

Shit. We were going to be running for miles.

***

I settled down at an empty table in the library and unpacked my things. After a quick check over the designs, I put them away again. I needed to let my brain work on them subconsciously. I eyed the book.

"Where the hell did you come from?" I muttered,

fingering the edge of the cover.

Maybe we should have called the police, but no damage had been done. Nothing had been taken. Just the opposite, in fact. We'd have been wasting their time.

Would I still be able to read it today? Even if I could, I didn't think it would get me any closer to working out how it could have been left in the house. I pulled out my notebook, drew a deep breath and flipped the book open. It took a few moments, but slowly, the runes made sense and a story emerged.

Rebellion

Aegyir had form and substance but he was not satisfied. He wanted strength. If a spirit would bind to him, he could draw on its vitality. And so he walked abroad until he found another host – a man in his prime – and when he found the man, he touched him lightly over his heart and walked on. The bond between the man and the spirit dwindled and the spirit was forced to form a weak bond with Aegyir.

Aegyir looked at the spirit. "Give me the man's vitality."

"No. You will keep it and not shepherd it to a new host, the way the Elders intended you to."

"Give me the vitality."

"What about the character?"

Aegyir spat. "What use do I have of the character? Give me the vitality."

The spirit knew that when all of the man's vitality had flowed into Aegyir, the man would die. If Aegyir wouldn't shepherd the spirit to a new body and give both the character and the vitality to it, there would be nowhere for the character to dwell and it would be cast into Chaos. The spirit tried to break the bond with Aegyir.

"You think that you can return to the man?" said Aegyir. "I am a Guide. Once I have come to you, you must leave your host and join with me."

"And you are to take me to a new host. Will you do that?"

"Perhaps."

The spirit did not trust Aegyir and held on to his bond with the man, hoping to find another Guide to transfer him to a new host. Aegyir laughed. The man's vitality seeped away, as heat seeps from a fire allowed to go out, and eventually he died.

"Will you transfer me to a new host?" asked the spirit.

"No."

The spirit's vitality and character were in Aegyir, but the character could find no space to exist and became cast into Chaos.

I leaned back in my chair. This Aegyir seemed like a nasty piece of work and I wondered what happened to these energyless characters, floating around in Chaos, wherever and whatever that was. Did they ever find a new body? Or were they destined to stay in limbo, without any energy to allow them to give life to a new body? By the time I'd finished reading the next section, I thought that Aegyir was even worse. Not satisfied with the slow seep of vitality from host to him, he began ripping it out of people, killing them quickly. But he wasn't designed to keep the energy he stole from people and it ebbed away over time, meaning that he had to kill again and again, just to keep the form he had. If he didn't, he slowly reverted back to being a wraith – the ghostly form I'd seen outside the gym the other day.

I grimaced. This Aegyir sounded like some kind of vampire, sucking the life out of everyone, going on a murder spree, just to keep something he shouldn't have. Greed was the cause of far too many evils in the world – people wanting something they didn't have but taking it anyway.

I hoped someone had stopped the bastard.

***

The gym was fairly quiet when I started my shift and I wished I'd brought either my design or the weird book with me. Having neither, I let my mind run potential interview questions, mentally rehearsed my defence of why I'd chosen the design I had, and planned what I would wear. Between Maggie's comments and the feedback I'd had from Finn, Rick and Billy, I was happier with the 1940s style of font – reminiscent of old London Underground signage – and the colour palette of pinks and greys felt right. Finn popped by when his shift finished and said he was off to pump iron until I knocked off at five. We agreed to meet in the foyer once my shift on reception was over.

"I've got a backpack with me so I'll take everything home," he said.

"Thanks." Rather him than me.

By quarter past five, Finn was stowing the last of my bits and pieces in the rucksack and levering it on to his shoulders.

"No hills, no intervals. You promised," I said. "And to be honest, I'm not in the humour for miles and miles, either."

"Too many toxins still circulating?" There was a distinct lack of sympathy.

"Mm."

He laughed, fastened the straps on the rucksack so that it wouldn't bounce around on his back and we set off.

"Where are we going?" I asked as we jogged through town and out towards the hills.

Finn outlined a route we'd done a few times and I was relieved that although there was one hill, the circuit was fairly short. All things are relative of course. It was a brief foray for Finn but about as much as I could face today.

We passed the last of the shops and cut through a

children's play park to get to a footpath which ultimately led to the quiet roads near our cottage. As we turned on to a country lane, lined with hawthorn hedges, Finn picked the pace up. "Manage this?"

"Uh huh."

It was Finn's bliss-pace. After about a mile of it, he would be on an endorphin-high and happy to eat up the miles. I'd yet to experience a runners' high and thought they belonged in the same category as unicorns. We were running at a pace too fast to talk, but not so fast that I would be breathing out of my arse after a few minutes. I'd manage to keep up with him for the circuit. Probably.

We settled into a steady rhythm. I tried to keep my core strong and my limbs loose, the way Finn always told me to, but however much I did, I never made it look as effortless as he did.

"You gonna manage the hill?" Finn squinted at me.

I glanced ahead. A track led off the tarmac road and climbed steadily for a few hundred metres before eventually levelling off. "Maybe."

"Choice is short and sharp up the hill, or round the long route."

"How long?"

"Another mile."

"Short and sharp it is then. Don't leave me behind."

The hills near the back of the cottage made a fantastic running route, if you didn't decide to sprint up them when you were hungover. I would pick trail running over running on tarmac any day and the only things you encountered up here in March were amber-eyed sheep and other runners. In the summer there might be a rambler or two but most of them walked the more scenic side of the fell.

After the rain of the previous few days, a rivulet of water ran down the track making it muddy. And slippy.

Finn, with his ability to impersonate a mountain goat with his sure footing, charged up it. There was no way I would manage to match him, even if I hadn't been hungover as hell. Three quarters of the way up the hill, my legs screamed and my chest burned and we still had the steepest bit of the hill to come. Finn had barely broken sweat.

"Nearly there!" he lied, running ahead, loose-limbed, his scruffy blond hair ruffling in the breeze.

I scowled but he couldn't see me.

I made it to the top of the hill without dying, but only just. Finn grinned at me, already part of the way down a bottle of water. I leaned on my knees, breathing hard, trying to pay off an oxygen debt of my own making.

"Don't get comfy," he said. "We're running to the bench.".

The bench was probably only about four hundred yards away but to my legs it felt like four miles. Finn was already sitting on it by the time I joined him. He pulled on the hoodie he'd had tied round his waist, his legs stretched out, his feet caked in mud. I flopped on to the seat next to him.

"Put your top back on; don't get chilled," he said.

I yanked it back on, drew the cuffs over my hands and flipped the hood up.

"Told you the view was worth it."

"Ah, Finn, Finn. You're always right. At least in *your* mind."

He was right – the view *was* worth it, though would be even better in summer. The bench – provided by the wife of someone who died thirty-odd years ago who had loved the view – faced out over the valley towards the south-west. To the right lay a thin track down to a quarry; to the left lay a valley clothed in crops. Dead ahead, in the distance, a high fell loomed, craggy and atmospheric and clamouring for someone to stand at the top, yelling, "Heathcliffe!" The sun was sinking fast but the light, even at this gloomy time of the year, was delicious.

Finn passed me the bottle of water and I drank deeply.

"Did you manage to read any more of that book?" he asked as he took the bottle back.

"Yeah. It talked about one of the Guides going rogue and murdering loads of people so he could stop being made of shadows and have a body."

"Nice! Anything else?"

"No. Reading it gives me a screaming headache, so I left it."

Finn wrinkled his nose. "How the hell can you read it?"

"I don't know. I look at the words and in my head I hear this weird language, and then it all makes sense."

Finn cocked one brow at me, but I had no better explanation.

"Ready to go back?" he asked.

"Yeah."

We set off and turned down a beech-lined road, the umber leaves still clinging on, ready to be ousted when the new shoots finally emerged. A light breeze rustled them, sounding like a whisper, and the birds tweeted and sang to one another across the road. Maybe Finn was right. Maybe running was the perfect panacea.

"This is not your place."

I blinked. Surely that was just the wind in the leaves. But it had sounded exactly like a voice.

"You need to return. This is not your place."

My pace slowed and Finn turned. "Okay? Stitch?"

"No. Nothing. Sorry."

We ran on.

"Aeron, this is not your place. You must return."

I stopped in my tracks. "Finn, can you hear that?"

He jogged back to me. "All I can hear is you breathing

like Darth Vader."

I shook my head. "Forget it. Sorry."

We started up again. So did the whisper.

"Aeron. You must return."

"Seriously, Finn, did you not hear that?" I stopped and stared at the hedge, seeing only dead leaves and the splintered ends of branches from where the hedge had been cut back badly.

"Nope. Still just you breathing. And birdsong and country stuff. What did you hear?"

"It sounded like someone whispering."

I stepped forwards, peering at the hedge, my head tilted, listening.

Nothing.

I reached out one hand and rustled a few leaves.

Still nothing.

Finn frowned one brow and arched the other, making his face completely lopsided and I stepped back.

"Okay. Forget it. Let's go," I said, shaking my head and setting my shoulders.

I set off again. Finn caught me up and I could tell from his face that he was listening out to try to hear whatever it was that I had heard. The whispering had gone though.

***

Back home, after a hot shower and some left-over bolognese, Finn and I were curled up together on the sofa, catching the end of the main news and then the local news. The headline on the local news was about a woman's body being found up by the quarry. Police were treating it as suspicious and were asking if anyone had seen anything there.

"Oh, shit," said Finn. "That's close."

The quarry was barely a mile away. One end of it was

still working; the other had been allowed to return to nature and was loved by dog walkers and runners and those just wanting a ramble in the countryside. We'd run within 200 yards of the path to that end this evening, and frequently went running there. It was at this end of the quarry that the body had been found. A picture of the woman flashed up on the screen – a snapshot taken at a wedding given the hat she was wearing. I sat up.

"I recognise her."

Finn rolled his head towards me. "Yeah? Who is she?"

Her name was given as Elaine Cooper and I screwed my nose up. "I don't recognise her name but I'm sure I've seen her before. Recently."

Finn turned back to the screen. "You've probably seen her in Tescos or round the town."

"Maybe."

It felt like I'd seen her more recently than that, but I couldn't place her. It would come back to me once I stopped thinking about it. I twitched my shoulders, trying to shake off a feeling of unease.

My mobile rang. Polly, our immediate neighbour. I frowned. We weren't especially friendly with Mike and Polly, mostly because they saw only the tattoos and the motorbike and made a lot of unfounded assumptions. The couple in the cottage nearest the road, Ösk and Lena, were both nearer our age and better friends.

"Hi, Polly."

"Reagan? Sorry to bother you. There's a man outside your cottage, just staring at it. He's been there for a while and he seems really creepy."

"A man?" Next to me, I felt Finn tense up. "Describe him?"

"Tall. Chunky. Rough-looking."

Stephen?

My heart galloped and I wriggled away from Finn to scoot up the stairs and peer out of the bedroom window. I prayed it was nothing. After all, Polly would describe Finn as "a bit rough-looking" and I shuddered to think how she described me. But given that random objects kept appearing on the kitchen table, I didn't like the idea of *anyone* staring at the house.

"Okay. Thanks for letting us know," I said as I reached the bedroom door, Finn hard on my heels.

"No problem. I heard from Lena that your brother was coming out of prison, that was all."

"Step-brother. No relation. But thanks." My voice was clipped and I forced myself to breathe. "Thanks, Polly. I appreciate it."

"It's okay. Is Finn home?"

"Yeah. He's right here."

"Good."

Finn cocked a brow at me as I rang off.

"Polly," I said.

I kept the light off and sidled to the window, bile rising and my breath catching as I recognised the figure outside. Finn stayed in the doorway, frowning. "What's did she want?"

"She said there was someone looking at the house."

Finn made as if to join me but I held my hand out to keep him back. I peered out at the lane below the window, keeping my body hidden from view.

"Is it Stephen? Feck, he'd better not come near this place!"

I wasn't sure what to say. My hands shaking, I fished my phone back out of my jeans pocket to snap a picture of Stephen before calling Helen. "Helen? Yeah, it's me." I crossed the room to Finn, grabbing the back of his sweatshirt and stopping him from pounding down the stairs to get to Stephen. "Stephen's here, staring at the cottage. You'd better get John to come and get him, or I'll call the police... Yes, Finn's with me... Helen, just get Stephen away from the house before something happens."

Pulling Finn after me, I went back to the window and peeked out again. As my eyes adjusted to the dark, I realised there were two figures opposite the cottage.

"Finn? Who's that next to Stephen?"

Finn looked out, still thrumming. "I don't see anyone else. Just Stephen."

"Next to him. About three feet away on our left, Stephen's right. He's wearing black. About the same height as Stephen. Is it one of his pals that came to the gym?"

Finn's head dipped closer to the glass, his breath misting it. "I don't see anyone else, Rea. I'm gonna go and ask Stephen to leave."

My hands tightened on his sweatshirt. "No, you're not, because I'm not sure you'll manage to ask nicely. And how can you not see the other guy?"

He was as clear a figure as Stephen. Was he the fucker breaking in and leaving things in the cottage? My heart lurched and my breathing faltered.

Finn frowned at the dark. "I don't see anyone else. Where is he?"

"On Stephen's right, almost directly opposite Mike and Polly's."

Finn shook his head. "Nope. Not seeing anything." He moved to where I was standing but still shrugged.

I took a harder look at the figure next to Stephen. As I did, he lifted his head and locked eyes with me. They were red.

I caught my breath, making Finn curl an arm around me. "It's okay, Rea. He comes one step closer to the house and I'll kill him."

I rested my palm on his chest. It wasn't Stephen I was suddenly scared of. The shadowy figure next to Stephen looked exactly like the thing called Aegyir in the weird book. *After* he'd killed the man.

Headlights swung into the lane, picking out Stephen's features. The light didn't illuminate the thing next to him. The car parked up and John got out. There was a muffled conversation and Stephen moved towards the car, his gait belying how drunk he was. As he turned, he walked straight through the other figure as if it wasn't there, though he staggered fractionally as he did so. John bundled him into the car and reversed back out of the lane. The shadowy figure gazed up at the cottage again – straight at me – and I shrank back from the window.

Finn coiled me against him. "It's okay. He's gone. I think we should tell the police he was here though, just in case."

"Mm. Thank you for not losing it and going out there."

He kissed the top of my head. "I was tempted. He shows up again, I may not manage to resist."

I pulled up the picture I'd taken to see if it showed Stephen clearly enough to send it to the police. It did. It also showed the murderous creature, Aegyir.

"*That's* the thing I was trying to get you to see." I held my phone out to Finn.

He squinted at it. "What?"

"The thing next to Stephen! It's the thing from the book!"

He took my phone from me and expanded the picture. "It's just black, Rea."

My breath huffed and I held out my hand. "*Here*. Head. Body. Legs." I stabbed at the screen. "*Here*!"

Perplexed blue eyes lifted to me. "Rea, it's just black."

I trembled. Someone kept breaking into the house. I was reading books written in runes. And now I was seeing invisible people. I rubbed my brow, tears prickling my eyes.

Finn took my phone back, saying nothing. I leaned against him as he called the police and sent them the picture, wondering if *they'd* be able to see Aegyir.

The call over, Finn bunted me. "Come on. Let's turn in; try to get some sleep."

I nodded but I didn't want to sleep. If I did, I'd open a window into my brain and Stephen would come marching in, trying to kill me again.

As we were settling down in bed and I was fighting to keep my eyes open, I remembered where I'd seen the woman whose body had been found at the quarry.

She was the woman who'd been glaring at me in the library, yesterday.

9

His fist connected with my cheekbone, whipping my head around.

"Slut! Traitor!"

Flecks of spittle landed on my skin. I opened my mouth, desperate to explain, but he raised his hand to me again.

"Save it. No one wants you here. No one.*"*

My eyes sought my husband, standing beside him, but he turned his back on me, lips pinched. My arms were wrenched behind my back and I was cuffed tightly and shoved forwards. I needed to explain. "Please? Please look at me?"

His broad back remained a wall of black leather. If only he would look at me, he'd realise that everyone was wrong about me. Surely?

"No one can bear the sight of you, Aeron," said the older man. My husband stalked away, stiff-backed.

I couldn't take my eyes off him. He had to turn and look. He wouldn't let me be taken away without one final glance? Could he?

He could.

I was marched down to the cells. Long hallways full of hatred and misunderstanding. I passed the body of Torfan – my little brother – being dragged away, his dead eyes staring at nothing. Aegyir had plucked his life-force from him, killing him instantly, but leaving him unmarked. Along with everyone else in my family. My tears caught in my throat.

So many dead. Orian should have told them.

Tears tracked down my face. I was hurled into a small, windowless cell, my knees banging on the rough stone floor, the sour tang of stale air filling my nose. One of the guards wrenched my arms back to remove the cuffs.

"How much do you weigh?" he asked. "The hangman will need to know."

I sat up, snatching at my breath, my heart thudding, sweat prickling my skin. Finn reached out and pulled me back to him, startling me, and I lashed out.

"Ow!" he said, voice thick with sleep. "Come here. Go back to sleep. It's just a dream."

Finn held me firmly against his bare skin, making small, drowsy, mumbling sounds. I nestled back against him and he was instantly asleep, as if the only thing that he needed was for me to be close. I rubbed my cheek against his chest, waiting for my heart rate to settle, wishing I could go back to sleep so easily, knowing I wouldn't.

It was only a dream. I knew that. The problem was that it was a frightening dream about the Realm. I could normally rely on it to provide comforting dreams – ones where I was respected and felt at home. Not ones where I was cuffed and being told I was about to be hanged. It had all felt so horribly real. I could almost feel the spittle as I'd been taken past those people. My arms hurt from being pinned behind me by the guards. Maybe I was just blending the nightmares I had about Stephen into the Realm. Maybe the sight of the shadowy figure had triggered this.

Finn shifted comfortably next to me and I smiled. He was the only man who had ever made me feel safe, valued, important. Even in his sleep he was protective, his arms coiled around me, his legs knotting with mine. I hoped that Stephen wasn't stupid enough to come back here, not even to stand and stare at the place, never mind batter his way in. I closed my eyes, trying to erase images from the backs of my eyelids, glad that the room wasn't pitch dark.

***

At work, only a few hours later, part of me was thankful it was busy because my brain was in overdrive. What the hell was that *thing* outside last night? However much I wanted to believe I'd imagined it, I hadn't.

Finn and I were both on early, finishing at two, and I'd taken my designs in, hoping to do snatches of work on them in quiet moments. But Saturdays were always busy, with a near constant flow of clients stopping to chat on their way in or out. The reception desk had a chest-high section facing outwards, with a desk area behind it. Separating the main entrance from the members-only area was a turnstile, right next to reception. Members and staff only needed to blip their card to go through, but invariably, someone would have left their card in their kit before washing it and need to get a replacement from me, which was a pain to sort out.

Eventually, I abandoned the design and tucked it back into my bag. I'd finalise it all in the afternoon, once we were back home and Finn was watching the footie. It was almost right. I hoped.

At just before noon, Finn sauntered up to the counter. "Lunch?"

"Yeah. Once Stacey arrives."

Finn leaned his forearms on the desk and dipped his head down to speak privately to me. "Has that guy been bothering you?"

"Which guy?"

"Behind me. Black t-shirt. Black jeans. Every time I've come past, he's been staring at you."

My gaze flicked over Finn's shoulder and back. "Yeah,

right enough, he's still staring at me, but no, he's not bothered me and I hadn't noticed him until you pointed him out."

"Okay. Call me if he does anything? I don't like the look of him."

I smiled. I was six feet tall with black spiky hair, multiple piercings, tattoos and heavy black eyeliner. In comparison, the staring guy could be a caricature of a maths teacher. I didn't like the fact he was just sitting staring at me though.

"Your charm's glowing," said Finn. "That's weird. Or is it like those mood rings in the crystal shop that change colour with temperature?"

I glanced down. The charm was bright blue like a gas flame. I looked at the man and felt ice inch through me as a slow smile crept across his face.

Blue for danger.

My breath caught shakily and Finn's attention snapped to me. "What?"

"Nothing. Just had one of those funny feelings."

"Someone walked over your grave?"

"Er. Yeah. Something like that."

Finn looked at his watch and pulled his phone out.

"Who are you texting?" I asked.

"Stacey. Telling her to get her arse over here. She's late. As usual."

We only had forty-five minutes for lunch and it wasn't flexible. Finn put his phone away and turned to face the staring man.

"Problem, mate?"

Staring-man shook his head, still smiling enigmatically. I moved so that Finn's body blocked the man's view of me, my skin prickling. Finn glared at him, but he didn't look away.

Finally, Stacey bounded up. "Hi guys! Sorry I'm late!"

She flashed a million megawatt beam at Finn, all teeth and tits. I rolled my eyes, slid from behind the desk and tucked my arm around Finn.

"Okay, we're off for lunch. See you in a while." I leaned on Finn to ease him away.

We had to pass the man to reach the food service area of the cafe. He maintained eye contact with me until I was level with him and then looked down at a newspaper on the table. I could feel Finn bristling next to me.

"Finn, leave it. We only have an hour and a bit to go after lunch and then we're out of here. He's just staring."

Who was I reassuring? Me or Finn?

***

As we turned on to our lane, my feet stumbled to a halt. Parked opposite our house was a police car.

"Finn."

He flashed me a quick look.

The door to the car clicked open and I nodded at the officer climbing out.

Finn's eyes widened. We made our way past Ösk and Lena's, and as we drew level with Mike and Polly's place, I saw why the police were here. Our front door hung from its hinges, the wood splintered to matchsticks. I bunched my hands, my short nails digging into my palms, a tremor that I couldn't fight working its way through my body.

"Shh. I'm here," murmured Finn. "And anyway, there's a dirty great copper here."

"Are you Finn Cullen and Reagan Bennett?" asked the policeman, meeting us outside Mike and Polly's. He wasn't dirty, or great. He didn't look much older than me and Finn, and barely reached Finn's shoulder. He was in uniform, though.

"Yes," said Finn. "Did Stephen do this?"

"Stephen?" The officer raised his brows.

"Stephen Gray."

The policeman flipped through his notebook to a clean page and wrote the name down. "Why do you think it's him?"

Finn's arm tightened around my waist. "Because he's just been released from prison after serving a conviction for breaking the door down and assaulting Reagan. And because he threatened Reagan as soon as he was released. And because he was hanging around here last night, drunk, staring at the cottage. We did report it."

More scribbling in the notebook. My gaze drifted to the door. The landlord had replaced the last one with a decently sturdy one after Stephen had kicked it in. Not sturdy enough, obviously.

We followed the policeman inside, tiptoeing past the splintered wood, the cottage freezing now it was open to the elements. Nothing was missing, as far as we could tell, though we barely had anything worth stealing. I wondered if we could get the door fixed that day or if we'd have to go and camp out at Rick's or someone's. The police had finished up – the forensics team had been and gone and the house was covered in fingerprint powder – so maybe we could make the house secure today. I didn't like the thought of it open to the world overnight.

A sledgehammer had been found on the strip of garden next to the cottage and had been bagged up and taken away. So the officer said. He also said it looked new. Bought specifically to smash our door in, then. I tried not to be sick.

"Did any of the neighbours see anything?" asked Finn, perching on the sofa next to me.

The policeman sat on the chair, leaning forward, his notebook on his knee. "The chap next door called us when he heard something, but he didn't see who it was."

Finn rolled his eyes, and I almost joined him. How very Mike. He probably hid when it was happening. At least he called the police.

The officer – PC Harrison – asked more about Stephen, made more notes and eventually left us to the remnants of our afternoon.

As soon as he left, Finn hugged me hard. "Hey, don't cry. Come on."

But his face was tight and his body taut, and my sanctuary couldn't, by any *stretch* of the imagination, be described as a sanctuary any longer. Snot bubbled out of my nose as I tried to stifle my sobs.

"Oh, nice!" Finn laughed, handing me a tissue. "Look on the bright side. Stephen's just broken the conditions of his parole. He'll go back inside."

"I hope so."

"Come on. Chin up. I need to get this door fixed. Help me measure up."

Finn was always better keeping busy. We measured what size door we needed, and he called Rick and Billy, who both left their work to come over. After a flurry of hugs that managed to make me feel worse, Rick went with Finn to get a new door leaving Billy with me. Despite Billy's assertions that violence wasn't the solution to problems, he brought a baseball bat with him. Finn's shoulders relaxed for the first time when he saw it. So did mine.

While Finn and Rick were out getting the new door, someone banged on the door-frame at the front. Billy scrambled to his feet, reaching for the baseball bat.

"It's okay. It's only Mike. I saw him pass the window," I said, staying his hand.

Billy headed out to the hall, returning a moment later with a shame-faced Mike.

"Oh, Reagan, I'm so sorry." Mike stood, wringing his hands, his floppy dark hair almost in his eyes. "I heard all the banging and smashing and looked out to see what was happening and saw a guy swinging a hammer at your door, so I called the police."

"What did he look like?" I asked, my throat tight.

Mike took a seat, wiping his palms on his ironed jeans. "I didn't really see. Tallish. Not as tall as Finn though."

He dried up. Billy narrowed his eyes, his lips a hard line.

"I didn't see!" said Mike, shrugging his shoulders up to his ears.

"Did he come into the house?" I asked. There'd been no evidence he had – nothing was missing and there weren't even any muddy footprints in the hall.

"I don't think so. The noise stopped and then he ran past the house. I didn't see his face. He had a black hoodie on with the hood up. Was there any damage inside?"

"No. Just the door."

Mike nodded, then met my eye defiantly. "I tried to call you."

My brows shot up, and I yanked my phone out of my pocket. Dead.

"Oh. The battery's gone." I slid the phone on to the table. "Did you try Finn?"

"I don't know his number."

To be honest, I was surprised he knew mine.

Mike jiggled his foot. "I'm really sorry I didn't see anything. Maybe Ösk and Lena did?"

I shook my head. "They're away today." Would Mike still have hidden if I'd been in when the door was broken down. I'd like to think that even Mike would have tried to stop Stephen from killing me. Ösk and Lena certainly would.

"Oh," said Mike. "Do you think it was your brother?"

I couldn't be bothered to correct him over the total lack of relationship. "Probably. Hopefully the police found some evidence."

He got to his feet. "I should leave you to it. I just wanted to pop over and say how sorry I was. Tell Finn I came by?"

"Will do. Thanks for calling the police."

Billy showed him out, stiff-backed and unimpressed. About ten minutes later, Finn and Rick's voices floated through the window, and I peered out to see the two of them carrying a door down the lane between them. They had it balanced on their heads, their hands steadying it from the sides, and I smiled despite everything.

By early evening, after much banging, swearing and mess, we had a brand-new door with fresh locks, a chain and two sturdy bolts. Rick had paid for it all, but both Finn and I were sure the landlord would pay him back. If not, we'd need more than the toaster-fund to cover it. Finn had added a chain and a bolt to the back door too.

"You two need an evening out," said Rick, sweeping up the last bits of crap from replacing the door. "Flicks or ten-pin bowling?"

"What's on?" I asked, preferring the cinema.

Rick listed a couple of things, neither of which would have been my choice, but they were better than staying in and fretting.

"Which is the least chick-flicky?" said Finn, threading his new keys on to his keyring.

We settled on a thriller that started in just under an hour. Rick gave the front door a final check while Finn fastened both the bolts and the chain on the back door, and we set off, the three men making an enclave around me.

As we all walked down the lane together, I hoped to God that we'd made the cottage impregnable. And not just from Stephen.

10

Sunday morning. The good news was that we got back from the cinema the night before to find the house intact. The bad news was that Finn was on early again, we'd both slept in, and were now trying to grab a hasty bite in the staff-room, at stupid o'clock. Well, *Finn* was grabbing a hasty bite. I wasn't working, so had all the time in the world. I was only there because Finn didn't want me in the cottage on my own. In fairness, I had no great desire to be in the cottage either, given everything that had happened over the last week.

I sat at one of the tables, the aroma of coffee displacing the gym's usual smell of perspiration and body spray. I had a bowl of some kind of healthy cereal in front of me that tasted of cardboard. Finn shovelled microwave-porridge down as fast as he could in between slurps of coffee.

He had a bug up his backside about *something*. Despite only having five minutes to eat his breakfast in, he was eyeing me as he chewed, clearly weighing up his words, and I knew him too well to think that what he wanted to say was something I wanted to hear.

"Just spit it out, Finn. What's up?"

He gulped down his last mouthful of porridge and bit his lip. "I'm worried about you. The dreams. All the nightmares. Do you think you should go to the GP? Maybe go back to counselling?"

His Irish accent was bursting through thickly. Was he worried about me or more worried how I would take his suggestion?

"I'm fine."

He blinked hard, his breath hissing, before looking at me, the blue of his eyes startlingly bright. "You're not fine. You're getting nightmares almost every night and even the nice dreams you used to have are now violent."

I opened my mouth to argue, and he glared at me. "Think about it? I'm only saying it because I love you and because I'm worried about you."

I swallowed my words. He reached across to hold my hand, his thumb rubbing my knuckles.

"Yeah okay, I'll think about it."

"Thanks. When are you meeting Lena?"

"Eleven."

She was coming over to help me choose my outfit for the interview. My nerves were shot to pieces and I could barely concentrate on what I needed to do for the interview, but I was also determined not to let Stephen spoil anything else if I could help it.

"Okay."

I ran my fingertip down the kink in my nose. "I'm sorry if I'm keeping you awake at night."

He sighed, shaking his head. "That's *not* why I want you to go to the GP!"

I finally looked at him properly, taking in the tension in his jaw and shoulders and the bruised look under his eyes, and regretted being snappish. "I know. But I'm still sorry."

His posture softened. "You taking the bike back?"

I shook my head. "You have it. When are we meeting your mum?"

"Half two. At the Farmers' Market."

He downed the last of his coffee, flinching at the

temperature, scruffed my hair up, and kissed the top of my head.

"See you at home. Call me if *anything* happens."

As soon as he'd gone, I pulled out the weird book, a pen and my notebook. It was too early for anyone sane to be here on a Sunday unless they were working so I had a couple of hours to myself to try to read some more. I made myself another coffee, poked at the soggy cereal in my bowl and opened the book.

After the parts that I'd already managed to translate, was a shortish chapter with no illustrations. Further on in the book were the pictures of me, my 'husband' and the man who'd assaulted me in my recent nightmares. I fingered my brow. The headache that had made my head scream each time I'd read the book was already poking at my brain. I leaned my chin on my knuckles, wishing I had some aspirin in my locker. I needed to know why there was a picture of me in the book; why there were pictures of the other people from my dreams. One similarity I could write off as a coincidence, but not all of this. Nausea poisoned my guts and I pushed the cereal away. How the fuck were my dreams in a book, written in runes? And *how* had it appeared on our kitchen table?

I turned to a new page in my notebook and studied the runes, waiting for the words to make sense, then read the next few pages.

Anarchy

Aegyir continued to kill, ripping the vitality out of those he came across and laying waste to the people. The Elders tried to reason with him but he would not listen. He had listened to their lies for too long, he said. He could have been powerful for millennia but instead had followed their rules and been nothing more than a weak slave, bound to do their bidding with no reward.

He told other Guides that the Elders had been misleading them for centuries and that they could stop being ethereal mist and be solid and powerful, if only they began breaking the code of the Guides that had been forced on them by the Elders. Aegyir showed the Guides how to take vitality and so become corporeal. Many of the Guides followed him, though many more stayed true. Those that followed were insatiable, killing anyone they came across, tearing the vitality from them. People fled, able to see the Guides now that they had form. The corrupt Guides needed to find a way to disguise their true identity.

One of the Guides found that if they sacrificed some of the vitality, they could adopt a different form and resemble the people. At first, they chose to resemble those still alive, but soon they began to hide the bodies of those they had killed and mimic their form. Now they could walk abroad in disguise, it became easier for them to form a weak link with the spirit of their victims and gain their vitality slowly. Many of the population were killed in this way and those that remained did not have the knowledge or the strength to defeat them. The people blamed plague and pestilence for the deaths.

I leaned back in my seat, chewing the end of the biro. How did you defeat a *thing* that looked like your neighbour and who could kill you by doing nothing more than placing a hand over your heart? How easy would *that* be? You would run away from something that looked like a monster – you'd be pretty wary of something like that – but your neighbour or a family member? I shuddered as I realised the implications. I took a big gulp of cold coffee to wash down the sick feeling I had.

What had happened to Aegyir? Had someone stopped him? Or was he still out there, ripping the energy out of people and then walking around as some kind of evil doppelgänger?

I massaged my temples and turned to the next section of the book.

The Realm

Many Outside were dead or dying and they could not stop what was happening. There were too few people Outside to tend to the farms. Harvests remained ungathered; animals were not fed. Men starved. Those that remained, feared that they would be annihilated. The people blamed a plague for the deaths but even if they had known it was the Guides, they could have done nothing. No one Outside was strong enough to take the vitality from the Guides and force them to become wraiths again.

Within The Realm, the Scouts brought news of the deaths. The Council was convened to determine if the Guardians should intervene. The Guardians were strong enough to free the vitality from the rogue Guides and trap them, but to do so was not without risk. There was debate, long into the night. The Realm and Outside had been separate for many years. Only the Scouts entered Outside. No one from Outside could enter The Realm. The Guides could not cross into The Realm and the lives of those inside The Realm were not in danger. Some on the Council believed it was The Realm's duty to help those Outside who were too weak to help themselves. However, many on the Council followed the stance of the First Lord, Eredan, and believed that The Realm should remain separate from Outside; that the affairs of men were of no importance to The Realm. The Seers warned of war within The Realm and urged caution.

I broke off, fuming. Thousands of people were dying and these guys in The Realm, wherever that was, didn't want to get involved. Sure, there was some risk to them, but their moral duty was to help, wasn't it? My mind ran over the various wars raging across the world, and realised that maybe it was *our* moral duty in the here and now to help, but that little was done.

Was Outside the Earth? The Black Death that had swept across Europe in the middle of the fourteenth century had killed millions. There'd also been Spanish flu after the First World War. I remembered that there'd been major changes to the social structure in England after the loss of so many people. During the Black Death, there hadn't been enough people to bring in the harvest or tend to animals and so as well as the deaths from the plague, there had been starvation. Was this book describing what had happened almost seven hundred years ago? Or the problems after the war?

I shook myself. The Black Death was caused by a bacterium wasn't it? Or a virus or something. Flu was a virus. It wasn't caused by some supernatural beings going rogue and ripping the life out of people. Even if it *did* relate to the middle of the fourteenth century or the beginning of the twentieth, it was merely a story, made up to explain why lots of people died.

I studied the picture again. It was the man who had sent me to be hanged in my nightmare – First Lord Eredan. He seemed a thoroughly horrible piece of work all round. He wasn't prepared to help defeat the rogue Guides who were decimating the population and had hit me and wanted me hanged in my dreams. Reading over this section again raised more questions than it answered – what or where was The Realm? What were Scouts and Seers and Guardians? Who was the Council? Why did only Scouts go Outside and why could no one from Outside go to the Realm?

My eyes were squiffy from focusing on the strange letters in the book and my head pounded. Maybe I should call it a day and do some more tomorrow. My gaze danced over the pictures of me and my 'husband', piquing my curiosity. What was their role in all this? Perhaps if I knew that, it would explain why First Lord Eredan wanted me to be hanged. Because *clearly*, my dreams were related to the place in the book.

I stretched my back, flexed my shoulders and read the next few lines, my heart racing.

> One Seer saw the war more clearly. Lilja was a minor Seer of the family Keriell but she said that she could see the coming war.

I stopped, my mouth suddenly like the Sahara. Lilja. In my dreams there was someone called Lilja. We'd talked about her forthcoming marriage. She was the one warning me of blue for danger. I read on.

> Lilja said that she could see Aegyir in The Realm. The Council was reconvened. No one knew if Aegyir would be able to force his way into The Realm if he gained enough strength. The Elders had always told us that only those from The Realm could cross. Anyone from Outside had to be invited in, before they were able to cross the portal. But who from The Realm would invite in Aegyir?
>
> The Council was split. Some believed that Aegyir would be able to cross if he gained enough vitality. Others thought that The Realm would remain impregnable. As time in The Realm passed and the arguments flowed from one side to the other, many died Outside.
>
> Aeron, wife of Faran, was distressed at the rising death toll Outside and the threat to The Realm. She petitioned her husband to speak to the Council and urge them to help the Outsiders to defeat Aegyir and the other rogue Guides. Faran spoke passionately to the Council about the plight of those Outside. He also warned that if Aegyir and the other Guides became strong enough to force their way into The Realm, they might be too strong to be defeated by the Guardians, and that Realm lives could be lost. The Council was split and voted. The majority of the Council chose not

to intervene in the affairs of Outside.

Aeron – me. Faran – my husband in The Realm, and also for years in my dreams. I fingered the pictures of them. I'd heard the names before, in my dreams, but I'd also heard the name Aeron being whispered somewhere else. I wracked my brain, trying to place where, then I remembered. When I'd been out running with Finn, by the beech hedges. *"Aeron, you must return."*

I closed the book abruptly. My headache had settled in for the morning and none of this made *any* sense. Here were people from my dreams, appearing in what read like historical tales, but my dreams weren't *memories*. I hadn't *lived* this.

I hesitated, a thought clanging loudly. Perhaps I *had* lived this. Didn't some people claim they could remember past lives? Perhaps I dreamed of mine.

I shook my head. I was always about the same age in my dreams as I was now in reality and had been throughout all my dreams, even when I was a child. Maybe I just didn't remember any other parts of that life.

I gave up. Reading the book gave me an unholy headache and didn't solve any of my questions. I needed to clear my head before meeting Lena. I packed everything away and rinsed out my mug and bowl.

Finn was right. I should see my GP; go back to counselling. Concentrate on the interview.

Leave all of this alone.

Except I knew I wouldn't.

***

Just after eleven, Lena banged on the door and tried to walk in, just as she always did. The door jammed on the chain. I hurried through to open it.

"Sorry. After yesterday..."

She swept me into a hug. "Polly told me! God, are you okay?"

"I'm fine." I extricated myself. "Finn and I were at work when it happened. Mike called the police. Polly was out."

I closed the door behind her and debated putting the chain back on. In the end, I just dropped the snib on the Yale lock.

"Polly said Mike hadn't seen who it was." She shot me a look. "Useless twat!"

I laughed.

Lena was wearing a long, sage-green skirt and knee-high lace-up brown leather boots. Bangles clanked at her wrists and a multitude of long necklaces hung around her neck, cascading over a frilled shirt. She'd put her white-blonde hair up in a messy bun but strands made their bids for freedom from every angle. I smiled to myself. Her personal style was a world away from the dark skirt-suits and crisp shirts she wore for her job as an accountant.

She and her partner Ösk had moved into the first cottage in our row of three a few months ago. Ösk had joined the gym and knew Finn pretty well.

"Kettle's just boiled. Want a coffee?" I ushered her down the hall to the kitchen.

She grinned. "Go on then. You on your own?"

"Mm. Finn's at work. He'll be back soon."

An odd expression flitted across her face. I was never entirely sure how Lena felt about Finn. Sometimes I got a vibe from her that she fancied him; other times I wondered if she disapproved of him for some reason.

She followed me to the kitchen and sat at the table while I started to make coffees.

"So, what are you planning on wearing tomorrow?" she asked.

Had we been closer in size, I'd have been tempted to ask if I could borrow something, but Lena stood a good six inches shorter than me and was at least a size skinnier. There was barely a scrap of fat on her, but then, there was barely any muscle, either.

"Some black trousers I have and a white shirt, and a jacket I got from Oxfam." I didn't own many professional clothes and couldn't afford to buy any new ones.

She wrinkled her nose. Lena most certainly didn't buy her clothes from Oxfam. "What's the jacket like?"

"Kind of a soft grey. It's nice!"

"Okay. Go put it all on. I'll finish the coffees."

Two minutes later, I was back in the kitchen and Lena was scrutinising my outfit.

"I don't like the white shirt. The trousers are good and you're right, the jacket's lovely. Good find! But the top... I can lend you a shirt that would be perfect."

"It wouldn't fit me. The sleeves would barely make it past my elbows! Ösk's shirts would fit me better!"

"True. Never mind then. It'll be fine. I'll lend you some bling though." She caught my expression. "Work bling. Not stuff like this." She jangled her necklaces, then paused, fidgety. I waited. "Who was it outside, the other night? Polly said that there was someone staring into your cottage. Was it Stephen?"

I sat down at the table, opposite her. "Mm. I called Helen and his dad came and took him away. He was drunk. Stephen, not his dad."

"And Finn was okay about it?"

I snorted. "Finn was Finn. He was mad as a hornet's nest but saw enough sense to wait for John to come and take Stephen away."

"Do you ever get worried that Finn will totally lose it and end up in trouble?"

I laughed. "Every day."

Lena bit her lips together, her gaze flitting over the mugs on the table. Eventually, she took a deep breath. "Ösk said he saw Finn squaring up to someone on Thursday night. Was that your brother too?"

"Stephen's not my brother. He's the son of the man my adopted mother married. I don't even know if there's an actual term for that. But yes, he and Finn had words on Thursday. Why?"

She scratched her ear. "I don't know how to say this."

I eyed her, wondering what this was all about. "Just say it."

She took a long breath before answering. "You don't ever worry that Finn will hit *you*, do you?"

I burst out laughing. "Christ, no! The *last* person on this earth to hit me would be Finn. Where's this coming from? Polly?"

Lena tipped her head in acknowledgement. "Mm."

"Well, Polly should know better! She lived next door when Stephen almost killed me. No, *Finn's* never the one I have to worry about."

I tried to blank the image of the door smashed to smithereens only yesterday.

"Okay. It's just with Finn's reputation—"

"His reputation? What reputation?"

She shuffled in her seat, her fingernail picking at a scratch in the table's surface. "I'm not sure you'd want to meet him in a dark alleyway."

My temper made my skin prickle. She may only have known us for a few months, but she surely didn't think *that* of him. "*Finn*? Trust me, you'd be safer than houses with Finn in a dark alleyway. Is this what Polly's been saying?"

"Mm."

That figured. I breathed steadily, trying not to snap at

her. "Lena, you know me and Finn better than Polly and Mike do, even though they've been our neighbours for *years*. Neither of them can see past the tattoos and the motorbike. Yeah, Finn has a temper, but it would *never* be directed against me. Or any other woman. His dad, or Stephen... well, that might be a different matter, but only because they've hurt people he loves, not because Finn's any kind of thug!"

Her posture softened. "That's what I hoped, but Polly was pretty certain he wasn't such a nice guy. And he's chunky... If he lost it..."

"You think I'd stay with a guy for seven years if I thought even for a *moment* he'd hit me?"

As soon as the words were out of my mouth, I thought of Alison Cullen who'd stayed with a man who hit her for well over twenty-five years now.

Before Lena could answer, the front door banged and the man in question arrived home.

"Hi, Lena. How are you?" He tossed his kit-bag into the corner of the kitchen and leaned over to kiss the top of my head.

"Fine thanks. How are you?"

She blushed. Guilt at having just accused him of potentially hitting me? Or *did* she fancy him?

"Oh, I'm grand thanks. We're going to the Farmers' Market this afternoon. You and Ösk coming?"

"Maybe."

"Is that your outfit?" Finn nodded at me.

"Mm. Lena's not sure about the shirt. She offered me one of hers but I don't think it would fit."

"What don't you like? The fact it's all black and white and grey? No, I'm not sure about that either. I think your green one would be better. Bring out the colour of your eyes." He touched the side of the kettle and flicked it back on.

"Since when have you been a fashion guru?" I said.

"Since about a minute ago." He grinned at me, getting a mug out and spooning coffee into it.

"Actually, I agree with him," said Lena. "Green's good on you. And you need a splash of colour."

I held my hands up. "Fine. Stop ganging up on me. I'll wear the green top!"

Lena stood, squeezing out from behind the table and shimmying past Finn. "I should go. Good to see you both. Maybe see you at the market?"

Finn showed her out while I scooted upstairs to change out of my interview outfit and hang it up. I put a bottle-green green top with it and stood back to look at it at it. Yeah, they were right about it needing a splash of colour.

Finn joined me in the bedroom to change out of his work clothes and into jeans and a t-shirt. I debated telling him about what Polly had been saying to Lena, but decided against it. Finn would be hurt that she'd even considered it.

"No sign of Stephen?" Finn pulled a dark sweatshirt on over his t-shirt.

"No sign."

"Good."

I hoped we wouldn't come across Stephen at the market. I needed a normal, stress-free day for once.

***

The Farmers' Market was held once a month in the centre of town and Finn and I strolled down to it after lunch. There were usually about twenty stalls, with offerings from a local micro-brewery alongside a number of food producers selling meats, jams, bread and cakes, and cheese. Down one aisle, away from the generators, were stalls selling hand-made crafts – pyrography, turned wood bowls, and leather work. I wasn't entirely sure if any of the stall-holders were actually farmers, but there was always something to look at and usually small samples of the food to nibble on.

Rick was waiting where we'd arranged to meet him and the three of us pottered around the stalls, happily trying out small cubes of cheese, pieces of bread, slices of sausage on cocktail sticks, and bits of cake. Finn and Rick were impressed with the micro-brewery's offerings but both of them were far too distinctive to be able to get more than one free sample, however many times they walked past.

Just before three, I caught sight of Alison across the other side of the market square and leaned against Finn to get his attention. He waved to his mum and the three of us moved towards her. Finn dragged his feet.

"Um. Would you mind if I had coffee with Mum on my own?"

Presumably, he needed to talk to her about me. Or about us. Neither option made me all that happy but I nodded.

"Sure. I was going to ask her about what I'm wearing tomorrow, but Lena saw it and anyway, Rick can give me his ideas."

"Me? What do I know about women's clothes?" said Rick, surprised.

"As much as I do," said Finn, peeling away from me. "Catch you in about an hour?"

Once he was out of earshot, I glanced across at Rick. "What's that about? Finn trying to get ideas for my birthday?"

"Maybe."

I hoped it was all it was, but after Finn saying he was worried about me this morning, maybe it wasn't.

"Did you want to grab a coffee?" I said.

"What, at the next table, so you can listen in?"

I laughed. "No. Different place. We've been round all the stalls and if we leave it a while, the brewery might forget that you've already had a sample of each of their beers."

As we made our way towards a small cafe at the corner of the square, I felt there were more people than normal gawping at me. That said, people did stare at me quite a lot. Several heads swivelled to me as I passed, their expressions making me shiver. I strode into the cafe with relief, only to realise that the sole free table was next to the window. As we sat down, I noted that four or five people in the square marched purposefully towards the cafe, glared in at me and continued past. None of them stood out as the kind of person to have a beef about me – just a middle-aged couple, one woman with a toddler in tow, and a man about my age. But all of them walked straight towards the cafe, staring at me through the window all the way, then veered off when they were about two metres from the glass.

"Rick," I said, grabbing the menu and partially hiding behind it. "Am I being paranoid or are loads of people looking at us?"

He glanced around, frowning. "No more than usual. You okay?"

"Yeah. A bit jumpy since Stephen came out. Especially after yesterday."

Rick ran his nail along the checked tablecloth. "I didn't want to tell Finn yesterday, given the funk he was in over the door, but Stephen came in yesterday morning, asking about getting a new tat."

Any lightness I had, disappeared. "You going to do it?"

"Why not? I can't bar him, just because you and Finn have history with him."

"He smashed our fucking door down yesterday. You could bar him on principle."

Rick paused, his focus still on the table. "Any news from

the police on that?"

"No. No witnesses, other than Mike who couldn't give any real description. No fingerprints on the sledgehammer, apparently. I suspect there'll be no fingerprints from him in the cottage, either. Mike didn't think he'd gone in."

The waitress came over and took our orders for coffee. As she left, I tucked the menu back into its holder, scanning the square. Everyone seemed to have moved on.

Rick shuffled the packets of sugar in the bowl on the table. "The parole board wouldn't agree to his release unless they thought he was no longer a danger. He would have to have shown remorse and they would have to believe that he wouldn't re-offend."

I sucked down a deep breath. "Yeah, well, Stephen's always been good at getting people to believe his version of things. Manipulative little fucker. I mean, how long did Helen and John take his word over mine and Sarah's? It took him nearly killing me before they realised what he was capable of. Anyway, he's broken the terms of his parole by smashing our door in."

"Except there's no proof he was the one who did it." Rick's gaze finally lifted to my face.

"You think it wasn't him?"

Rick shook his head. "No, I'm pretty sure it *was* him. But if there's no evidence against him, there's no reason to put him back inside."

I caught my breath, a lead lump forming in my guts. Would I ever be free of Stephen?

"Did Finn tell you Stephen came to the gym on Thursday? Threatened me," I said.

"Finn didn't. Billy did. Said he wasn't sure Finn would have kept his cool if he hadn't gone out."

"Yeah, I think it was a close call."

Rick breathed steadily. "I told Finn he needs to be

careful. He throws a punch at Stephen and it'll be Finn who's inside, not Stephen."

I sighed, dipping my head and rubbing the back of my neck. "Tell me something I don't know."

The noise levels in the cafe rose as a group of women with their kids arrived and filled up two tables behind us. None of the kids seemed to have been taught how to sit still. One banged a spoon on the table, repeatedly, another was bellyaching about not having been allowed to have an ice-cream, while the other two were squabbling about which seats they would each have. Two of the women were chatting as if they were the only two there. The other was bent over her phone, ignoring the kid banging the spoon.

Rick fiddled with the sugar, making small piles of the packets. "Finn told me that you found a weird book."

My eyebrows shot up. "Er, yeah. When did he tell you?"

"This morning. I popped in to the gym to see Billy and grabbed a coffee with Finn."

Why the hell had Finn told him? And what else had they talked about? "What did he say about it?"

Rick didn't answer for a while, his focus on the table as he shifted the packs of sugar around. "He said it had pictures in it that looked like the pictures you draw – of that place you dream about. And that the writing was in runes." More building. More fiddling. "And that you said you could read it."

"Mm." Why was Rick so cagey?

"Do you still sleep-walk?"

I blinked at the change in direction. "Um. No. Why?"

Again, no reply for a while. I pieced it together. "Does Finn think that *I* made the book?"

Rick finally looked up. "He's not sure. He's worried about you. Said you were having bad dreams all the time. And you *used* to sleep-walk when you were really stressed, and you have painted things in your sleep. He wondered if you could have drawn it in your sleep and not remembered."

He'd certainly like that explanation better than one that involved someone being able to enter the cottage when it was locked up.

I opened my mouth to deny it, and then stopped. *Could* I have made the book? I couldn't remember ever buying a blank book like the one I'd found, but it *was* the kind of book I liked. The pictures showed scenes that could have come from my dreams, and despite the fact the writing was all in runes, I thought I knew what it said.

But although the pictures *looked* like mine, I knew it was a different artist – the technique was different. And the runes were printed. And when I'd done all those paintings in my sleep before, they were at best described as abstract, but more accurately described as looking like someone blind had done them.

"He's just worried about you," said Rick, brushing my knuckles with his and snatching my attention back to him. "Don't be mad with him."

I chewed the edge of my lip. "Is this what he's talking to his mum about?"

Rick's face softened. "No. That's something else."

"What?"

"Rea, I can't tell you. But it's nice. Don't stress about it."

I fixed him with a beady stare. "Is it about my birthday?"

He grinned. "Sort of. Seriously, I can't tell you. He'd kill me."

I let it drop, my head running back over what Rick had said. "Does he really think I made the book?"

"Yeah. Though he thinks you did it in your sleep and don't remember doing it. He thinks the stories in it are what you've been dreaming about. Rea… go to the GP. Tell them about your nightmares and that you can't sleep."

"Yeah. Finn and I had this discussion this morning."

Our coffees arrived and we made space for them. Sighing loudly, the waitress tossed all the sugar packets back into their bowl and glowered at Rick before clumping off. Rick smirked.

I took the chance to change the topic. "Anyway… when are you and Billy going to get a place together? You've been together for ages now."

He rasped his palm over his stubble. "Oh, I don't think we'll ever move in together. If it ain't broke, don't fix it."

"Cheaper to run one place than two."

"Not the most romantic of reasons."

I smiled. Rick always looked far more like he'd play a thug than a romantic lead, with the tats, dreadlocks and heft. "Do you and Billy do romance?"

"Fair point. But I don't think we'll ever live together."

I peered at him. "You and Billy are okay, aren't you? Nothing's happened?"

"No! No, we're fine. I just like my space."

"Have you two talked about it?"

"Yeah. Billy would quite like us to get a place, but…" He shrugged and turned to peer out of the window. "Jeez. You'd think no one had ever seen a tall woman and a black guy before."

I followed his gaze. The people who'd been staring before had now gathered next to the cafe. They locked eyes with me for a moment before moving on. My heart race picked up and I swallowed hard.

My eye caught a glimpse of the man who'd been in the gym yesterday – the man who looked like a maths teacher. His attention was on me as he walked, and he collided heavily with someone, making them stumble. He caught the man's elbow, steadying him. The man's body sagged and I tried to see what had caused it. The maths teacher man had his hand on the other man's chest, his head bent as if speaking to him. Slowly, the crumpled man straightened and looked straight at me, before the pair parted and went their separate ways.

"Do you know them?" Rick must have seen all of this, too.

I turned back to him. "No. But the guy in black was in the gym yesterday, sitting in the cafe, staring at me."

"Stalker?"

"Dunno. Hope not."

Behind us, banging-child and bellyaching-child ratcheted up the volume. I flinched, looking across at Rick.

"Time to go?" I said, nodding at the group.

"Yeah."

We downed our coffees and paid up. From the scowls being hurled at the noisy table, the waitress would quite like them to either leave or pipe down, before they drove everyone out.

We were pulling our jackets back on outside the cafe and contemplating going back around the market when Rick caught sight of Finn and Alison making their way across the square. Rick waved to them and a couple of minutes later they joined us by the cafe.

"Had a good chat?" I asked, pointedly.

Alison gave her son an enigmatic smile and Finn blushed.

"Are you ready for tomorrow?" she asked me.

"Ready as I'll ever be."

"Well, they'd be stupid not to give you the job."

I hoped she was right.

The four of us headed out and said our goodbyes at the edge of the market. Finn draped his arm around my shoulders and I tucked my hand into the back pocket of his jeans.

"So, what were you talking to your mum about?" I said, as soon as we were out of earshot.

He squeezed me. "You'll know soon enough."

I cast my mind back to the discussion we'd had a few days ago. "Please don't get me a dog for my birthday."

"It's okay. I won't."

"But it was about my birthday?"

Finn shook his head at me, eyes bright. "Wait and see!"

"I don't like surprises."

"I know. You might like this one. I *hope* you'll like this one. But stop fretting about it; it won't be for a while. I just needed to sound Mum out about something."

"Finn! Tell me!"

"Patience, woman! You'll know in a couple of months."

I still wish he hadn't waited to tell me.

***

That evening, we were at our other favourite once-a-month treat – the "Eat All You Can For A Fiver" buffet at the local Indian. They might have run it more often than once a month if Finn and I weren't such regular customers to the event. I mean, Finn can pack it away like it's going out of fashion, but I'm not far behind him.

The restaurant was busy – we weren't the only cheapskates in town – and we managed to get the last available table. The place had an unfashionable feel, with lots of red and gold decor that had faded past shabby without ever being chic. The tables all had crisp white tablecloths on, but the paintwork on the walls was scuffed and the chairs were all dinged. Tacky tea-light holders dotted every table, though their light didn't add to either the atmosphere or the brightness of the room. I don't think any of the lightbulbs in the place were more than a 40W equivalent. But even if you could only barely see what you were eating, it always tasted amazing.

The buffet was laid out according to spiciness of the dishes, with the milder curries near one end, progressing to the vindaloos at the other. Finn would, of course, always head for the hot end. I restricted myself to the milder end, with occasional forays to the middle of the table, not having Finn's lead-lined gullet.

We sat down, plates piled high. I don't know why we both did that – there were no restrictions on how many times you could refill your plate – but we always loaded our plates, just in case anyone changed their minds.

"Do you honestly think I made the book?" I said, stirring some of my korma into the rice.

Finn chewed slowly and swallowed, blue eyes full of caution. "Ah. Rick told you."

"Yeah." I'd been stewing since the afternoon.

Finn put his knife and fork down and took a swig of his beer. "It's crossed my mind."

"Except I'm not sleep-walking any more."

He put his glass down, positioning it carefully. "You never knew you were when you did. I'd just wake up and find you somewhere random, saying weird things like you needed to wash all the tar off your hands. You tried to make a fried breakfast once, despite the fact neither of us would have eaten it."

He had a point.

"Anyway," he went on. "It's a more sensible reason for where the book came from than it came from the Realm!"

I narrowed my eyes. "Did you tell Rick *that*, too?"

He arched his brows at me. "No. Cool it."

"I'm cool. I'm just pissed off with you that you talked to Rick about me."

"He's my best friend. And I'm worried about you."

"I know. But why didn't you talk to me first?" I stabbed at my dinner.

He sighed. "Because I knew I'd get this response. Rea, I don't want to fight over this. It was only Rick! And he's your friend too!" He reached across to hold my free hand. "Seriously. I don't want to fight about this."

I glared at him, shoving the piece of chicken I'd speared around my plate, making tracks through the rice. "You really think I'm sleep-walking again?"

He rubbed his thumb across my knuckles. "Rea, we've lived together for six years. *Every* time you've got stressed in those six years you've started sleep-walking. Every time. So, yes, I think the reason the pictures and the stories in the book are like your dreams is more likely to be because you drew them in your sleep than because someone is able to break into the house, magically arriving from your dreams."

"Why the runes?"

He gulped back another swig of beer. "Who knows? Why the fry-up at three in the morning? Why the idea your hands were covered in tar? Or that the walls were about to fall on the bed? Or *any* of the bat-shit crazy things you've said or done while you've been sleep-walking."

"But a whole book? Even if I wrote and painted all night, every night, it would have taken me weeks to make that. And anyway, the runes are printed."

My voice had risen and heads turned to us. Finn bowed his head slightly, shooting looks at me.

"*And*, I didn't do the pictures," I said, trying but not quite succeeding to lower my voice. "The style's different from how I draw."

"Even when you're asleep?" he said, his voice low and urgent. "When you did all those paintings three years ago, they looked nothing like what you normally draw."

"Yeah, because I had my eyes shut when I drew them!

They looked like shite!"

His eyes widened, imploring me to quieten and I turned away, biting the inside of my lip.

"Rea." He tweaked my fingers. "Rea?"

"What?" I snapped.

"Look at me."

I did.

"Let's not fight. I'm sorry. I love you. Let's enjoy the curry."

I rubbed my eye. "I didn't make the fucking book... I am going to see the GP though. Maybe he'll give me something to help me sleep."

"Thank you."

Behind the serving area in the restaurant was a telly, tuned to the local news. I frowned as I recognised our town. Subtitles scrolled across the bottom, and I screwed my eyes up to read them. The main headline said that another two bodies had been found at the quarry, near the place the woman had been found on Friday. Both were men and one had been named as Simon Fraser, a local man who worked at a nearby cafe. All three deaths were being treated as suspicious.

Simon Fraser's picture flashed up as the subtitles asked for anyone who might have seen anything at all, however trivial, to come forwards. Finn had seen me looking at the telly and turned to see what was on.

"Hey. That's the guy who was staring at you. Yesterday."

And the guy who I'd seen from the cafe this afternoon. My stomach flipped. First the woman in the library, now him. I peered at the screen. "Are you sure it's him? I thought I saw him this afternoon."

"Yeah. I'm sure. That's so weird. Where did you see him?"

"He was at the Farmers' Market."

Finn looked sceptical. The news indicated that Simon Fraser's body had been found that morning so the man in the square couldn't have been him. I breathed steadily. I must have been mistaken. He *had* been quite far away when I saw him.

The news moved on to announce that four people in a local hospital had died of flu and asked people to be vigilant. Viewers were also reminded that the seasonal flu vaccine was still available for free to those over 65 and to people with various health conditions.

"You wouldn't need a terrorist event to bring the country to its knees," said Finn, turning back to his food. "You'd just need a flu epidemic. Imagine if ten per cent of the population couldn't go to work for over a week because of flu. What if schools closed because there weren't enough teachers available? Then loads of people would have to be off work to look after the kids. Or if there weren't enough staff to run the power stations? The vaccine should be given to everyone, not just the ones with health risks."

He had a point, but my brain was still on the fact that two people who'd been staring at me were now dead, presumably murdered, and their bodies dumped within a mile of our house, and my appetite vanished. I poked at my food while Finn cleared his plate.

"More?" he said, nodding towards the buffet table.

"I'm not all that hungry. You get my fiver's worth."

I forced a smile. A slight frown flitted across Finn's brow, but he said nothing, just scraped his chair back and headed for the buffet.

Three plates of curry later, I wondered if Finn was going to come apart at the seams.

"You're not going to be able to *move* tomorrow," I said, grinning at him.

"Yeah, I may have overdone it tonight." He leaned back

in his seat, rubbing his belly and belching, before belatedly bringing his hand up to his mouth. "'Scuse me."

I laughed.

We settled up and staggered out of the door. The restaurant lay on the same side of town as our cottage and we started back down the street, past the shops and towards the spit-and-sawdust pub on the corner. Just after we'd passed, an all too familiar voice hailed us.

"Cuckoo!"

"Keep walking," I said, leaning on Finn.

"Hey! Cuckoo! I'm talking to you."

Despite my best efforts at keeping Finn moving, he stopped. Stephen stood just outside the pub, but he looked clear-eyed, not drunk. He must have seen us as we passed the pub window. He'd obviously managed to get some clothes that fitted him as the sweatshirt he wore looked new, under an equally pristine jacket, and clean trainers poked out beneath better-fitting jeans. His belly still flowed over the waistband though.

He held both his hands up and waggled his fingers at us. "Great invention. No fingerprints."

Black leather gloves clad his hands. Finn bristled and I pressed against him, trying to get him walking again. Stephen reached into a pocket and a phone glowed in his hand.

"Finn, keep moving," I urged. "He's filming us. You so much as look sideways at him and John will use it against you."

With difficulty, I propelled Finn towards our cottage. As soon as our backs were turned, Stephen called after us, his voice ringing down the street.

"Don't think you're safe, Cuckoo. Someone even worse than me wants you dead."

My blood turned to ice in my veins. It was Finn's turn to

keep me walking away.

Who the hell did Stephen mean?

11

Monday afternoon found me waiting to be called in for my interview. The room was bright and airy with comfortable seats upholstered in a vivid turquoise that reminded me of pictures of the Caribbean. A drinks machine sat on a counter at the side, gurgling occasionally. The last candidate to go in had been a man a few years older than me. He was now back and had taken off his jacket and made himself a coffee. He'd offered to make drinks for everyone, which was nice, but no one else wanted anything. An older man was pointedly ignoring everyone else. The first woman in hadn't returned to the room and another woman, a similar age to the aloof guy was now being interviewed. Everyone looked at least ten years more experienced than me. My designs were clutched on my lap and I felt stiff and uncomfortable in my clothes. I tried to remember to do my breathing exercises and hoped my antiperspirant would hold out.

The interview with the older woman finished and she too decided not to come back to the room. I wondered if it would be me or the other man up next.

Me, apparently.

"In you come, Ms Bennett."

A woman with blonde hair cut in a sharp bob that emphasised her cheekbones ushered me in. I felt naked without my war-paint and nose-ring and although I was confident that I looked good in what I was wearing, it wasn't as natural to me as jeans and a t-shirt would have been. I plastered a smile to my face, thanked the woman and followed her into the room.

There were two other people on the interview panel – another woman, slightly younger than the one who had brought me in, and a man about twenty years older than me with dark, piercing eyes.

"Let me introduce everyone. This is Lucy Ashcroft and Toby Hall, both senior designers here, and I'm Heather Green, head of human resources. Do have a seat."

I perched nervously, my mouth dry. Lucy Ashcroft had shoulder-length wavy hair of a colour best described as mousy, dark blue eyes, and a welcoming smile. She was dressed as if she modelled for Vogue – a blend of classic, well-tailored skirt-suit in grey, with a quirky twist of a loudly patterned cerise scarf and over-chunky jewellery – and seemed utterly relaxed. Toby Hall was a different matter entirely. His bitter-chocolate eyes gave the impression he was reaching into my soul and not liking what he found. He wore light-coloured trousers and an open-necked shirt, and his salt and pepper hair was cropped short, making him seem older than his line-free face suggested.

Like the room we'd been asked to wait in, the interview room was bright and airy, with pale walls and focal splashes of turquoise. The chairs were grouped around a light beechwood table, with the three of them clustered together on one side and me on the other.

Heather Green slid into the vacant seat. "Ms Bennett, did you get the brief we sent along with the invitation to interview?"

I nodded and pushed the folder I was clutching on to the table. We had begun.

The interview went on a lot longer than I'd expected but seemed to go well. They asked me how I'd come up with my original designs, whether I'd sought help, and what had influenced the changes from the original work I presented to the finished product. I answered as truthfully as I could. My partner hadn't much liked the initial colours; a friend from the college had offered advice and suggestions; I'd amended the colour scheme in light of their feedback. Yes, I was pleased with the final design. Yes, I would be open to further feedback. No, I wouldn't be offended if my designs were rejected by the team-leader though I would seek further feedback on why they hadn't been accepted. No, my partner wasn't in the design industry, he was a personal trainer but he was after all a member of Joe Public so his view was important too. There was much nodding from Ms Ashcroft and some meaningful glances exchanged between the three though I didn't know what the meaning was.

"Thank you very much, Ms Bennett. I've appreciated your candour," said Lucy Ashcroft at the end.

Was that good or bad?

Heather Green got to her feet. "We will be making our decision today and letting all candidates know. You're more than welcome to wait back in the other room if you want, but if you need to leave, that's fine. We'll call you with our decision."

"Oh, I'll wait, thank you." I had nothing better to do.

I returned to the waiting room. The guy who'd made the coffee was scrolling through his phone. I gave him a tight smile that he didn't return and went back to the seat I'd been in before.

I could see the main working area of the company through large plate-glass windows on one side of the waiting room. A small team of people sat at work stations and it seemed like a happy place to work. The staff all had smiles for each other and chatted together. At one point they all gathered around one person's computer screen, talking animatedly for a few minutes, though I couldn't see the screen to know what was being discussed. One woman moved away, returning with what looked like a large board with a minimalist design on it that reminded me of Japanese calligraphy, and pointed at it, her hand making large sweeping gestures as she talked. There was much nodding and agreement and then the group broke up and returned to their own work places full of good humour. I wanted the job more than ever.

My room was far less convivial. Silent-man had been called in, leaving only me and coffee-man who was still playing with his phone. I wasn't hypocritical enough to pass pleasantries with someone I neither knew nor wanted to get to know, so I stayed silent. Anyway, which would be worse? Finding out you liked them or finding out you hated them? I picked at my nails and waited. No one else seemed to have been in for as long as I had. I stole a better look at coffee-man. He ticked all the trendy boxes – the right kind of glasses, just the right amount of product in his perfectly cut dark hair, expensive clothes and a swanky phone that he was glued to. Mine was on silent but it flashed to indicate a new message. I sneaked it on to my lap and read it surreptitiously. It was from Finn asking how it was going. I texted back that I thought it was going okay but that everyone else seemed a lot more experienced than me so I didn't think I would get it. Almost immediately a message flashed back: you never know. I smiled. The man across the table raised his head, a slight curl to his lip and I looked away.

Ten minutes or so after the final candidate had come out and left, Ms Green returned to call in smug-coffee-man. My heart sank. He must have been given the nod in his interview.

I waited, fiddling with my phone, chewing my lip. *Fuck*! I had so wanted this job.

A few minutes later, the door opened again and smug-coffee-man stomped out. I frowned.

"Ms Bennett?" Ms Green smiled warmly at me.

I stood up, my heart racing. Ms Green ushered me back into the interview room.

"Ms Bennett, we would like to offer you the job."

My jaw hit the floor. Seriously? Belatedly, I realised Ms Green was still talking.

"Although you are clearly at the start of your career, we were highly impressed with your work. We were equally impressed with your candour over who you'd liaised with."

I tried to stop gawping.

"Uh, thank you, Ms Green. I'm delighted," I managed to stammer out.

"We need to discuss the starting salary with you."

What? I had *no* idea what to ask for. Thankfully, they opened the negotiations. Their first offer was at the low end of the range in the job advert, but was better than I got working part-time at the gym. My gaze fell on the papers in front of Mr Hall. A large figure was scribbled there, above the upper end of the range advertised, with an exclamation mark next to it. Had smug-coffee-man just priced himself out of the job?

I drew a deep breath and swallowed.

"Would you be prepared to go a little higher?" I asked.

Glances pinballed between them, but Ms Green nodded and offered another grand. I accepted. I wasn't going to push my luck, especially given their opening line, pointing out how near the *start* of my career I was.

There were smiles all round. Not least from me.

"The job starts at the beginning of next month if you're

available," said Lucy Ashcroft. "Heather here will get you sorted out with various bits of paperwork and so on, but let me welcome you to the team." She leaned over to shake my hand.

I was in danger of resembling a complete idiot with a grin splitting my face in half but I mustered some composure. Heather Green also shook my hand and said she could give me some of the paperwork now, but that she would need to send some things out to me. To be honest, I was so shell-shocked that I wasn't taking much in.

Toby Hall seemed far less happy about the decision. His gaze bored into me and he hadn't yet smiled. Perhaps he was one of those people who never did.

"I look forward to working with you," he said, a curious light in his eyes that was borderline sinister.

"Thank you."

There was a flurry as various pieces of paper were put in a card folder and handed to me and then Mr Hall was standing in front of me, his hand extended.

"Ms…" He hesitated. "Ms Bennett."

I took his hand. Instantly his face changed from the somewhat severe-looking mid-forties guy to a monstrosity with red eyes, dark wrinkled skin and a cadaverous face. Inside my head, a snarling, malevolent voice said, "You made me a lot of promises, Aeron. I *will* make you keep them."

I caught my breath and he released my hand. Immediately, he was the guy who had interviewed me. His focus dropped to my wrist. "That's an interesting charm. Where did you get it?"

I blinked. The bead was glowing a bright blue colour. "Um. It was a gift. From a friend."

"Indeed."

I was ushered out before I could say anything else. At

my wrist, the charm lost the blue light and was opalescent again.

I dug my phone out and sent an elated text to Finn. One pinged back almost immediately claiming he'd never had a shred of doubt over it.

I smiled, the charm-bracelet catching my eye.

Blue for danger.

I rubbed my lips, my smiles gone. What the hell had I seen just now?

***

Back home, the image of the thing that Toby Hall had morphed into still flooded my head. Finn wasn't due to get in from work for an hour, so I made myself a coffee and fished out my sketchbook. I pencilled a picture of Toby Hall, and next to it, an image of the demonic monster that had appeared while he was shaking my hand. Underneath, I wrote out what I'd heard in my head. I could swear that I'd never seen Toby Hall before, but the demon was exactly like the picture of Aegyir from the book, *and* the thing that had been staring at the house.

As I put the finishing touches to my drawing, doubt crept in. Had I *actually* seen the man change? Was I merely getting muddled with the things I'd read in the book? But if I *had* drawn the book while sleep-walking, I must have seen the thing before I'd drawn it. Unless I was imagining everything. The circular arguments were doing my head in and I packed everything away, frustrated.

Finn arrived home with the biggest bunch of flowers I'd ever seen.

"Either you've had an affair or I've just landed my dream job," I said, taking them from him with a grin.

He picked me up and swung me around, kissing me hard. "Well, I've not had an affair, so I guess you must have landed your dream job. Well done, Rea. I knew you'd do it."

"Ha. Well you knew better than me then. The other people there for interview were *far* more experienced than me, and I think they offered it to another guy first! I think he asked for too much money, which is why they gave the job to me. I'm cheap."

He stuck his bottom lip out. "Maybe, but you got the job, and it's better money than you get at the moment. *And* it's what you want to do. When do you start?"

"Beginning of the month. Sorry, I haven't made any dinner."

"Thai takeaway?"

"Ooh. Expensive. We *must* be celebrating!"

He kissed me again. "Seriously, well done. I am so proud of you. Choose some takeaway then tell me all about it?"

***

After dinner, I clicked the telly on and surfed the channels until I found the national news, wondering if there was any update on the bodies found at the quarry. Our town was the main bulletin again. Yet another body had been found up at the quarry, three days after the body of Elaine Cooper had been found and in a spot not far from the two found yesterday. The police were saying the deaths were suspicious and that all were thought to have occurred where the bodies had been found.

"Police locally have named the victim as Toby Hall, a forty-four year-old man with a wife and twelve year-old son."

I almost dropped my glass of wine as a picture of the man who'd interviewed me flashed up on screen.

"What?" said Finn.

"He interviewed me. He was the one who creeped me out."

"Police think that Mr Hall was attacked while walking his dog and are asking for anyone who was in the Wood Lane Quarry area between lunchtime and eight o'clock this evening to come forward," intoned the newsreader, before moving to a new topic.

I put my glass down on the table before I spilled it. "I can't believe it. I met him this afternoon."

"Are you sure it's the same guy?" said Finn, turning the sound down on the telly.

"Mm. Here. Look." I dug my sketchbook out and handed it to him, open at the right page. "I drew him when I came back."

Finn scanned the pictures and frowned. "What the hell's the thing on the right?"

I hesitated, tucking my legs up on the lumpy sofa and fiddling with my charm-bracelet. "Okay. Don't think I'm mad. When he shook my hand at the end, after they'd offered me the job, his face changed so he looked like that."

He quirked a brow up. "A demon? And what's this underneath?"

"That's what I heard in my head when he was looking like a demon."

"Who's Aeron?"

"It's the name everyone calls me in my dreams," I said slowly. The name I kept hearing being whispered around me.

I recognised Finn's expression. It was the one he always gave me when I was drunk and spouting nonsense.

"I swear! I saw his face change and I heard him say that in my head. And now he's dead!"

He rubbed his hand over his hair, leaving it spiked up. "Rea. You sound utterly deranged. You're just sleep-deprived and mixing up your dreams with stressing about Stephen and the job, and then the relief at getting the job has made you hallucinate or something. It's a bit alarming that he's been murdered though." He hesitated, his eyes drifting back to the telly, even though the news had moved on to something else. "Hang on, they said they were looking for people who'd been in the Wood Lane Quarry area between lunchtime and eight. You saw this guy in your interview and you weren't out of there until after four. You should call the police and tell them that."

I curled my toes up. "I'm pretty sure that his colleagues will be able to tell them that."

"Call them."

"And say what? That their timeline is wrong because he was interviewing me? They were asking for people who'd been in the Wood Lane Quarry area over that time presumably because the murderer could have been there before the attack on this guy. Maybe he'd tried to attack someone else. Maybe they think he lay in wait for ages or was scouting the area out or something. They must know he was at work today."

"Just call them!"

I sighed, pulled out my phone and called 101.

The call over, I poured myself another glass of wine, unsettled. Was this going to come back and bite me in the arse? The charm that had turned up out of nowhere had glowed blue three times now and every time, the person nearest me had been described as a murder victim within hours.

Blue for danger.

Maybe the danger was me.

12

"Aeron, you must return."

Lilja was standing in front of me, her face full of concern. Mist swirled around us, making it impossible for me to locate any landmarks. Her rose-pink jacket matched her cheeks and her eyes were bright with unshed tears.

"Aeron, listen to me! You must return. Lord Eredan will forgive you... Lord Eredan will need *you."*

"And Faran?" My heart lurched at his name.

"He'll want you to return."

I turned away, snorting. "Are you saying that as a Seer or because you think I want to hear it?"

Lilja caught my hands, her hair falling forwards. "Aeron? Please! You have to return. Make your peace with Lord Eredan and Faran. Aegyir will kill you. He wants revenge."

Panic rippled through her voice but I turned my head away. How could I return after all that had happened?

"It isn't a plague."

Her voice was suddenly calm and I looked back at her. "What do you mean?"

She bit her lips together. "Just like last time. The Outsiders think it's a plague, but it's Aegyir, gathering vitality the slow way. He's going to kill you. Come home."

"I am *home."*

She grasped my hands so hard it hurt. "Read the book. If you won't come home, you'll have to stop him, before he kills everyone."

Her voice ricocheted around my head as I woke. I rubbed my palm over my face and peered around the bedroom. The night light was on and the room was bathed in a comforting glow. There was no one in here with us. How could there have been?

Aegyir. The Guide who had turned into a monster and begun stealing people's life-force. The thing Toby Hall had turned into. Toby Hall who was now dead.

Aeron. My name in my dreams. The name Aegyir had called me at my interview. The name whispered by the beech hedges. The name in the book.

How did Reagan Bennett fit in?

I had to finish reading the book. Work out what the hell was going on. Whatever Finn thought, I hadn't written it myself while sleep-walking.

***

I'd been on a short shift spanning lunchtime and was now back home. Finn and I had already had a fight about this, but I couldn't spend every minute I wasn't at work cowering in the staff-room or hiding out at the library, or Stephen had won. That said, I locked the door and put the bolt and chain on. My dreams still circled my brain, so I grabbed the laptop and a large mug of tea and settled in the bedroom, where no one could see me if they peered in the windows.

I spread out the laptop, my notebook and the mysterious book on the bed and sat cross-legged on the faded duvet, chewing the end of a biro. I definitely hadn't made this book and nor had Finn, so someone had brought it to the cottage. I had to believe they'd done that for a reason, along with leaving the charm-bracelet. Who though? Lilja? How did someone from my dreams manage to leave me things? But who else could have left them? I ran through my thin list of friends, discounting all of them. None of them apart from Lena would just walk in and leave things – certainly not without also leaving a note. And no one knew about my dreams apart from Finn.

Okay, so if I accepted that these had come from Lilja – however that was possible – could I also assume that what it said in the book was true and that what she told me in my dreams was linked to it?

"The plague is not a plague. Just like last time. Aegyir is gathering vitality the slow way."

Aegyir could steal your life-force either from a light touch that drained you or by ripping it out which killed you instantly. If he was gathering it the slow way, people would be dying from what seemed like a plague. The only plague I could think of was the Black Death, but people were covered in sores or lumps with that, weren't they? I fired up the laptop and searched for information on the Black Death. Much of it was as I remembered from history lessons in school – millions of people died, the population was decimated, it was indiscriminate in who it killed. Then my eye snagged on a link to 'pneumonic plague' and I clicked on it. No buboes; people died within a few days; symptoms very similar to flu in many ways. I caught my breath, my heart missing a beat.

Flu.

I pulled up some news pages to see how bad the current flu outbreak was. Bad. And centred around here.

"You wouldn't need a terrorist event to bring the country to its knees. You'd just need a flu epidemic."

A link at the bottom of one of the articles took me to the major flu outbreak in 1918. Unusual in that it killed the young and the fit. I chewed my pen, feeling queasy. If I was going to steal someone's vitality, I'd go for those who seemed to have the most. Was the 1918 outbreak actually Aegyir? And now Aegyir was taking vitality again and was coming to kill me. According to Lilja.

If I had to choose, which would I go for? Quick and painful? Or long and lingering? Probably long and lingering. Give me a chance to say all the things I wanted to say to people before I died. But there would be several days of fear; of knowing this was it. I wasn't sure how I would cope with that, so maybe quick and painful was better after all. I fingered the drawings in the book. Aegyir ripped the ball of light out of a person and then they were dead.

The bodies at the quarry. They'd all made my charm glow. And then Toby Hall, who should be dead by the time of my interview, turned into Aegyir.

I rubbed my eyes. This couldn't be real. I tried to see it all how Finn would. I was tired. I'd been stressed about the job interview and about Stephen. Okay, the charm and the book were more than a bit weird, but the rest was surely the result of an overactive imagination colliding with a lack of sleep. Of *course* I was dreaming about evil things coming to get me and to get revenge – I'd had Stephen put away in jail and now he was out and threatening me. The book was a collection of myths and fantasies, nothing more. My head was muddling my fears about Stephen being released with these weird stories. But however hard I tried to write it off, questions stung at me like a swarm of bees.

How was Toby Hall still alive in the afternoon of my interview? The police seemed to think he was dead before then. And why did the charm-bracelet keep glowing blue? The temperature hadn't suddenly changed while I was in the library, or any of the other times it had glowed, so it wasn't temperature-dependant like a mood ring. What was the danger?

I turned to the picture of me – Aeron. Everyone had a doppelgänger, didn't they? Perhaps Aegyir just *thought* I was this person. Perhaps Lilja did.

So why did I dream of her and of the Realm so much?

I stretched out my legs and punched the pillows into a heap behind me.

"Come on, Reagan, you're smarter than this," I muttered to myself.

I sipped my tea, staring at the book and the laptop. It felt as if I had all the pieces there, but I didn't quite know how to put them together because I didn't know what the picture was.

"Well, I don't know where Aeron is supposed to be returning to and I wouldn't go, even if I did, so apparently I need to kill Aegyir and stop him from stealing everyone's energy. Should be simple, right?" I mocked.

The Black Death lasted a few years with odd outbreaks afterwards, but it came in phases. I pulled up the pages on it again, navigating to some citing documents from the time.

"Oh. You thought *cats* were the problem," I said, scanning the pages. "Anything more useful? Like red-eyed demons being involved?"

I clicked on links to manuscripts in the British Museum, hoping there would be translations, since my knowledge of medieval Latin was zero. Nothing. I kept reading. My tea went cold.

There was nothing in the least bit useful linking to the Black Death so I went back to the 1918 flu epidemic. Spanish flu, though it had nothing to do with Spain. I found pictures of enormous rooms containing hundreds of people lying on camp beds. As I flicked through them, a shadow caught my eye, and I enlarged the picture. Was it just a smudge on the lens? Or a flaw in the negative?

My mouth went dry as my brain made sense of the

shadowy mark. A Guide, with its hand over the chest of a man. A ball of light being stretched thin, emerging from the man's chest, bony fingers pulling it towards the Guide. The more I looked at the pictures, the more of them I saw – Guides stealing from the men, the nurses, the doctors… I swallowed. Was another epidemic as terrible as 1918 about to hit Britain?

A hammering on the door coincided with my phone pinging, making me jump.

"You need to take the bolts and chains off," yelled Finn from outside.

I checked the time, surprised to see just how many hours had passed. I closed everything down and bellowed down the stairs to Finn that I was coming, then pounded down to open the door.

"Hey," he said, giving me a lopsided grin and a kiss.

"Hey."

He paused in the hall, sniffing. "What have you made for tonight."

Shit! Shit, shit, shit! I was supposed to have been making a cake to take over to Billy's.

I winced. "Um. Nothing. Sorry. I clean forgot."

Finn dropped his kit-bag on the floor, still studying me. "Oh. Okay. Maybe we can pick something up on the way over." He shrugged out of his jacket and put it and his bike helmet away. "So what *have* you been up to all afternoon, if you weren't baking?"

"Erm…" He wasn't going to like the answer.

He leaned back out of the kitchen, looking down the narrow hall to me, a frown crossing his brow. "Rea?"

"I was trying to work out something." He was still staring hard, and I stretched my back. "I think Aegyir is behind the deaths at the quarry. And the flu outbreak."

Finn still hadn't moved. He stood in the doorway, one

hand on the door-frame, his eyes locked on mine. Slowly, his posture tightened.

"So, instead of making the thing we promised to take to Billy's tonight, you spent the afternoon thinking that a mythical creature, that only you can see, and only you can read about, is murdering people and giving people flu?"

I scratched behind my ear, screwing my toe into the thin beige carpet of the hall. "Er. Yeah."

"Is this all because of that book?" He sounded calm, but from the tightness in his shoulders and jaw, I knew he wasn't happy.

"Mm."

"You do know the book isn't actually about you. It isn't *real*."

"Except the woman in the book who looks just like me is married to a guy called Faran, who looks just like the guy I'm married to in my dreams, who is also called Faran."

His gaze didn't waver. "Says the only woman who could have drawn the pictures and who can read the book."

I strode towards him, breathing hard. "I swear to you, I did not make that book. Are you calling me a liar?"

He held his hands up, standing his ground. "No. I just don't think you *know* you made the book."

"I didn't make it, Finn! The runes are printed and the drawings only *look* like mine."

Finn leaned his broad back against the door-frame as if scratching his spine. "So what are you suggesting? That the book was brought here by someone from your dreams? That it *is* you in the pictures? That there *are* life-stealing demons going around murdering people?" He rubbed his hand over the back of his neck, closing his eyes. "Are you drunk?"

"No, I'm not fucking drunk!"

His eyes opened wide and his brows rose. "For real? So

you *genuinely* believe all that?"

"Yes! No... I don't know." Cold, logical reasoning said it couldn't be true. But I didn't seem to be running on logic any longer. My face scrunched. "I'm sorry I forgot about dinner at Billy's."

He sighed, his head dropping back against the door-frame. "Yeah, well, it won't be the first time we've taken a bar of chocolate from the late-night garage to pot-luck." He reached out a hand and caught hold of my fingers. "I'm sorry I snapped at you. I don't know how the book got here, but it's still just a book and your dreams are still just dreams. Real life is me and you and the gym and your new job. Don't lose sight of that."

"I won't."

He drew me to him, his body warm against my cheek. He smelled of the gym, and I tilted my face to him, wrinkling my nose. "Don't take this the wrong way but you need a shower before we go to Billy's."

He laughed. "You saying I stink, woman?"

"Yep."

I went to move away, but he held on to me. "Serious question. *Have* you been drinking?"

"No!" I shoved him away from me.

"Good. 'Cos then you can drive and I can have a beer." He grinned at me, ducking away from the mock punch I aimed at his head.

***

Half an hour later, I turned the bike into the supermarket car park and waited while Finn scooted in. Every few weeks, Finn and I had a pot-luck dinner with Rick and Billy, where we took it in turns to make either the main course or the dessert. It rotated through the three houses. I hoped Billy wouldn't mind that we were going to bring a rubbish cake from the supermarket.

It turned out not even to be that good. Finn jogged back out a few minutes later clutching a multipack of Mars bars.

"No cakes left," he said as he slid his leg back over the bike and tucked the pack into his jacket.

"Not even a pudding in the freezer?"

"Oh." He took his helmet from me. "I didn't think to check that. Oh well."

His arms settled around my middle and I set off.

Billy lived on the opposite side of town. I cut away from the town centre which could get snarled up, even at this time, and looped round the outskirts, going through the streets where the less well-heeled shops were – the bookies, the cheap phone places and the shops selling vaping stuff. Much as I liked taking the bike out on my own, I preferred it with Finn on the back. The bike behaved differently – more weight going into the corners for a start – and the feel of his arms tightening as his body shifted with the movement of the bike always made me feel snug and secure.

We reached Billy's and I parked on his drive, surprised that Rick's car wasn't there. Maybe he walked. He lived closer than we did.

Billy's house was a typical suburban semi: door to the right of a bay window downstairs; two windows upstairs; front area paved as parking with a few pots of plants clinging to the periphery. Some early dwarf irises poked out blue heads next to yellow miniature narcissi. Since Billy didn't have green fingers, I suspected he'd bought the pots ready-planted from the garden centre.

Finn rang the doorbell and pulled the pack of Mars bars out of his jacket, shaking his head at me.

"Don't give me that face," I said. "We could have brought ice-cream!"

Billy swung the door open and welcomed us in. Inside, we stashed our helmets and Billy took our jackets. Finn handed over the chocolate bars. "Pudding. Sorry."

Billy poked his tongue into the side of his mouth, mirth wreathing his face and Finn shook his head, closing his eyes. "Don't ask."

Billy looked from Finn to me and back again. "Trouble in paradise?"

Finn gave me a pained look, then glanced around. "Rick not here yet? Isn't he meant to be doing the main course?"

"No." Billy's tone was curt, his posture rigid, even for him. "He's not coming."

Billy ushered us through to the lounge, and we sat on a beaten leather sofa to one side of the wood-burning stove.

"Everything okay?" I asked, frowning. Rick never missed these evenings.

"Dinner will be a few minutes yet. Let me get you guys drinks," said Billy. "Who's driving?"

Finn pointed to me with a smirk.

"Beer or wine? Or something soft, even if you're not driving, I guess." Billy smiled, but it was faked and tight and didn't reach his eyes.

"Beer, thanks."

I opted for an elderflower cordial, and Billy left us to go and get them, his back straight, his broad shoulders tense.

"Where's Rick?" I whispered. "What's happened?"

Finn shrugged. "Dunno. He didn't say anything to me. I thought he'd be here."

Billy returned with the drinks before we could talk any more and plonked himself down on the matching sofa on the other side of the fire.

"To Rea, and her new job," he said, too brightly.

"Yeah, cheers." I lifted my glass. "Billy, what's happened? Where's Rick?"

Billy's gaze dropped to the floor, and he breathed deeply, rubbing his thumb over the side of his glass. "Have either of you seen him since Sunday?"

We both shook our heads. Had *Billy* not seen him, either? They might not live together, but they saw each other most days.

"What's up?" I asked.

"He's been weird over the last couple of days. Like he doesn't know me." He ground to a halt, and his shoulders hunched. "He's not been to work. The place is all locked up."

"What, he's not got Bruce to cover?" asked Finn.

Billy shook his head. That *was* different. Rick loved his work. Bruce worked in a town about an hour away and came in if Rick was ill or wanted some holiday, and both of those were pretty rare. Maybe Bruce wasn't free. But in that case, why would Rick *not* be there, and why would Billy not know?

Billy sipped his beer. "Do you think he's taking drugs?"

Finn's head shot up. "Who? Rick? Er. *No*."

There was no doubt in Finn's voice, and I wondered why Billy was asking. "Billy, do *you*?"

"I don't know. I thought it might explain why he seems to barely know me and be acting so weird. He hadn't replied to any texts, so I went over last night to see him. It was as if he didn't even recognise me. He stood in the door and looked completely blank. He was really odd. When he finally let me in, he asked loads of questions he knows the answers to. About you two."

My brow creased. "Us?"

A log popped in the stove, releasing sparks and Billy glanced across at it before replying.

"Mm. How long you'd been together. Who Stephen was. How I knew you... it was completely weird. The way he was talking... it was like he was someone else entirely. If I didn't know better, I'd have wondered if he had a twin. I didn't stay long. When I went to kiss him, he backed off and was horrified. I've tried texting him today and he hasn't replied. I'm almost hoping he *is* on drugs in some ways. Otherwise, it seems like he's had enough of us and doesn't have the guts to tell me."

Rick had his faults, but running away from something that needed to be said wasn't one of them.

Finn shook his head vehemently, stretching his long legs out over the blood-red rug in front of the fire. "I can't see it. He's always been anti-drugs."

"And he's not talked to either of you about anything?"

I shuffled in my seat. "I talked to him on Sunday about whether you two would ever move in together and he said he needed his own space," I replied. "But I certainly didn't get the impression that he was wanting to call things off."

Finn leaned forwards to put his beer down on the low glass-topped table in front of him. "He hasn't talked to me. And if he was gonna break up with you, he'd talk to me, Billy."

Billy nodded, but his shoulders were still bowed. "If you see him, let me know?"

"Of course," said Finn. "I'll try to catch up with him and see what's up."

Billy put his beer down and stood up briskly. "Okay. Well, dinner's probably ready."

He shot out of the room, and I turned to Finn. With half an eye on the door, he sent a text to Rick, then slid his phone away again just as Billy invited us through to the kitchen.

The house was modern in decor – neutral walls, though more taupe than cream, and with splashes of bright colour throughout. It was nowhere near as tidy and stripped back as Rick's house and was all the more homely for it. Pictures of Billy's time in the army scattered the walls – groups of soldiers laughing to the camera, taken during his tours overseas.

I glanced through the window. It was dark outside, but there was a good view of the garden from the extension normally, and Billy had pots of scented plants near the doors that filled the extension with perfume in the summer.

Dinner was awkward without Rick as a social buffer between Finn and Billy. When all four of us were there, we were a group of four friends. Tonight, it felt like two employees having dinner with their boss. Neither Finn nor Billy seemed able to put that aside for Billy to open up fully, leaving the conversation stilted. By the time we'd each nibbled on a Mars bar over coffee, I knew Finn was as keen to leave as I was. We made our excuses as soon as was decently possible.

In the hallway, Billy handed us our jackets and helmets. Finn stayed in the hallway while I stepped over the threshold and from the murmurs between them, I assumed Finn was reassuring Billy that things with Rick might change.

The front door closed, and Finn pulled out his phone.

"Rick got back to you?"

He shook his head. "I always thought he and Billy were solid. And I think Rick would have said something to me the other day if he wanted to call things off."

"He seemed okay about everything on Sunday."

Finn wrinkled his nose. "Well, if he *is* getting so stoned he's that out of it, I can't see him and Billy lasting. Billy won't stand for that."

He called Rick, nodding at me to wheel the bike down the drive, out of earshot of the house. His call went straight to voicemail. "Hey, Rick. Only me. Everything okay? Billy's a bit stressed about you guys. Catch you tomorrow?"

He hung up, rolling his lips inwards, and I rubbed his

back. He joined me on the bike and jammed his helmet on. "I'll see if I can catch up with him tomorrow. I don't want to get caught in the middle if they *are* splitting up."

I kicked up the stand as Finn settled his arms around me, a horrible feeling of unease settling between my shoulder blades. Rick would never take drugs, so why the hell was he asking about me and Finn like he didn't know us? And how could he not know who Stephen was?

***

The next morning, I trudged down our lane back to the house, the paper bag from the pharmacy clutched so hard in my hand it was starting to go soft. The GP appointment had been exactly what I'd expected – all too brief with a prescription handed over at the end and a promise to refer me back for counselling. He'd prescribed something to help me sleep and something else for anxiety. I'd had the prescription filled, but I wasn't convinced I would take them. Well, not the pills for stress. Some sleep would be good, but if a murderous demon was planning on killing everyone, including me, being anxious about that seemed entirely appropriate. I'd been on the same pills before and they'd made me feel dissociated and zombie-like. I wanted to feel sharp.

I unlocked the door, kicked off my shoes when I got in and locked the door, sliding the bolt across and putting the chain on, too. I shrugged my coat off, heavy-limbed with fatigue. I hadn't slept well. No surprise there. The old, familiar nightmares about Stephen had marched through my brain, blending with new versions that incorporated Rick and demons and the Realm in a confusing mix. Then Lilja had popped up again, telling me not to trust anyone, but she'd vanished before explaining any more.

I had until just after lunch to myself. Finn finished at

two, and we were trying out a session at a climbing wall when he got back. It was something both of us had fancied doing for a while and there'd been an online voucher that made it cheap enough for us to sign up for. Mind you, we'd signed up before the break-in and we now owed Rick shed-loads for the door. The session was non-refundable though, but at least the landlord had made positive noises about covering the costs of the door when Finn had called him.

The cottage was cold. Putting an electric fire on just for me seemed extravagant. Since I was knackered, I decided to snuggle back under the duvet upstairs while Finn was at work. I'd be cosy and warm and if I fell asleep that would only be a bonus. I bunched the pillows together and tucked under the covers, still fully dressed. Right enough, I was toasty, but my brain was too busy for me to sleep so I fetched the book and took some painkillers, hoping to prevent the screaming headaches I got whenever I tried to read the runes. Back upstairs, I flopped back on the bed. Something twitched in my brain that I couldn't ignore.

The book had said that the Guides began to hide the bodies of those they had killed, so they could resemble their form without suspicion. Hence the woman in the library. Hence the man in the market square. Hence Toby Hall in my interview. All managing to be strolling around and making my charm glow blue, long after they were dead. Blue for danger – the danger being that these weren't people, but rogue Guides *looking* like their dead victims.

My heart rate stuttered.

Was Rick dead?

"The way he was talking... it was like he was someone else entirely. If I didn't know better, I'd have wondered if he had a twin."

No. *No*! Not Rick. Kind, funny, caring Rick who'd kept Finn together when I fell apart. Who might look like a big scary guy but who was as soft as butter. Who would do *anything* for me and Finn.

I closed my eyes, my stomach knotting, and I ground the heels of my hands into my cheekbones. This was madness. Did I seriously believe this?

My head said no.

My heart knew it was true.

An image of Rick's body, abandoned in a corner of the quarry, flooded my brain and I swallowed hard, scrubbing tears from my eyes. Were we going to tune into the news and see our friend's face flash up on the screen as the latest body to be found in the quarry?

I needed answers. I reached for the book and flipped it open to the section where this had been described. The runes settled into words and phrases and I re-read the section greedily, hoping desperately to find something that gave some wriggle-room.

"At first they chose to resemble those still alive, but soon they began to hide the bodies of those they had killed and mimic their form."

I drew in a deep breath. Okay. So they *could* just resemble living people. I fought my stuttering heartbeat. Maybe Rick was still alive, but Aegyir had been pretending to be him when Billy saw him.

Except Billy said he'd been at Rick's place. Rick wouldn't let a stranger walk around his house as if he owned it, any more than Finn would.

Why Rick? Why did Aegyir want to resemble *him*? Why not keep looking like the woman from the library? Or Toby Hall from my interview? Or even the guy who'd been staring at me the other day?

Because their bodies had been found. Presumably Aegyir needed a new victim because he couldn't appear as the others without raising suspicion. I grabbed my phone and checked the local news. My heart lifted a little to find there were no reports of new bodies. I clung to the hope that Aegyir was just pretending to be him and that Rick was still alive somewhere, though deep down I knew I was clutching at straws.

I scraped my hair back from my face and drew the duvet tighter around me, shivery with stress. Even if Aegyir was just pretending to be Rick, it had to be linked with me, didn't it? No one else was seeing demons or wraiths shepherding spirits from a dying person as far as I knew.

Why the woman from the library? Or the others? Were they just in the wrong place at the wrong time? I closed my eyes, trying to remember if I'd seen any of them *before* my charm had glowed. I was sure I hadn't seen the woman in the library or the guy who'd been staring at me in the gym, but there was a possibility I'd seen Toby Hall. Or that Aegyir had connected him with me. On Friday, on my way to the library, I'd walked to the place where my interview was, so that I could check how long it took to get there. If Aegyir was following me, he could have thought the people there were important.

I screwed my face up, queasiness roiling in my gut. How long had he been following me? Who else was in danger? Not Alison. *Please* not Alison.

He'd been watching the cottage. He'd seen me any number of times. Why not attack me directly?

Because I was never alone? With Stephen being released, neither me nor Finn had wanted me to be anywhere vulnerable. Maybe he'd never had the chance.

I gnawed on my knuckles, thinking. If the man staring at me at the Farmers' Market *was* Aegyir, he'd seen me with Rick in the cafe. Did he think that Rick was a way to get close to me? But he'd also seen me with Finn a lot more. Perhaps Aegyir could only adopt the form but not all of the character. The book said the character always got lost to Chaos. That would explain Rick not knowing about me and Finn or who Stephen was, and seeming like a different person to Billy. Maybe Aegyir wouldn't choose to mimic Finn because I'd spot the difference instantly. He clearly didn't realise how well I knew Rick, then.

Cold fear settled in me as the pieces fell into place. Lilja said that Aegyir wanted *me* dead. And to get to me, he had to get through Finn. And Finn would never believe that Rick was being impersonated by a life-stealing demon and would let him into the house without qualm.

My hands shook and my skin turned clammy. Finn had said he was going to stop by Rick's on his way home. I snatched my phone up. My fingers shook as I dialled. Shit. It cut through to voicemail.

"Hey. It's me. Um. Just come straight home? Don't go over to Rick's. I'll tell you why when you get in. Just, please... don't go over to Rick's."

I hung up and texted him the same message. He was pretty good at checking his phone as soon as his shift was over and I prayed he would today.

Why did Aegyir want me dead? Presumably, he wanted *Aeron* dead. A few pages on in the book was another picture of Aeron/me. Should I skip ahead and read that bit? What if it only made sense if I read it all sequentially? Also, a few pages on from where I'd left off there was a gruesome diagram of a body with knives sticking out of it, next to one where the head had been lopped off. The images turned my stomach. Fuck. I hoped that wasn't the only way to defeat Aegyir.

I braced myself for the searing pain in my head and started to read.

Slaves

Aegyir was hungry for power. The stronger his victim, the more vitality it had and the stronger Aegyir would become if he took the vitality.

One day, Aegyir went to take the vitality from a man who had a great amount of strength. Aegyir placed his hand over the man's chest and started to remove the vitality. The man fought Aegyir and bit his arm and Aegyir's life-fluid entered the man's mouth. Immediately, the man was calm and obedient to Aegyir and Aegyir took his vitality and the man died.

This intrigued Aegyir. Why had the man become docile? Aegyir began to experiment with victims, trying to recreate the conditions that led to the victim becoming obedient. After many victims had been killed, Aegyir learned that he could enslave his victims in life and receive their vitality when they died. The victim had to consume some of Aegyir, while Aegyir had contact with the person. The vitality would flow into Aegyir when the victim died. Until then, he would be obedient to Aegyir.

Aegyir was furious with The Realm for denying him strength and form for so many years. He went to the portal and tried to cross but he was not strong enough to enter The Realm. In his anger, he began to enslave those Outside, building an army so that he could enter The Realm by force.

The Seers could see that some of the Guides were planning to overthrow The Realm. Scouts were sent from The Realm to find how many Guides had been corrupted by Aegyir. Aeron urged the Council to act.

That was the end of the section and I studied the pictures accompanying the story. They depicted Aegyir enslaving his victims. The first drawing showed black fluid being dripped into the mouth of someone pinned down with Aegyir's hand on their chest. The black liquid came from Aegyir's hand. I assumed this was the life-fluid that had been mentioned and that it was the equivalent of blood. The second image showed pretty much the same thing except that instead of his hand being pressed against the victim's chest, Aegyir had his index finger in the centre of the person's forehead while he knelt on his chest. Both pictures showed three drops of black life-fluid falling into the victim's mouth.

I nibbled the inside of my lip. Enslaved during life, then Aegyir got your vitality when you died. Double win for Aegyir. At least this looked like it would be more difficult to accomplish than merely touching a person's spirit for a slow-steal of their vitality. In the pictures, the person looked to be fighting back and was being pinned down by Aegyir.

I re-read the final line. Aeron urged the Council to act. Is *that* why Aegyir hated her? Did she put a stop to him?

I read the next section, the runes resolving into words more easily, though a headache still brewed. Only some of the Realm-dwellers could cross the portals that connected Outside and the Realm. The Guides from Outside *could* force their way into the Realm, but they needed to have a corporeal body and a lot of strength to do so. The Realm Guides couldn't cross to the Outside, as far as anyone knew. Anyone could be invited into the Realm, however, if the invite came from a Guardian.

I paused.

"I invite you in."

That's what I'd heard when the black mist had rocked me backwards, up by the fracking site. It had felt as if *I'd* said it when I'd heard it in my head.

I rubbed my brow and read the next bit, trying to reconcile what I was reading, with my dreams and the vision up at the fracking site.

The Council was split over how to deal with the rogue Guides. Some argued for a group to go Outside to dispatch them; others suggested that the Guides should be invited into the Realm and be dealt with there. Votes were taken but no decision was made.

I let my gaze settle on the window, my brain trying to piece everything together. Just as I was about to read the next part, my phone buzzed. Finn. Thank God.

"Hey, just me. Why don't you want me to go and see Rick?"

From the way his voice faded in and out, he had the phone clamped to his face with his shoulder as he packed up his things.

"Tell you when you get in. Just, please, don't go and see him."

There was a scuffling sound and then Finn's voice came through clearly. "Why? If he and Billy are splitting up—"

"Finn, please? I think something really odd is happening with Rick."

There was a long pause. "Why? What's happened?"

I held my breath for a moment. I could hardly tell him my fears over the phone, not least because he'd laugh and go and see Rick. "Nothing. Just come home?"

Another pause. "Okay. Oh, I went past his tattoo place on my way in and it was still all closed up. Not even a sign on the door saying when it'd be open again."

"Oh. He's usually pretty good about that."

"Yeah. Okay. I'm on my way."

We rang off, and I tossed my phone down on the bed. If Finn was just setting off, he'd be back in about ten minutes. Maybe I had enough time to read a bit more before he got back.

The next couple of pages of the book described how to dispatch a corrupted Guide. They needed splitting into various components in order to be 'dispersed'. There appeared to be three phases a Guide could have – a wraith that shepherded a spirit from body to body, a physical form once the wraith had stolen a person's spirit, and a dispersed form that resembled mist or smoke. I exhaled slowly, forcing my emotions to calm and my mind to focus. I was pretty sure the wraith-form was what I had seen with the old man who had been hit by a car and in the grainy pictures from 1918. The physical form was just like Aegyir in his raw form – cadaverous, with leathery skin and red eyes. Even the thought of him made my skin crawl. I wondered if what I'd seen that day when I'd taken the bike out – the black ball of mist – was the dispersed form. If the Guide was dispatched by a Guardian, it was turned into the dispersed form and could be sealed in a vessel.

I paused, thinking back to the day on the bike again. If a dispersed form was trapped in a vessel, how had it got loose in the countryside? I closed my eyes, re-running the afternoon. There'd been a tractor in the field. The fracking had boomed and made the earth shiver.

Goose bumps chased across my skin. Had the mini-earthquake from the fracking released a dispersed Guide somehow? The ball of mist had appeared immediately afterwards. Had it been buried where the fracking was taking place?

The way in which the Guide was dispersed was what the diagrams with the daggers and the beheading indicated. It wasn't pretty. The vitality needed to be separated from the body. To do this, three daggers needed to be driven into the Guide in specific places – one in each side of the chest and one into the diaphragm. Once they were in, the Guide was then beheaded, at which point all the stolen vitality would exit the body, leaving the Guide resembling smoke or mist. The Guardians could then trap the mist in a special jar and seal it. For reasons not made clear, this went better if it happened on Realm soil, and all of the stabbing, beheading and trapping had to be done by a Guardian.

I moved to sit cross-legged, frowning. If all this had had to happen on Realm soil, why was the mist out *here*? This wasn't the Realm. Not enough leather for a start.

The vitality that was released could be collected by another Guide and taken to Chaos to be reunited with the character. Presumably, that was by a non-corrupted Guide. I wondered what happened if you killed a rogue Guide in the vicinity of other rogue Guides. Did the others gobble up the released vitality before it could be retrieved? What if there weren't any friendly Guides nearby? Did the vitality just float about until one came along?

Is this how any of it worked, anyway? I had no deep faith in any religion. When you died, you died, and that was it. Was I really made up of three parts, the way this book described? The idea that my character would come back in someone new was quite comforting, though. The idea that bad characters also came back was somewhat *less* comforting.

If the Guide wasn't dispersed by a Guardian and didn't continue to steal vitality, the energy it had taken would slowly leak away, making the Guide less and less powerful. Eventually, it would revert to being a wraith. From the wraith-like form, it could either behave and shepherd spirits as intended or it could go back to stealing the life-force out of people and become corporeal again. A wraith couldn't be dispersed. Only a Guide with corporeal form could.

Before I could read any more, the roar of Finn's bike sounded in our lane. I scooped the book up and hurried downstairs to take the bolts and chain off the door just as Finn's key turned in the lock.

"Hey," he said, taking off his helmet. "What's up? And why are you so pink?"

He hooked his arm around the back of my neck and

pulled me into a kiss.

"Um. Hot. I was cold, so I went up to bed. Oh. The GP gave me some stuff this morning."

"Yeah?" He smiled, peeling off his jacket and hanging it on the hooks in the hallway. "And counselling?"

"Yeah, but that'll take time to come through. Have you eaten?"

"Mm. Stop deflecting. Why didn't you want me to see Rick?"

I turned away, the book still clutched in my hand, and walked into the lounge. Finn followed me. I scrunched myself into the corner of the sofa, wondering how to tell him what I was worried about, without sounding as if I'd lost the plot. He sat next to me, peering at me from beneath furrowed brows.

"Come on. Shoot."

His gaze drifted down to the book and his jaw bunched.

"Promise to hear me out?"

"Yes," he said, slowly.

I told him. With every sentence, his brows crept higher. Eventually, I tailed off. "You're not buying this, are you?"

He pushed his shoulders up. "Do I think there's a demon out there killing people, that currently looks like Rick and that I shouldn't talk to my best friend about his relationship going tits-up in case he murders me? No. I think there's an outbreak of flu at the moment and that some bastard is killing people and dumping the bodies at the quarry, which is bad enough, but not fantastical. What did the GP give you?"

Tears stung my eyes at his dismissal. "Sleeping tablets and anti-anxiety stuff."

"Okay. Get a good night's sleep tonight, take some of the other pills and see whether you still think all this tomorrow."

I gritted my teeth. "Finn—"

He held his hand up. "Nah. I love you... to the moon and back... but that doesn't mean I have to buy into you saying there are demons murdering people and impersonating my best mate."

I blinked hard, wanting to cry with frustration. Finn coiled an arm around me and drew me against him.

"Shh. Come on. You're tired and strung out, that's all." He kissed the side of my head and leaned back, taking me with him.

I punched his chest. "That's not all! How do you explain the book?"

He held my gaze, saying nothing. He *still* thought I could have made it.

His thumb rubbed the groove of my spine at the small of my back. "Come on. Get changed and let's go climbing."

I nodded, giving in rather than fighting over it – for now. I knew that I hadn't written this book. There was no corner of my imagination that could have invented this, even if I *could* have been printing runes and drawing in my sleep. Maybe one of the Scouts would spot that Aegyir was free again and some of the Guardians would come and sort it out. Maybe some of the Guardians were already here and would take Aegyir into the Realm to disperse him.

After all, I wasn't a Guardian and all the stabbing and beheading worked better on Realm soil. According to the book, we were Outside with no way to cross into the Realm without an invitation.

13

"Reagan."

I was walking back from the gym the following afternoon and I turned, surprised to see Rick next to me. I hadn't heard him approach. I'd had a good night's sleep for once and the idea that Aegyir was anything more than a myth, never mind impersonating one of my friends seemed less credible today. Nonetheless, I scoured him, trying to see *any* sign that he wasn't actually Rick, but he looked just like he always did – jeans, black t-shirt, leather jacket, heavy stubble. The only difference was his dreadlocks were wild this afternoon, rather than fastened back in a bandana.

"Hi. How are you? Everything okay?"

He fell into step with me. "Everything is fine. Why would it not be?" He smiled, but it didn't reach his eyes and a cold feeling zipped through my body.

"Well, you didn't come to pot-luck on Tuesday and Billy's a bit worried about things between you."

His brow creased as if he was trying to recall something he'd forgotten, and he didn't reply. I tried to see his pupils but his eyes were naturally so dark it was difficult to see if they were pin-point or not.

"Rick, can I ask you something?" He didn't say no, so I ploughed on. "You're not taking drugs are you?"

"Why?" He shoved his hands in his pockets, smiling at me.

“Because you seem pretty spaced. And Billy wondered if you were stoned when he came over.”

Instead of turning to cross the end of the main shopping street to head home, I half backtracked on myself, cutting down a side street so that we emerged back on the road leading towards the gym. This part of town was busier than the walk home and Rick was making me feel uneasy. For the first time in my life, I didn’t want to be in a quiet alleyway with him and the realisation sent cold goose bumps over my skin.

“As I have said, everything is fine. I have not been stoned. Are you going home? I will walk with you.”

“No, I’m going to the gym.” I strode determinedly back towards the safety of work.

Rick’s stride lengthened to match mine. “But you have just come from there.”

How did he know? Had he been watching me?

I tried to shake the thought away, but it clung on stubbornly.

“I forgot something,” I lied.

“I will walk with you. I want to speak to you.”

This wasn’t the Rick I knew and loved. His speech patterns were all wrong and it wasn’t due to drugs. It was like he was someone else entirely.

Shit.

“I have a copy of Finn’s dragon for you,” I said, my heart racing.

“Finn’s dragon?” He frowned, narrowing his eyes.

“Yeah. You’re always on at me about it. I’ll let you have a copy.”

“Thank you.”

He had no idea what I was talking about. As we turned back towards the gym, I checked I knew where every CCTV camera was en route.

"What did you want to talk to me about?" I said, my thoughts tumbling.

"Finn."

I hadn't expected that. "Finn? What about him? He's worried he's going to get caught in the middle between you and Billy."

"I wanted to talk to him. Can I come over?"

"Since when did you need an invitation, Rick?"

His eyes glittered and he smirked as if I'd said something funny. "I need to see him. Perhaps I will just come over one day."

The way he said it, it sounded like a threat.

We'd reached the gym and I squinted through the glass door, hoping to see someone I knew. "You coming in to see Billy?"

"No. Not today." He held my gaze, face hard.

And then he flickered.

It was as if there were two images, superimposed on one another. One was Rick. The other was the thing I'd seen in my interview.

Aegyir.

I took a step back, increasing the distance between us, my heart lurching.

Aegyir smiled. "Say hello to Finn for me. I will see him soon. I know where to find him. And you."

He glanced at my wrist. In my peripheral vision, I saw that the charm was glowing. Before I could say anything, Aegyir morphed back into Rick and strode away.

I hurried into the gym and prayed that a boxing bag was free. I needed to kick the shit out of something.

***

I was still punching and kicking when Finn found me an hour later. Sweat poured off me and I felt like over-cooked spaghetti, but however much I hit, nothing erased the monster I saw in every blink.

"What's up?" Finn steadied the bag against his shoulder as I pummelled it.

"Tell you at home."

"Okay. Shall we go? You look like you're running on empty."

I stopped, my arms instantly hanging limply at my sides. I tipped forwards and rested my head on the bag.

"Go hit the shower. I'll meet you in the cafe," said Finn. "You look beat."

I eased myself upright. He was still there. Every blink. I felt sick, his last words ringing around my brain.

"Rea?" Finn caught me around the waist as my vision swam. "Okay. Never mind the shower. Let's get you home."

"Sorry. Bad afternoon."

"Yeah, I can see. What the hell's happened?"

He peered closely at me, his eyes clouded with worry. I had no words of reassurance for him.

"Right. You gonna manage the bike? 'Cause if you're not, I'm carrying you."

"I'll manage. Sorry."

Finn supported me out to the bike. I hadn't been expecting to be on it and had no leathers or Kevlar or helmet. Finn handed me his jacket and I shrugged it on. It swamped me and left him in just a hoodie and jeans. Then again, I was in a t-shirt, sweatshirt and tracksuit bottoms.

"You'll freeze," I said.

"I'm not gonna go that fast! And I'm certainly not wearing my jacket and leaving you to freeze."

I didn't argue. I was already beginning to chill from the sweat. He thrust his helmet at me and I slid on to the bike, wrapping my arms around his middle when he got on. Finn drove back with one hand clutching my clasped hands against his abdomen. I hoped we wouldn't get clocked by the police or any traffic cameras.

"So, what's happened?" he said as soon as we were in.

"In a bit. I need a shower."

I had no idea how to tell him what had happened without sounding like I was losing it completely.

"Okay. Share? I need one and anyway, I don't trust you not to collapse."

Upstairs, I stripped off my sweat-soaked things and left them where they fell. The shower was over the bath and Finn switched it on and helped me step in. My legs were barely holding me up and I leaned my weight back against him.

"Tell me what happened?" he said, steering me under the water to wet my hair before rubbing some shampoo through it.

"Promise not to think I'm going mad."

"Do my best."

I told him. I could tell from the silence that he didn't believe the last bit. The bit about Rick turning into the demonic figure I'd seen in my interview. As I talked, he rinsed my hair, soaped my body and kept me upright as the water cascaded over me. When I ground to a halt over what had happened, he turned the water off and scraped his hands over his face and body. He handed me a towel, and held my hands as I clambered out of the bath.

"And," I said, remembering something I hadn't told him. "I told Rick I had a copy of your dragon for him and he had no idea what I was talking about!"

He rubbed a towel over himself, saying nothing. The expression in his eyes told me he was biting something back and I gritted my teeth.

"Finn, you do believe me? About Rick changing?"

He picked up his kit off the floor, scooped up my things

and tossed the whole lot into the washing basket in the bedroom. "I believe that you think you saw that. Do I believe that Rick is a demonic figure, wrapped in the body of Rick? Nope. Sorry." He hugged me against him and kissed me tenderly. "Come and talk to me while I cook."

Solid, sensible, down-to-earth Finn. Some of the many qualities I loved about him, but they infuriated me tonight. I followed him down to the kitchen and watched the muscles of his shoulder flexing as he chopped an onion. I picked at the label on the bottle of beer I nursed, frustrated at my inability to get him to believe me.

I knew I was tired. I knew I was stressed about Stephen.

I also knew I'd seen Rick morph into Aegyir and that Aegyir knew I'd seen it.

And that scared me more than Stephen claiming unfinished business.

***

While Finn would run off any stress, my solution was to draw. Finn was finishing the washing up after dinner and I leaned against his back. "Can I sketch you this evening?"

"Can I have clothes on for it? It's cold."

"Yeah. Some. Keep the shirt off?"

He peered over his shoulder at me, one brow raised. "You just want me for my body."

"Can't deny that's partly true. You are *very* sexy, my man. But you know I love you for more than that."

He turned and pulled me into a long kiss, soapy hands dripping suds down my neck. "Oh, Rea, I love you."

"I love you too. To the moon and back."

"And then all the rest."

He kissed me again before drawing back and gazing at me, his eyes so full of love I felt as if I would burst. "We can't just go to bed?"

"No. I need to draw."

"Aagh. Alright. What do you need me in? Jeans?"

In the lounge, he peeled off his top and I put the electric fire on. It *was* cold.

He sat on the floor, his back against the edge of the sofa and smiled at me. "Come on then. Pose me."

I arranged him how I wanted him – sitting on the floor with his arms along the seat of the sofa and his legs stretched out in front of him, crossed at the ankle – and took up a position to his left, sitting cross-legged on the chair. He looked across at me but I shook my head.

"Focus on the telly?"

"Can I *watch* the telly?" he said, sounding grouchy.

"No, because then you won't sit still. I'll be as quick as I can be."

"You've had enough bloody practice."

He sounded as if he was grumbling, but I caught the twinkle in his eye. "Yeah, well, you're a mighty fine specimen to draw. Sit still!"

He did, allowing me to sketch the curve of his shoulder muscles and the tattoo that swirled over his upper arm, its image distorted both by the position of his arms and by the angle I was at. I had to force myself to forget that I knew it was Celtic knotwork and concentrate on the pattern I could see. I moved on to draw the notch in his collarbone at the base of his throat, then his torso. I finished the rest of the drawing as swiftly as I could, aware that even with the fire on, it was chilly, then flipped the cover of my sketchpad closed and put it at my side. Immediately, Finn wriggled, rolling and flexing his shoulders and hands as if he'd been motionless for days.

"You done?" He sounded more brusque than he was.

"Yeah. I'm done." I laughed.

He pulled his rugby shirt back on and sat on the sofa. I

crawled up beside him and tucked against him. "Thank you. You are a very patient man."

"Stretch out with me?"

He lay along the length of the sofa, before pulling me until I was lying on him, his hands resting lightly at the small of my back.

"Have you phoned your mum yet today?"

"No." He arched his hips up against me as he pulled his phone out of his back pocket.

"Hi, Mum. It's me." He touched the screen of his phone as he put it on the arm of the sofa. "You're on speaker-phone and Rea's here. How are things?"

"Fine. Fine."

"Dad in?" Code for *"Are you able to talk?"*

"He's at the pub. Any news on the break-in?"

"Nope." Finn shifted under me, wincing. I sniggered. I'd been lying on his tackle. He mouthed a shush at me, a smile lifting one side of his lips. "The police have said there were no fingerprints either in the house or on the sledgehammer. It was Stephen though. We saw him on Sunday night and he was bragging about wearing gloves."

"Did you keep your cool?"

I could imagine Alison's face as she said it – raised brows, worried the answer might be 'No'.

"Yeah, of course." He rolled his eyes at me but I was with Alison on this.

His mum started into a long tale about Mrs Davies from down the road who was getting her bathroom done, but Finn wasn't listening. He dipped his head to kiss me softly, but not silently it would seem.

"Finn, are you still there?" said Alison, breaking into her own train of words.

"Yep." Finn pulled a face at me.

I swallowed a laugh and blew on his neck, making him

squirm. He unceremoniously dumped me on the floor and grabbed his phone, taking it off speaker-phone.

"No, no. Sorry. Rea fell off the sofa." He planted his foot on me to stop me getting back up. Bad move. His feet were even more ticklish than his neck. He snatched them back up to the sofa out of my reach and held a hand out to me, palm out.

"Hang on a sec, Mum... Rea, cut it out! Hi, I'm back... No, she was tickling me... Yeah, she's fine... Though she might not be fine if she doesn't quit tickling me."

He only had one hand free whereas I had two, allowing me to attack his feet with impunity. Finn was now laughing too much to be able to talk properly.

"Mum, I'm gonna have to go. I'll see you soon. Sorry! Love you."

He finished the call, tossed his phone on the side, and caught my other wrist. "Reagan Bennett, get your sorry ass back up here!" He hauled me steadily towards him, eyes light, kissing me soundly.

I eased back and propped myself up so that I could look at him. "Have we missed the news?" Lovely as it was to be lying here with Finn, I had to know if we'd just lost our best friend.

Finn held his wrist up behind my head. "We've missed the main news. Local is just about to come on."

I squirmed over him, eliciting huffs and squeaks from him as my bony joints caught tender parts of him, and retrieved the zapper from the floor next to the arm of the sofa.

"Christ, woman. You could have just asked *me* to reach it!" He rubbed his palm over his thigh where I'd accidentally kneed him.

I clicked the telly on and wriggled a bit more until I could see the screen, prompting more sighs from Finn. The only silver lining in the headlines was that no more bodies had been found. The death toll from flu had risen to fifteen, though. The murders were still the main article. The police said they were keen to speak to a man who'd been seen with the last victim – Toby Hall – and showed some CCTV footage of him with a man about six foot two, with dreadlocks and thick stubble. I kicked Finn. "That's Rick."

The TV had paused on a fuzzy still from the footage. Finn squinted at the image, frowning, his bottom lip stuck out. "Yeah, it does look a bit like him."

"It's not just *like* him. It *is* him."

Well, I would swear that it was Aegyir, shape-shifted to look like Rick. The clip finished and the hotline number came up on the screen. I elbowed myself up, grabbed a scrap of paper and a pen and scribbled it down. Finn's eyes widened.

"Rea? You're not gonna call them are you? That's not Rick. I know he's been acting weird, but he hasn't turned into a murderer! If it had been *Stephen* I'd be phoning the police myself, but for one, I don't think it is Rick and for two, I *know* Rick wouldn't kill someone."

"*Rick* might not. But he's not Rick. He just *looks* like Rick."

Finn stared. "Are you fucking kidding me?"

"Finn, it's not *Rick*. It's Aegyir."

"Jaysus. I don't believe I'm hearing this. Are you *seriously* saying you believe Rick's been taken over by a demon? Can you *hear* what you're saying?"

"Finn, I'm telling you, it's Aegyir. And he's going to try to kill you, and me."

I picked up my phone but Finn reached across and snatched it from me. "Rea, *stop*! Think about it. You're honestly saying you think there are these *things* that kill people and steal their bodies?"

"Yes! And it looks like Rick!"

"Jaysus. You have completely lost it."

I could feel tears of frustration springing. "How can I make you understand? He killed Rick, and he's going to kill you."

Finn held my gaze, his jaw bunching as he clenched his teeth. "How can you make me believe my best friend's been taken over by a demon and is killing people? You can't! You've lost your mind!"

I glared at him. "You have to admit that it looked like Rick. If he's *not* been possessed and he's *not* involved, then he can be eliminated from the police enquiries."

"Let's watch the clip again." Finn held my phone out of my reach. "If you're still sure it's *Rick*, my best friend, the man you've known for years, then phone. But you are not phoning the police with some fantasy about demon possession. They'll have you committed!"

He tipped my feet off his lap to retrieve his laptop, booted it up and navigated to the police pages. We watched the clip, stared at the still, and watched the clip again.

Finn screwed his eyes up. "I accept that it's a bit like Rick, but I don't reckon it *is* him. He's not wearing his bandana for a start."

"He wasn't today." I gulped, my breath catching in my chest.

Finn stared at me, breathing steadily, then his eyes slid back to the frozen image on the screen. He tilted his head, his face scrunched up, then he replayed the clip, watching closely.

"It's not him. That's not how he walks," he said. "Rick doesn't walk as stiffly as that. He's always a bit loose in the joints."

I peered at the image again. The more I looked at it, the less certain I became. It *might* be Rick but the posture was all wrong.

"Okay. You win," I said begrudgingly.

"Thank you."

He put the laptop to one side and I tucked back against him, scared.

I was losing my mind.

14

It was Saturday morning and Finn and I were both at work. I was on the door and Finn was on a break in the cafe and grabbing a glass of water when they arrived. I didn't know who scared me more, Rick or Stephen.

"Morning, Reagan," said Rick.

I didn't like his smile. Stephen was wearing a sleeveless t-shirt and the upper part of his left arm displayed a new tattoo. The two of them leaned on the counter, their shoulders almost touching. I took a step back. Why the hell was Rick here with *Stephen*?

Except I didn't really believe it was Rick.

"Morning," I said. "Are you here for a coffee?"

The way the gym was laid out, if you wanted to use the facilities, you needed to be a member and go through the turnstiles. The cafe was open to all and needed no membership card to get access. Rick was a member. Stephen certainly wasn't.

"Just here for a coffee," said Rick.

Out of the corner of my eye I saw Finn straighten. As soon as Stephen and Rick moved away from the desk, I buzzed Billy.

"Hi. Billy? Rick's here. Er, with Stephen. They're in the cafe. So is Finn. Can you come down?"

Sensibly, Finn was staying on the far side of the cafe, though he was hurling daggers at them. They sat at the table closest to me, Stephen sprawling in the seat, his pasty face sullen, his doughy middle cinched in by his jeans. He had an expression on his face that left me in no doubt that he would happily finish what he'd started all those years ago. Rick sat up straight, his posture precise, his dreadlocks loose. He had a slight smile on his lips as he stared at me. I didn't need to look down to know that the charm on my wrist was glowing. Blue for danger alright.

Billy arrived, all military bearing and watchful eyes. "Rick! Always good to see you. Stephen. You're barred. I'm going to have to ask you to leave."

Stephen sneered at Billy. "Why am I barred? I've not done anything."

"You threatened one of my staff. You're barred. Are you going to leave willingly or will you need throwing out?"

"I'd like to see you try."

So would I. Stephen might have an inch of height over Billy and a lot more bulk, but I'd back Billy any day. Unfortunately, Rick intervened before I had the pleasure of seeing Billy physically throw Stephen out.

"No, it's fine. Stephen is going."

Stephen opened his mouth as if to protest and immediately his face blanked, as if someone had thrown a switch in his head and put him on autopilot. He nodded dumbly and got to his feet. He didn't even say anything to me as he passed my desk. I watched his back as he disappeared out of the door and away from the gym, thinking about what the book had described.

Billy sat where Stephen had been, his back straight, his hands folded on the table in front of him. "Rick, you know you're always welcome here, but don't you ever bring Stephen into my gym again."

Rick said nothing.

Finn joined them, his posture belying the fact he was

about to explode. Billy stood again, imposing himself into Finn's space and standing between Rick and Finn.

"Calm down." He stared at Finn.

"I'm calm."

"Like hell you are."

Rick canted his head. "Are you on a break, Finn? Come and join me?"

Billy pressed his palm against Finn's chest. "Keep your temper."

"I will."

Rick's gaze swung to Billy. "I need to speak to Finn. You are not needed."

Billy's eyes widened. Finn dipped his head. "It's fine. I'll talk to you afterwards."

Billy walked back towards me and leaned on the counter, facing Finn and Rick, his meaty arms crossed tightly across his chest. "I'm not convinced Finn's going to keep a lid on it."

Nor was I. Mind you, from the tension in Billy's shoulders, I wasn't sure *he* was, either.

"And Rea? Don't get in the middle of them. I know you'll do anything to protect Finn, but you'll get hurt. I'll be just over there. I can deal with both of them if it kicks off."

Could he? All Aegyir would need to do was reach into his chest and yank out a ball of light. Sweat gathered in my armpits at the thought of Rick doing that to Finn and I swallowed hard.

Billy took up a seat a few tables away, his arms crossed, a scowl making itself at home. When I looked back, Finn had his glass of water clasped between his hands, his knuckles white. If he had a lid on it, it wasn't fastened down tightly.

"What the hell, Rick? Why are you hanging around with Stephen? You *know* what he did to Rea. You *know* how both Rea and I feel about him. What the hell? Are you going to throw all our years of friendship away over a piece of shit like Stephen?"

"He has served his time. Paid his tariff. That is the point of imprisonment. You are locked up for a period of time and once that time is served, you have finished your punishment."

"He nearly killed Reagan."

"And has been punished for it. You beat him, but have not been held to account. You beat your father and have not been held to account. Perhaps you should reconsider your attitude to those who *have* been punished for their crimes."

Oh, Jesus.

I sidled towards the edge of the reception counter. Billy's chin lifted, his eyes locked on Rick.

"I was protecting Reagan," said Finn. "I was protecting my mother. You *know* that."

Rick nodded slowly, steepling his fingers. "Ah yes. Finn. The great defender of women. How far would you go to protect Reagan?"

A muscle ticked in Finn's jaw and his face was like thunder. "Rick, what the fuck's got into you?"

"You would fight for her," went on Rick, who *so* wasn't Rick. "What else? Would you die for her?"

"Yes," said Finn without hesitation. My heart sank.

Rick smiled beatifically. "Would you kill for her? *What* would you be prepared to do for Aeron?"

Finn blinked. "Who?"

Rick bowed his head fractionally. "Reagan. Forgive me. I always think of her original name."

Finn stared at Rick. "What do you mean, her *original* name? Why did you just call her Aeron?"

"A slip of the tongue. Forgive me."

Rick pushed his chair back and stood. Finn sprang to his feet, breathing hard, his hands flexing. Billy also got up and took two steps closer to them. I scampered out from behind the reception desk, visions of Aegyir snatching balls of light through people's chest walls flooding my brain. I interposed myself between Finn and Rick just as Billy flanked Finn's other side.

"Rick," I said, my heart hammering as his eyes settled on me. "I think you should leave. Go and be friends with Stephen if that floats your boat. I think you've probably blown your friendship with us."

His gaze travelled slowly from me to Finn and back before he moved towards the door. I followed him. Billy put a restraining hand on Finn's shoulder.

At the main door, Rick turned to face me. "So… you would do anything to protect him and he would protect you with his life? Interesting." He smirked at me as he pushed the door open. "Very interesting."

***

"He called you Aeron."

"I know."

"Didn't you say that was what you were called in your dreams? And in that book?"

"Yep."

"What the hell?"

The conversation was on repeat. We were halfway home and Finn was still in a complete funk about Rick and had been since he'd seen him. We turned to cut through a play-park, hugging the path at the edge under the street lights.

"How does he know that? Stephen?"

I dug my hand deeper into the back pocket of Finn's jeans. "No. Stephen wouldn't know that. He only ever calls me Cuckoo."

I knew damn fine why Rick had called me it, but Finn

was no more likely to agree that Rick's body was now holding a soul-stealing demon than he had been before.

Finn marched straight ahead, his arm tight around my shoulders, his back taut. "Is it in your sketchbook?"

I tried to visualise my books. *Was* the name Aeron in my sketchbook? *Could* Rick have seen it there?

"Have a look when we get in." We emerged from the park and turned on to the suburban road leading back towards the cottage. "More likely there than Stephen. He certainly doesn't know."

Finn chewed, his face serious. "I don't get why Rick's suddenly hanging out with Stephen and spouting all that shit about him having served his sentence. He *knows* the history. He *saw* the state of you after Stephen attacked you. He's my best friend! Jaysus. He *knows* how I feel about Stephen. Why would he do this?"

"It's not worth trying to fathom it out. He's decided to be friends with Stephen, despite knowing it will wreck his friendship with you and me, and will probably make Billy end things with him."

Finn strode on, pushing our pace up until we were home in half the time it normally took. As soon as we were in, he headed for the lounge to find my sketchbooks. I followed him and sat on the chair, fingering my hairline. A headache was beginning to tap away behind my eyes, like I had a resident woodpecker. Even with sleeping pills, my nights were shattered. Either Stephen was haunting me and I was reliving the day he nearly killed me, or everyone in the Realm wanted to have me hanged as a traitor.

Finn flipped through my sketchbooks and I raised a brow in query. Finn worked right the way through each book and then started again at the beginning before stopping on a page.

"When did Rick last see your drawings?"

"When he was last over. Two Wednesdays ago. Before my interview. Why?"

Finn turned back a few pages. I dated every sketch, so he'd know exactly which drawings had been done by the time Rick and Billy had come over.

"Well?" I asked. I knew the answer from his face.

He shook his head. "No mention of Aeron until *after* he'd have seen your drawings. The first time you mention it is in the drawings from your interview. What the hell?"

***

I was back in the misty, featureless place. Lilja was with me, her face lined with fear. Her hair tumbled in soft waves to her shoulders and her finely drawn mouth was pinched. "You need to return to The Realm."

"I can't."

She grasped my hands, her eyes full of pain. "You are in great danger Outside. You'll be safe in The Realm. Please. You must return."

I tried to pull my hands away. "They won't let me back in! Or had you forgotten that I've been banished for all eternity?"

She held my fingers tightly, her eyes pleading with me. "Faran would forgive you. He still loves you."

"And what about Finn? Can he come to The Realm?"

Lilja said nothing and I dipped my head towards her, demanding a response.

"No." She closed her eyes. "He would not be allowed to cross the portal."

"Not even if I invited him?"

She sighed. "What would he do in The Realm? He is not a Guardian or a Seer or a Scout. You are married to Faran."

"He'd be safe."

She tugged at my hands. "Aeron, he cannot enter. You know that. Faran—"

"Faran banished me! If Finn stays Outside, I stay Outside."

She bowed her head, her hair falling forward and shielding her face. "I know that you love him, but Aegyir is coming for you."

I snatched my hands free. "Aegyir has found *me!"*

The mist swirled around us and Lilja gazed at me, her eyes bright with tears. "Aegyir will kill you. Please come home."

"I'm not leaving Finn."

Lilja bit her lip, blinking at her tears. "Then you will have to kill Aegyir, before he has his revenge."

"Will you help me?" Lilja had been my closest friend for all of my life, despite our different statuses. We'd got each other out of endless trouble over the years – a devastating combination of Seer and warrior.

Lilja smiled sadly. "I'm not a Guardian. But I'll do what I can. I wish you would return to The Realm. Killing Aegyir will not be easy."

15

Rat-tat. Rat-tat.

I glanced over to Finn, frowning. Neither of us had seen anyone pass the window. We were the last cottage in the row and you couldn't reach our door without us seeing.

"I'll go," he said.

I leaned back in the sofa, listening to see who was at the door.

"Rick."

Finn's tone was flat. I could imagine him blocking the doorway, a hand on each side of the frame. Rick would know not to mess with Finn when he was like that. But I was still convinced this wasn't Rick.

"Finn. I have come to apologise. May I come in?"

"Apologise for what?"

"May I come in?"

I scrambled to my feet and ran into the hallway. "No!"

Finn looked at me over his shoulder, one brow cocked. Rick smiled at me, making me think of a crocodile. "Reagan."

He took advantage of the fact Finn's grip on the door-frame had dropped and pushed past him into the hallway. I back-pedalled to the lounge and searched the room for anything that could possibly be used as a weapon. Against me. By me. I'd barely started my assessment when Rick came in and I shifted my balance, ready to fight or run.

Finn was hard on Rick's heels and invited Rick to sit. Rick took the chair, leaning back confidently.

"Rick's here to apologise," said Finn, his voice hard. He perched on the edge of the squashy sofa, and I sat next to him, keeping my eyes on Rick.

"I am sorry if you feel that I have jeopardised our friendship by associating with Stephen."

My breathing deepened. Rick's body. Not Rick's voice. Not his speech patterns. Not him.

"You know the history," cut in Finn. "I don't know why you're hanging round with him. He threatened Rea again, the moment he was out."

"I did not know that he had threatened you." A sinister smile inched across Rick's face.

"I told you last Sunday," I said.

Rick shook his head, amused.

"No. Maybe I didn't tell *you*," I added softly.

Rick's face darkened. "I also wondered if you wanted more tattoos?"

My brain scrambled through several things in a flash. Rick would have said tats; the black liquid that Guides used to bind their victims to them in life *and* in death; Stephen was sporting a new tattoo; the robotic way Stephen had obeyed Rick in the gym.

"No," I said, before Finn could have a chance to speak. "Anyway, you seem to have given up on the place. You've not been there all week. That's not like you."

"Business to attend to. But I should be there again soon."

"Well, we're both fine thanks. Neither of us need any more tats."

An awkward silence developed. I wanted Rick to go but he seemed settled. I could hardly bear to be in the same room as him, but if I left, would Finn be okay?

"I've got that hoodie of yours." Finn stood up.

My heart galloped. Was Finn going to leave me alone with him, after everything I'd said?

He was. He thought this was Rick, who might be acting weirdly, but would no more hurt me than Finn would. I opened my mouth to say something but Rick's gaze snapped to me and he shook his head almost imperceptibly, wriggling his fingers as if drumming them slowly on an imaginary table.

Was he threatening Finn?

"Yes. I would like that back. Thank you."

Finn shot him a puzzled look then looked at me. "Back in a second."

As soon as he was out of the door, Rick turned to me. "Let us stop pretending, Aeron."

I caught my breath as Rick's face and body morphed to reveal the demon Aegyir in his full cadaverous horror. His red eyes flashed. "I thought when I was released that it would have been impossible to find you, but it has been so *easy*."

I swallowed.

"It has taken me a few bodies to be able to get so close to you, but here I am. In your house."

In a smooth movement, he rose and crossed the room. I shot to my feet but he caught my wrist, holding me back, pressing the index finger of his other hand against my forehead.

I gasped, my head flooding with images of fighting. Blood; the clang of metal on metal; screams; shouts; men falling. I felt helpless. Unable to break away from Aegyir and unable to save anyone in the battle.

I staggered away the moment he released me. The door was immediately behind me and I rattled through it and sprinted to the kitchen. Aegyir followed. I backed away, before colliding with the worktop. Aegyir moved to stand directly in front of me, trapping me.

"You betrayed me, Aeron. You promised me The Realm."

I groped behind me, hoping there was knife I could grab. "I have no idea what you're talking about."

A sardonic smile inched across his lips. "Liar. You know exactly what I am talking about, Aeron. You made me a lot of promises. Time to keep them. You will open the portal for me."

"I don't know what or where that is and even if I did, I can't open it." I didn't know if I wanted Finn to come back and wallop Rick, or whether I wanted him to stay safe upstairs.

"You misunderstand me. It was not a request."

"I *said*, I don't know where it is or how to open it."

My fingers curled around a knife and I brandished it in front of me. Aegyir laughed. "Do you remember nothing? That will not have any effect on me."

My brain skipped over the image of the decapitated body with three daggers in it. Were there more knives within easy reach? Aegyir stepped closer. I saw a shadow move in the hallway behind him.

"Do *try* to remember, Aeron." Aegyir's face almost touched mine, his fetid breath coating my skin. "Your amnesia is most irritating."

"Your hoodie," said Finn from the hallway. "*Rick*."

As Finn entered the kitchen, Aegyir reformed as Rick and stepped back. I saw Finn blanch further. "Rea? You okay?"

"She is fine. There was a large spider that ran across her. I killed it for her."

Finn knew damn well that if a large spider had run across me, I'd have scooped it up and thrown it outside myself.

"Rick's just leaving," I said. I didn't know what would happen if Aegyir was determined not to leave. Would he kill us both right here, right now? Was there any chance that Finn could pin him down? Or that either of us could stab him? However much I knew he was Aegyir, he looked like Rick and there was no way either of us could kill him.

I was hyperventilating so much my fingers began to tingle. A cold sweat trickled down my spine.

Rick stepped back. "I shall see you around. *Reagan*."

I pushed past Finn to escort Rick out, fastening the locks and bolts as soon as the door was closed behind him. Finn joined me almost immediately. "What the *hell* was that thing?" He was chalk-white. "Aegyir?"

"Yes." My legs wobbled and I grabbed the end of the banisters to support myself.

"So where the hell is Rick?"

My legs gave way and I crumpled to the floor and wrapped my arms around my knees. "He's probably dead."

Finn gawped at me, his breathing juddering to a halt. "What?"

I rested my forehead on my arms, crying. "I think he's dead. All the other times my charm has glowed, the people were found dead. The bodies at the quarry. I've been hoping that Aegyir's just been *looking* like Rick and that Rick's okay, but…"

My sobs choked my voice. The only way Aegyir could be sure that only one person looking like Rick was walking around town was to remove the original. And he would want Rick's vitality.

Finn sat next to me, his arm sliding around my shoulders as I wept, his sniffs telling me that he was close to tears.

"Okay, so *now* do you believe me?" I said.

He cradled me tight against him, his voice thick when he spoke. "Yeah. Crazy as it is, I think I believe you. What the hell is it doing here? What does it want with us? How do we make it go away?"

I burrowed against him, feeling his heart thump against my cheek. "I don't know why it's here, but it's something to do with me. It thinks I'm this Aeron person. And I don't think we can make it go away. I think we have to kill it."

Finn tipped me back to look at me, his eyes wide. "Tell me everything you know."

***

Two coffees later, Finn knew everything I did. I wasn't sure if he believed all of it but he couldn't deny that Rick had morphed into some hideous demon and back, before his very eyes. I'd told him everything that Aegyir had said to me, everything I'd read so far in the book and what I'd seen in the visions, both just now when Aegyir had drilled his finger into my forehead and when the shadow had come over me when I was on the bike.

It was late on Sunday afternoon and we sat on the battered sofa, the book on the table in front of us. Finn blew his cheeks out, his gaze resting on the book. I knew what he was thinking. He had no way of independently verifying *anything* of what I'd told him. Everything had come from a book that only I could read, or from visions only I had seen. He thought I could have written the book, albeit subconsciously. The only thing that had brought him round to thinking I wasn't mad or hallucinating, was the fact he'd seen Rick shape-shift.

"So why do you think Aegyir is here?" Finn asked. "Why is he after *you*?"

"He wants me to open a portal, but I have no idea what or where that is. I assume it's a portal to the Realm." I shrugged. "He talked about me betraying him and him wanting revenge on me for that."

"But it's not *you* who betrayed him. It must be someone or something that *looks* like you. Whoever it is in the book. It's this Aeron person he really wants, surely? I mean, it *can't* be you! I've known you since you were fourteen. And you may have had a rough start in life, but it didn't involve life-stealing demons!"

He was right, but I wasn't sure we'd be able to convince Aegyir that I wasn't Aeron.

"We should tell the police," said Finn.

"What, that there's a shape-shifting demon marauding around the place? You think *they're* going to stick three daggers into him and lop his head off?"

Finn gaped. "You think *we* are?"

I closed my eyes, fingering my brow. "No. But what can the police do? If it *is* a shape-shifting demon?"

"Lock him up for murder? Let's call the hotline. Say we think that the person in the CCTV is Rick."

He didn't wait for an answer. He pulled his phone out and hunted about for the piece of paper I'd scribbled the number on, finding it bundled together with some receipts on the deep windowsill. He came back to the sofa, absently tucking an arm around me as he made the call. I waited, chewing my thumbnail. It was only as Finn rang off that I realised what a huge mistake we might have made.

"Suppose the police go and talk to Rick," I said. "They won't arrest him there and then, surely? So what's to stop him shape-shifting to another person? Then we'd never know what Aegyir looked like."

All we'd have done would be to make him angry and effectively invisible. Shit!

"We need to find out why he's after this person that looks like you," said Finn. "Maybe then we can work out how to convince him it's *not* you." He chewed the inside of his lip. "Answer me honestly, Rea. *Could* you have written that book?"

I breathed deeply. "Honestly? No. I don't remember ever buying a blank book like that and the runes are printed. And although the drawings look like mine, the style isn't right. It's hard to explain, but it's like when people are verifying paintings. Everyone draws or paints in a different way and that doesn't look like the way *I* draw. And although I fully accept I *could* have drawn stuff in my sleep, I'm not a tidy person. I'd have left stuff out. Or I'd have woken up. Or I'd have woken you up. And I'd have written it in English, not runes."

"So how come you can read the runes?" Finn tucked his feet up on the sofa and swivelled to face me.

I scrubbed a hand through my hair. "I have no idea. I didn't think I could and then as I looked at them, the stories came to me. It's not written in English. It's not that one symbol represents A or anything like that. It's like a different voice in my head, but although it's not English, I know what they're saying. I can't explain."

"Read it out to me? I don't know what any of it says."

"Okay." I flipped the book open to the next chapter.

Aeron

The Elected Successor, Faran, was married to Aeron of the house of Wymond. As wife of the Elected Successor, she was the second most powerful woman in The Realm but this power was not enough for her. She wanted to rule The Realm without her husband. She was not willing to wait, and left The Realm to make a pact with Aegyir. She betrayed The Realm by opening the portal for Aegyir to allow him to enter and overthrow the First Lord and the Elected Successor. She promised Aegyir that The Realm would be unprepared for his attack and that he would rule

The Realm with her.

Aeron invited Aegyir in and he attacked The Realm with thirteen other Guides and those from Outside whom he had enslaved. Many of The Realm were killed before the Guardians could control Aegyir. Most families lost sons and daughters, fathers and mothers. The thirteen Guides were dispersed and trapped in vessels. The slaves were killed. Eventually Faran, Lord Eredan and Aeron formed the triad and Aegyir was defeated. He was sealed in a vessel and cast from The Realm to be contained within the earth Outside, from which he would never escape.

The traitor Aeron was charged and tried for her crimes against The Realm. At her trial, Aeron confessed that she had invited Aegyir into The Realm and that she had promised him that he would rule The Realm with her after they had overthrown the First Lord and the Elected Successor. She swore that she had invited Aegyir in as part of a plan with Orian of the house of Hadwen, to trick Aegyir into entering The Realm so that he could be defeated. She swore that she had believed that Orian was preparing the Guardians so that Aegyir would be defeated when he entered The Realm. She accused Orian of treachery. Orian renounced all of her claims. The Council found Aeron guilty of all charges and she was sentenced to hang. Before she was hanged, the Elected Successor requested that her sentence be commuted to banishment. She was cast out of The Realm and forbidden from returning for all eternity.

The pictures that accompanied the text were of Aeron, who bore more than a passing resemblance to me, and Faran, the Elected Successor, who was the spitting image of my hunk in my dreams.

I closed the cover and put the book on the table.

"Well, I guess we know why Aegyir wants revenge on Aeron," said Finn, sitting back and scraping his hands over his face. "She sounds like a real piece of work!"

A horrible feeling wriggled in my belly. It didn't feel

right.

"But in earlier stories, she was worried about the Outside and wanting to help them to *defeat* Aegyir."

"She doesn't seem to want that any more!"

"She's being described by the people who banished her. The victor always writes the history." I folded my arms.

He cocked his head. "She invited a demon into their land and he killed a whole heap of the people there. They may have a point."

"Aegyir thinks it's me. That I'm Aeron," I said, my voice wobbly.

Finn bunted along the sofa and slipped his arm around me. "I know she *looks* like you, and you're not an average-looking woman, but how *can* it be you? I know you can be forgetful at times, but even *you* would remember if you'd invited a demon into another world and he'd slaughtered a load of people! He's seen a tall, black-haired woman with green eyes, and thought, 'I know someone like that'."

He smiled lopsidedly at me, trying to reassure me. I rested my face against his shoulder. The visions I'd had of the battles rushed back to me, only they felt closer to memories than visions.

Maybe Aegyir had put them in my head when he touched me. I rubbed my cheekbone against Finn. "What do we do?" I knew he wouldn't have an answer but I needed to ask.

"Let's see what the police do. They may lock him up."

"And if they don't?"

He kissed my hair. "Face that if we get to it."

***

After dinner, Finn sat on the sofa, hunched over his knees. "Rick's dead, isn't he?"

He chewed his lip, not far from tears and I scooted

down the sofa to sit next to him, sliding my arm around his back and leaning him towards me. His best friend, dead. I knew how that felt. It was years since Sarah's death and it still hurt me to my core. Was losing your best friend to a demon, better or worse than finding their body crumpled on rocks? Would Finn ever get over this? I could still see Sarah's battered shape, painted indelibly on the backs of my eyelids, even after all this time. Would Finn ever be able to forget seeing his best friend morphing into a demon and back? I wasn't sure I would.

I squeezed him, my voice catching. "I'm sorry, but I think so."

"I need to run."

The last thing I wanted right then was to go out running. Scratch that – the last thing I needed was for Finn to go out running on his own and for Aegyir to find him.

"Okay." My palm circled his back.

He straightened, dragging his hands through his hair and leaving it in unruly clumps. "No, Rea. I *really* need to run. I'll leave you behind."

"I don't want you going out on your own."

He faced me, his brow crinkling. "I can handle myself!"

I tried not to see the pictures of balls of light being ripped out of people's chests. "Against anyone other than Aegyir, I'd agree. But not him."

Finn scratched his cheek, his eyes on me. "And you reckon *you're* a match for him, if *I'm* not?"

"I didn't quite mean it like that. Maybe *we* are a match. And anyway, would you rather I was left on my own?"

A cheap shot, but it worked.

"Of course not!"

"Then I'll get my kit and try to keep up."

Boy, had he needed to run! We ran for miles, at a pace I struggled to manage. Only the fear of one of us being out alone kept pushing me on. Finn seemed as if he was lost in his thoughts and normally this would mean he was blissed out on a runners' high. I wasn't so sure he was in a happy place today.

As we turned down the path that led back to the cottage we saw Billy's red Honda parked next to our shed.

"Shit," muttered Finn.

We should have thought about what effect calling the police would have had on Billy. As we jogged to a stop at the door, Billy got out of his car. He looked as if he'd lost several pounds, the shadows in his face were so deep.

"Hi, Finn, Reagan. I'm sorry to bother you at home on a Sunday, but I need to talk to someone."

"Sure. Come in. Come in," said Finn, kicking the mud off his trainers.

I scanned my bracelet. Plain opalescent bead. No danger. This was actually Billy then.

Finn made coffee while I took a pint of water through to the lounge to sit with Billy. His usual bluff demeanour had been replaced by bewilderment and he hunched forwards on the seat, his hands clasped together on his knees. I listened to Finn clattering about in the kitchen, wondering what to say to Billy. There was absolutely no way I could tell him what had happened, but surely, if he'd spent *any* time with Rick recently, he'd know there was something seriously amiss. Aegyir might be conjuring Rick's image, but he had none of Rick's character.

"Things still difficult with Rick?" I asked, brows raised.

"Kind of. I've just spent half the afternoon at the police station."

My heart sank. Of course he would have.

"Have you seen much of him this week?" I hoped in many ways he hadn't. He was safer that way.

Billy shook his head. "He's still not answering any texts.

The only time I've seen him was when he came to the gym with Stephen and he didn't want to talk to me."

Finn pushed the door open with his hip and plonked Billy's coffee down on the table. "So, what's up?"

Billy scraped his hand over his face. "I've spent the afternoon at the police station. Someone thought the chap on the CCTV was Rick. They obviously pulled him in and asked him where he was on all these dates. He said he was with me for all of them."

"And was he? With you?" Finn asked.

"Not for all of them. Some of the earlier dates he was, and for one of them I knew where he actually was, though I don't know why he said he was with me." He drew in a long breath and met Finn's eye. Finn fidgeted. "And of course, now the police think I look suspicious."

"I'm sure they don't," I said, though he was probably right. I wondered how he'd react when he found out it had been Finn who'd called the cops.

Billy leaned back in the seat, his eyes closed, rubbing his brow. "Why the fuck do they think it's *Rick*?"

"Because I called them and said that I thought it was," said Finn.

Billy was up on his feet immediately. Finn scrambled up too.

"What?" Billy's face flushed and the muscles in his neck bunched.

"It looks like Rick on the CCTV they showed on the news the other night. And given who he's been hanging out—"

Billy punched him. Finn staggered backwards, licking blood off his lip. I saw his fists flex as he straightened and stepped between them.

"Enough! Billy, I don't care that you're still my boss for another few days and I don't care if you sack me. But you do *not* come into my house and throw punches."

He held his hands up in peace and I turned to Finn. "Cool it."

"*I'm* cool." He touched his lip gingerly.

"Sit down. Both of you!"

I waited until both of them were seated and joined Finn on the sofa.

"Why the hell did you say to the police that it's Rick on the CCTV?" asked Billy, glaring at Finn, breathing hard. His colour was still high, his body wound tight as if at any moment he would pop up again like a jack-in-the-box.

"Because it looks like him," I said before Finn could answer. "Billy, I'm really sorry if you've ended up with a shit afternoon, but if Rick hasn't been involved then the police will discount him. We don't even know that Finn was the only one who called. Rick's pretty distinctive."

Billy's scowl swung to me. "Did you call because he's hanging around with Stephen?"

Finn shook his head. I prayed that he would follow the line I'd laid out. "No. I called because it looks like him on the CCTV."

Billy's jaw clenched. "I spent all afternoon with the cops, raking through my diary, answering questions like how I knew Rick, what was the *exact* nature of my relationship with him, what we were doing on particular dates. Do you know how embarrassing that was?"

"I'm sorry. I should have thought to call you," said Finn, knotting his fingers together.

Billy glowered at him, then switched his focus back to me.

"Do either of you *seriously* think that Rick could have been involved with *any* of this? For God's sake, I've known him for years. I've *slept* with him for years. I love him! How can you *possibly* think he's involved?"

I swallowed, tears nipping my eyes. What could I say?

There was no body – as yet – and I *couldn't* tell Billy that I thought Rick was dead. It would crush him.

"When did you last see him?" I asked. "And I mean properly. Not just him popping into the gym like he did the other day."

Billy hesitated. "Not for a week. He hasn't been over and when I went over to see him, he wasn't in. The last time I saw him for anything more than a few minutes was Monday, when he was really off with me and hardly seemed to know me."

He'd calmed, marginally, and sat back in the seat, nursing his drink, his eyes full of pain.

"Billy, please be careful. I don't know what's going on with Rick at the moment, but he's not himself." It was as close to the truth as I dared to go. What I wanted to say was that I didn't think Billy should have anything to do with Rick at all. What if Rick killed him? Or made him into a slave? Jesus, how easy might *that* be?

He raised his head, frowning. "Be careful? What do you think he'll do to me?"

Finn wriggled his shoulders. "Rea's right. Rick's been really strange recently. Be careful. I don't trust him."

Billy stood up as if squaring up for another fight. "I'm not listening to this. I know he's been weird recently, but this is *Rick* you're talking about. My partner. Your best friend!"

"Billy, please," I said, holding up both hands, palms out. "Rick came over here this afternoon and wasn't at all like the Rick we know and love."

"Why? What happened?"

I struggled for words. What version of the truth could I say? Billy would no more believe me about Aegyir than Finn had originally.

"We were arguing about him hanging out with Stephen

and I told him that Stephen had threatened Rea. He seemed pleased about it," said Finn.

Billy looked stunned. "But he loves you, Rea. Both of you."

"He didn't seem to today," said Finn. "Seriously Billy. Please be careful. Give him a wide berth for a bit? Don't get hurt."

Billy laughed mirthlessly. "I suspect I'm going to get *very* hurt... I'm sorry he was like that with you though, Rea."

"Don't apologise for him. You didn't make him react like that. Sit down? Finish your coffee?"

Billy perched again. "Do you genuinely think he could be involved with what's happened up at the quarry?" He blew out a derisive snort.

Finn ran the tip of his tongue over the developing bruise on his lip. "I think he's been acting very oddly since Stephen came out of prison and that he looks like the guy in the CCTV," he said, taking care with his words.

"You think he could be covering for Stephen?" Billy's face cleared.

"Could be," said Finn. "Billy, he's either *not* involved, in which case the police will clear him, or he's got himself into something that's totally out of character, in which case he'll come to his senses pretty quickly. Yeah?"

Billy's eyebrows were still quirked up in the middle but he shrugged and sipped his coffee. "I'm sorry I hit you. I forgot everything I've ever tried to teach you."

Finn grinned. "Huh. It's reassuring to know that even *you* can lose your cool, oh zen master. I'm sorry I didn't call you and give you a heads up."

Billy said nothing. I hoped that the police would arrest Rick or that Billy would steer clear of him. He finished his coffee in a gulp before glancing from Finn to me and back again. "You guys need to stretch and change. I'm sorry I disturbed your night off."

We all stood and I rubbed Billy's shoulder. "I'm so sorry we didn't give you a heads up. Please be careful. I don't know what's got into Rick and maybe it will sort out soon, but just be careful. Don't end up dragged into something you don't want to be in."

Billy stepped back. "I'll leave you guys to your Sunday."

His voice was tight, but I thought we'd reached some kind of truce.

Finn saw him out. He blew his cheeks out as he returned and I half expected him to go straight back out for another run. Instead, he flopped down on to the sofa next to me.

"What the hell do we do?" he said, letting his head loll towards me. "How do we get rid of Aegyir? Keep Billy safe? I can't lose Billy as well as Rick." His voice cracked.

I tucked my toes under his thigh, my arms around my knees. "I'm kind of hoping that the guys from the Realm will come out and deal with him. I mean, it says in the book *what* to do, but it's impossible."

"Why?"

I caught my bottom lip in my teeth. "Because it involves sticking daggers in him and decapitating him and it has to happen in the Realm and it has to be done by a Guardian."

I shivered. How many of our friends would we lose before the Realm came to our help?

16

The next day, we were both on early at work. The alarm had dragged us from broken sleep and unfathomable dreams and we were still half asleep when we went into the kitchen to get breakfast. What was there woke us up pretty damn quick.

"What the hell?" said Finn, rubbing his eyes.

Sitting on the kitchen table was a roundish leather bag, the size of a head, held closed by a drawstring. Balanced across the top of it was a sword. We both gawped.

"What the hell?" said Finn again.

He rushed to the front door. Still locked. Still bolted. The chain was still on. Ditto for the back door.

"How the fuck did these get here?" he said, staring at them. "What the hell are they?"

The sword was fairly plain, the blade about a metre long and the hilt a sturdy cross. No fancy hand guard, just a big chunk of metal. I eyed the bag, a cold feeling in my belly. I didn't want to imagine what was inside.

Without touching either object, I leaned forwards and peered at the sword. It felt familiar.

Mine?

I closed my eyes. I knew this sword. It had a nick in the blade near the hilt and there were runes inscribed along the length of the blade. *"For Aeron, my mighty warrior."* It was from my father. A wedding present.

"It's mine," I whispered. "The sword – it's mine."

I shook myself. I didn't know who my real father was and this wasn't from *Paul*. Nor was I called Aeron. Nor was I married!

I opened my eyes to see Finn staring at me, mouth open. "It's *yours*? What do you mean?"

"I don't know. I just know this sword. From my dreams."

I checked the blade, confirming what I already knew.

If this was Aeron's sword – *my* sword? – then it came from the Realm. So what the hell was in the bag? I leaned over and picked it up, my hands shaking. It was heavy, but the contents shifted in a way that told me whatever was in it wasn't solid.

Not actually a head, then.

I breathed hard. The neck of the bag was tied with a leather cord and I pulled at it, loosening it until I could open the bag and peer in. My breath escaped in a rush. The bag was full of soil. I showed Finn who scrunched his face up.

"However stressed I am and however much I might sleep-walk, there's no way I've produced a leather bag of soil and a fucking sword!" I said, putting the bag back on the table.

"Where have they come from? How the hell are they getting in the house?"

"We don't have time to fret about this right now." I showed him my watch. We were running late. "Let's worry about it this afternoon."

We grabbed a quick breakfast, both of us transfixed by the objects on the table, and headed out to work on the bike.

As we put our helmets away in our lockers, Finn glanced across to me. "Rea, what the hell is going on?"

I smoothed my palm over his cheek and kissed him. "I don't know."

"Someone's getting into the house. While we're in it. I know I sleep deeply, but..."

And there it was. The thing that was stressing Finn more than anything. More than the fact there was a demon walking the streets, dressed in his friend's body. More than the fact the demon was after revenge on someone who looked exactly like me. The fact that someone could get into our cottage with a weapon and neither of us knew about it. Finn was terrified that he couldn't protect me, even in our own home.

I kissed him again. "I know. Let's talk about it at home." I planted my hand between his shoulder blades and propelled him out of the staff area, trying to jolly him. "Go on. Your adoring fans will be waiting. Try not to flirt too much."

I watched him as he made his way to the weights room and then turned to go to reception. It would take more than joking with him to shift the weight from his shoulders.

I'd brought the book with me again, hoping to find more clues in it on a second reading than I had on the first. In the quiet moments between calls and clients, I re-read it, but I was no closer to knowing how we could defeat Aegyir than I had been the day before. The bag of soil made a little more sense as I assumed it was soil from the Realm, wherever that actually was. The sword to decapitate Aegyir? Okay, but didn't we need three daggers and a special vessel as well? Even assuming that either me or Finn would be able to actually *do* any of that. Maybe they would be waiting for us when we got back.

Neither of us saw Billy to talk to, though he was in the building. I kept checking the charm on my bracelet but it remained steadfastly opalescent. If Aegyir *had* shifted to a new form after getting grilled by the police, it wasn't anyone in the building.

Mid-morning, Finn and I grabbed our break together, sipping coffees at the back door of the gym, away from everyone. I kicked the scattering of fag-ends off the step by the fire escape and sat down, my coffee steaming in the crisp air. Finn sat next to me, shoulders hunched.

"Has Billy talked to you?" He peered at me over the rim of his mug. "He's passed the weights room a couple of times but he's not spoken to me. Think he's okay?"

"He came past reception but didn't stop to talk. Just give him space. He's got a lot on his mind. Tough to wonder if your lover has got mixed up in something terrible and rough to have your private life raked through by the police. Not helped by it being your protégé who dobbed him in to the cops."

Finn smiled ruefully. I squeezed his hand. "He'll come round. He won't stay pissed off forever."

He stared into the depths of his coffee, his jaw bunching. "You think Rick will do anything? To Billy?"

I sucked in a long breath, thinking. "You know, I think he would have done it by now if he was."

He closed his eyes, nodding. "I hope you're right. I can't bear the thought of Billy getting hurt."

Billy was a big man, full of vitality. Billy wouldn't get hurt by Aegyir. He would get dead. I tried to swallow a lump in my throat, my chest tight. We needed to do something about Aegyir and sooner rather than later, but I still didn't know what.

One thing was for sure. Finn couldn't stick three daggers in something that looked like his best friend or lop his head off, and I wasn't convinced I could either.

***

Work over, Finn and I were back home and sitting in the kitchen, the bag of soil and the sword on the table between us.

"It feels horribly like whoever is leaving us this stuff, thinks we're going to kill Aegyir," I said.

Finn raised his eyes to me. "You can't be serious."

I shrugged. "Can you think of another reason why someone has so far left us a charm that glows in the presence of these rogue Guide things, a book that tells us how to deal with one if they go feral, a bag of soil and a sword?"

He clamped his lips shut.

"And what happens if we *don't* do anything?" I asked. "Who will Aegyir attack next? Billy? Me? You?" My breathing faltered at the thought.

His eyes clouded. "We let the police deal with it."

I sucked in my breath, my back stiffening. "Are you suggesting we take these to the police? And say what? That they appeared on our kitchen table through locked and bolted doors and that we think they might be needed to kill a demon?"

"Well, what are *we* supposed to do with them?"

I dragged my hands through my hair. "I don't think it's sensible to give them to the police. We've been left them for a reason."

Finn gaped. "Seriously Reagan, are you thinking that we're gonna chop Rick's head off?"

"You must be wound up. You never call me Reagan."

He folded his arms and leaned on them on the table, bunching his shoulders. "Yeah. I'm wound up. You're talking about murdering one of our friends."

I copied his posture. "If he's Aegyir, he's *not* one of our friends! What if we're genuinely the only people who could stop him from killing everyone?"

Finn exhaled sharply. "And what if we're wrong? Though I guess we'd be able to plead insanity in our defence!"

I backed down. My brain ran over something 'Rick' had asked Finn the other day. How far would Finn go to protect me? For that matter, how far would I go to protect Finn? Would I die for him. Certainly. Would I kill for him?

Yes. If I had to.

If Aegyir came for Finn, I would lop his head off before he could draw breath.

"What if he tried to take you?" I said, my voice shaking, my knees jammed against Finn's under the tiny table. "You know, drag your life out of you."

"I'd punch his lights out."

"You think Rick didn't try that? What if he came for me?"

Finn's face darkened but he didn't answer.

I fingered the edge of the leather bag. "Moot point. We don't have the rest of the stuff, so even if I could get Aegyir to stand on this soil while I decapitated him, I need three special daggers and a vessel to seal him in."

"You could do *any* of that?" said Finn, one brow up in disbelief.

"If he was coming after you, yes," I said, though there was more conviction in my voice than in my heart.

Finn shook his head. "I'm not letting him anywhere near you. I almost lost you once; I don't want you even in the same postcode as him." He pushed himself away from the table and picked up the bag and the sword. "Let's put these away and let the police deal with it. If Rick was involved in any of the deaths, they'll arrest him and lock him up."

He put the sword and bag in the cupboard at the end of the kitchen, tucking them behind the ironing board. I wished I had his faith that the police could do anything at all about Aegyir, but I didn't. He'd kill and shape-shift his way out of any detention.

My only hope was that the Realm would send some Guardians to deal with him, but there was precious little sign of that so far.

17

"You still will not leave Outside and return to The Realm?"

Lilja and I were back in the misty wasteland. I peered at her. As ever, she was dressed in dark leather trousers and a snug fitting pastel jacket, her hair loose and flowing over her shoulders.

"No. Not if Finn can't come too. I'm not leaving him Outside."

She sighed as if she'd known all along that this would be my reply. She probably did. She was a Seer after all – able to see the different versions of the future. I wouldn't have left Finn in any of them.

"Aegyir is planning to trap you. If you will not return, you will have to kill him. He will not be easy to kill Outside."

"Will you help me?"

"I am trying. I am forbidden from having contact with you. Everyone is. And anyway, I am not a Guardian."

"Nor am I," I retorted.

Lilja said nothing, her expression hard to read.

"Can you send the Guardians? Can't they protect the Outside? Aren't they supposed to deal with Guides who turn feral?"

Lilja shook her head. "The Realm is not in danger. Not yet. Outside is not in danger. Only you are in danger and the Guardians will not come to help you."

What did she mean, the Outside was not in danger?

"Aegyir is killing people! Surely the Outside is in danger from him? If he gets strong enough, The Realm will be in danger too."

"The Guardians are not concerned yet. The Seers see no threat to the Outside and no threat to The Realm. The Guardians will not be concerned until it is too late for you."

My head sank and my shoulders slumped. No one would help me. "Okay, so I kill Aegyir to protect Finn and myself and the Outside? Can you see that?"

Lilja turned away, her fingers plucking at the edge of her jacket, her breath shuddering as she exhaled. When she looked back, there were tears in her eyes. "I see you in battle, Aeron. I do not see you win." She brushed a tear from her face. "Come back to The Realm? Please!"

"No. I won't leave Finn and he can't enter The Realm, so I stay here and fight Aegyir. What else can I do?"

I stepped back from Lilja, watching as the mist engulfed her, feeling truly alone.

I woke with a jump. What if these dreams were real? What if the things that Lilja said to me in them were true? She could see me in battle, but she didn't see me win.

My mind slid out of the half-dream state and I woke fully, my mouth parched and my heart racing. They were only dreams. They were the way my brain processed stuff. How could they possibly be real?

I tried to get back to sleep but a single question kept rattling around my brain, keeping me awake.

If they weren't real, how could things be appearing in our kitchen?

***

"I wonder if you could help me?"

I was on early shift again. It was coming up to half seven

in the morning and I was the wrong side of a second mug of coffee. I looked up at the young woman in front of me. "I'll try. What's up?"

She leaned her elbows on the chest-high divider, moving in to speak softly. I assumed the tampon dispenser in the ladies' loos needed refilling.

"I need a portal opening," she said, flashing me a wide smile. "And you can open it for me."

I frowned. "I'm sorry?"

"Oh, Aeron. Aeron. You heard. I need a portal opening. And you will open it for me. Invite me in."

Her eyes flicked red, for no more than a fraction of a second. She was still smiling as if we were best friends and bouncing on her toes, long legs clad in fitness tights, her top half in a fluorescent pink t-shirt. I scanned the ground floor. Other than a couple getting a drink at the cafe, there was no one around.

"I don't know where this portal is you keep talking about, and even if I did, I couldn't open it," I said, fear trickling through me.

She sighed, pursing glossy lips. "Do you love Finn? Billy said that you do. More than anything."

I felt the blood drain from my face. "Leave Finn alone."

"Aeron, you will open the portal for me and invite me into The Realm. Or I will kill Finn."

"I'm *not* Aeron and I don't know where this portal is." My body flooded with adrenaline.

"I do," said Aegyir, flipping long blonde hair over narrow shoulders.

"Whose body are you in?" I asked, hoping to distract him. "Is Rick okay?"

"Rick was very useful. *Full* of energy." Aegyir shrugged. "This is just someone else I found. It is sufficient. She doesn't need it any more." A sneer marred his pretty face.

"The portal. You will open the portal and invite me in. Or I kill Finn."

My mouth desiccated. The young woman's features hardened.

"He is at home at the moment, I believe," said Aegyir. "About to come to work."

"Leave Finn alone. This has nothing to do with him."

I wasn't sure it had anything to do with me either, but Finn certainly wasn't part of it.

The woman pouted. "No."

No, Aegyir wouldn't leave Finn alone? Or no, it wasn't anything to do with Finn?

"It is a simple concept. Invite me into The Realm, Aeron. Tomorrow night. Or the day after tomorrow, Finn dies."

"I'm not Aeron. I'm Reagan Bennett."

The woman dropped her head on to her folded arms on the raised desk. "Reagan Bennett. That is only your name. Underneath, you are Aeron." She jutted her chin towards my bracelet. "You say you know nothing of The Realm, yet you wear a Seer charm."

"I found it."

The door opened behind her and Finn breezed in, grinning at me as he passed. He blipped his card at the turnstile and his gaze swivelled to the person leaning on the divider. "Hi there. You joining?"

The woman simpered. "Yes, if all the staff look like you." She looked him up and down lasciviously.

Finn laughed, blushing, and made his way towards the staff-room. And safety.

I exhaled slowly. Aegyir turned back to me, china-blue eyes flashing red again. "I hope for your lover's sake that your memory returns, Aeron," he snarled, making no pretence to disguise his voice.

I took half a step back, glad of the dividing barrier

between us. "If you hate this Aeron so much and you're so sure I'm her, why haven't you just killed me?"

The woman shook her head, blinking. "Are you as stupid as you sound? Because I need you alive to open the portal."

Did that give me a bargaining chip? "And if I *could* open it. What then? Are you going to kill me then?"

"Possibly. Though I want you to suffer for what you did to me."

I rotated the bracelet on my wrist, its bead burning bright blue. My heart raced as ideas jumbled in my brain. "Where's the portal? How do I open it?"

"Along the track from your house. Next to the boulder. You're a Guardian. All you need to do is invite me in. Tomorrow night. Six."

He morphed from the pretty young woman into Finn's mum. I gasped.

"Jesus, have you killed Alison?" My vision tunnelled.

Back in the form of the young woman, Aegyir smirked. "I could have. But I have enough strength to appear as whoever I wish. Tomorrow night, Aeron."

I watched as the young woman swung away from the counter and out of the gym. My hands hadn't stopped shaking by the time Finn appeared, killing time before his eight o'clock class started.

"She gone?" He leaned on the exact spot that Aegyir had.

"Yeah."

He dipped his head, squinting at me. "You okay?"

"Mm. I need more sleep, that's all," I lied. No point both of us being panicked and he was due to take a tough cardio class any minute. I'd tell him when we had a break.

He peered at me for a moment, clearly not believing me. "Okay. Sorry, I've gotta run. See you later."

How the hell was I going to stop Aegyir from killing

him? I couldn't open any portal. I wasn't who he thought I was.

Was I?

***

"Aegyir came to the gym."

Finn turned, pausing mid-action as he opened a can of Coke. "What?"

We were in the staff-room. Finn had just finished taking his early class and his hair was dark with damp after a shower. I'd meant to wait until we were both on a proper break before I told him, but I couldn't keep it in me any longer. I'd left someone covering the desk and dashed up here to catch him before he saw any of his individual clients.

"When?" he said, snapping open the can with a hiss. "I haven't seen Rick and I was keeping an eye out for him."

"He was there when you got in. He was the pretty woman leaning on the desk."

"What? Jaysus! Why didn't you say something?"

"Because he'd just threatened to kill you if I didn't open the portal to this Realm place for him. Tomorrow night." I reached behind me to grasp the table and perched on the edge of it.

He blanched, his eyes dark with fear and a pulse throbbed at his neck. "What did you say?"

"I said that I wasn't Aeron and that I couldn't open the portal for him but he wasn't having any of it. If I don't open it, he'll kill you on Thursday." I stopped before my voice squeaked any more.

"We have to call the police," he said.

I hauled in a deep breath and let it go in a rush. "And say what? That someone we can't describe has threatened you? I have no idea who that woman was, but I think she must be dead. And Aegyir said he can shift to look like whoever he wants. If the police go after him, he'll switch to a new body."

Finn's knuckles went white as he held the can. "So what do we do? Do you even know where he thinks this portal is?"

"Mm. Up the track towards the quarry. Next to a boulder. Where we run."

He leaned back, scouring my face. "You have that look you get when you're planning something."

I squared my shoulders. He wasn't going to like this. "I thought I would meet him. Take the bag of soil up there earlier and sprinkle it around and stash the sword. Then when he arrived, I would pretend to open the portal but kill him instead."

Finn's brows canted upwards. "I mean, apart from a whole heap of other points, like, I'm never in a month of Sundays gonna let you anywhere near this fucker, don't you need some special daggers and a jar to put him in? And do you honestly think you can chop his head off? Not that it matters, because you're not gonna go *near* that place, tomorrow night or any other time."

Before I could reply, one of the other personal trainers breezed in to grab a glass of water from the sink next to where Finn was standing. He looked from me to Finn and back again and hurried out, slurping from the glass. I assumed he thought we were in the middle of a domestic.

I wrapped my arms around my body, hugging myself tightly. "Finn, I have to. He's going to kill you!"

Finn screwed his nose up. "Nah. He might *try*, but nah."

"Finn, he could look like anyone. You wouldn't be able to stop him. All he needs to do is put his hand on your chest." Tears spiked my eyes and panic began to rise in me. "What if he looked like your mum? What if he looked like *me*? Do you think you'd fight back? Do you think you'd hesitate, even for a second, if he looked like me and went to kiss you and put his hand on your chest?"

I could hear the hysteria in my voice but I couldn't help it. The thought of Aegyir killing Finn, the only man I had ever loved, was more than I could cope with.

"Hey, hey," said Finn, pulling me towards him and wrapping his arms around me. "Come on. Come here."

"How can we be ready if we don't know what he looks like? I have to go to the rock face by the boulder tomorrow, otherwise he'll kill you and we'd never see him coming." I pulled back and scraped my hands over my face. "What would you do if it was *me* he'd threatened? You'd go to the rock face. You'd take the soil and the sword and you'd go there and try to kill him. I have to do that! How can I not?"

He drew me towards him again, rubbing his hands over my back, tracing the wonky line of my ribs.

"He'll kill you," he whispered, his voice catching.

"No. He needs me alive to open this portal. He might want to kill me *after* I open it, but since I'm not this Aeron woman, I *can't* actually open it, can I?"

"And then he might kill you because you can't. I won't let you go there."

"Finn, I have to."

I couldn't stop the tears. He was my world and I would protect him at any cost.

There was a long silence. I knew from Finn's breathing that he was crying, though if I moved so that I could see his face, he'd pretend he wasn't.

"If you really, *really* have to go, then I'm coming with you."

"No. You're staying at home, where it's safe."

"You know I can't do that."

I moved back, ready to remonstrate with him, but the defiance in his face silenced me. "Rea, there's absolutely no way that I'm gonna let you go up a secluded farm track to meet a demon, on your own. No way."

He wasn't going to back down and secretly, part of me was pleased he would be there to help.

"Okay. But only because I don't think I can stop you."

He gave me a lopsided grin and kissed me. "What kind of guy would I be if I let you go on your own?"

"A safe one."

18

Was this the right place? A lot rested on us having found exactly where Aegyir would be. I circled on the spot, examining every stone, every blade of grass. We'd walked up the track that started at the end of our lane, hugging the edge of a farmer's field. At the end of the field it changed to a thin stony path that wound its way towards the quarry. On the right-hand side was a sheer rock face, not far from the place Finn and I would picnic in the summer, looking out over the valley. This was the place where I'd heard voices before and I was sure it was the place that Aegyir meant.

The rock face was a wall of craggy limestone, its surface mottled with lichen and pitted with cracks. The path up to the top of the rise was strewn with boulders, but next to the rock face a larger, rounded boulder dominated the space. Unlike the rocks littering the path, its surface was smooth and had no moss growing on it. Yellow, grey and green splashes of lichen speckled one side; the other side, shielded by the crag, was clear. Scrubby gorse bushes ringed the edge of the path.

I walked along the rock face, letting my hands travel over the pitted surface. I don't know what I was hoping for. A door handle? A conspicuous keyhole? There was nothing. Finn stood next to the boulder, the bag in one hand, the sword clasped against his leg, the blade running down towards his foot.

"Is this the place?" His eyes scanned the area and he looked dubious.

"I think so."

I needed a better sign that it was. I moved further away from Finn, climbing the hillside before turning and picking my way back down, listening for the whispers I'd heard before. If Finn thought I was mad, he didn't say anything. I tried to remember exactly where it was that I'd had the vision of the Realm when Finn and I had done a night run, just over two weeks ago. It was near the rounded boulder, I was sure of it. I slowed my pace, concentrating.

Nothing.

I kept going until I was sure I was too far away and then retraced my steps. Finn fidgeted, shifting his weight from foot to foot and I tried to blank him out and focus on the limestone cliff.

"Do not invite him in."

I stopped, my heart in my mouth. I'd heard it. It was faint, but I'd heard it.

"You are not welcome."

I swallowed, listening for more, but there was silence again. I faced Finn. "Here."

"Sure?"

"Mm."

"Based on...?"

"The whispers. Same as I heard before. I can hear the Realm."

Finn peeled himself away from the boulder, holding the leather bag out to me. The grass was thin here, cropped short by rabbits. A stride away was a gorse bush where we could conceal the sword. It was here or nowhere. I pulled the neck of the bag open and prayed that I was right. Reaching in, I grabbed a handful of soil. It was gritty and had a different tang to it. Less earthy. I scattered it on the ground around me, covering an irregular shape that stretched from the boulder to the rock face, extending about a metre and a half in width.

Please let me be right. Right that this was the place. Right to be putting the soil here.

Right to believe I could kill Aegyir.

The bag empty, I took the sword from Finn and stashed it in the gorse bush. I circled around it, fiddling with it until I was convinced it would be easy to grab when we returned and had to face Aegyir, but was safely hidden from view until then. It wouldn't do to come up here and realise some yob had found it and nicked it.

Satisfied, I checked my watch. We had about an hour before we were due to meet Aegyir.

As we walked back down to the house, my brain churned. How did you prepare for meeting a demon? How did you prepare yourself for needing to chop its head off? My hands were already shaking at the *idea* of doing it. When it came to it, would I be frozen to the ground? A queasy feeling settled in my stomach and I had a sour taste in my mouth.

At the cottage, Finn made coffees and taped his hands as if he was about to have a training session on the punch bag. I raised a brow.

"Just in case I need to hit him," he said, working the tape deftly over his knuckles.

I wished we had body armour. We'd decided to go up wearing our motorbike jackets and trousers as at least they were made of Kevlar. I had no idea if they would be any protection against a demon reaching into your chest to rip out your vitality, but at least they were stab-proof.

As I sipped my coffee, I tried to prepare myself for what was ahead. I tried to imagine Finn was in danger and how I would react. Tried to lock that anger and hate into a useful shape that would allow me to slice the head off something that looked like my friend.

What terrified me was knowing that Aegyir could look like anyone. He'd told me that. I was unconvinced I would be able to chop off Rick's head, but I knew for certain I would never manage to decapitate something that looked like Alison Cullen. I prayed that Aegyir would drop all pretence of being anything other than what he was.

Finn caught my eye across the table. "Are we really doing this?" He clasped his hands around his mug of coffee.

"What choice do we have? I have no doubt that if we don't do something to stop him this evening, Aegyir will find a way to kill you tomorrow. He's going to work his way through everyone close to me until I meet him on that hillside and he finds out I'm not able to open the door. If I meet him tonight and he realises I'm not Aeron..."

I tailed off. I'd been about to say, "Maybe he won't kill you," but I knew that I would choke on the words. Finn blanched. I assumed he thought that if Aegyir realised I wasn't Aeron, he'd just kill me anyway.

"No heroics," I said. "I don't want you getting hurt."

He nodded, but I knew all too well what could happen when the red mist came down with him. I finished my coffee and checked the clock. "Time to go."

***

We were there first. The sun was sinking but there was a good half hour or more of light. I didn't want to contemplate doing what I had to do in the dark. I paced the area, checked that the sword was where we'd left it and listened for signs that Aegyir was approaching. Finn took up a position between the limestone cliff and the gorse bush. His hands were white from the tape around his knuckles, peeking out beneath the black of his jacket, and his face was etched with worry. He straightened, his attention locked on the path up from the field. Two figures approached. Rick and Stephen. I swallowed. I should have known that Stephen would come too, but it was an added complication I could do without.

Aegyir, still looking like Rick, stood before me, Stephen at his shoulder. My stomach knotted.

"Aeron. So glad that you came." His eyes flicked over Finn who stood behind my left shoulder, about three steps away from me and closer to the gorse bush than me. "And you brought him along too. Thank you."

Finn flexed his hands but kept his distance.

"I see no need for any pretence up here. We all know who I am and it's tiresome to waste vitality on this." The image of Rick dissolved from around Aegyir as he spoke, until what remained was a cadaverous figure, leathery skin stretched over bones, red glints in dark eyes, sinewy tendons showing clear along the backs of his hands. He wore a long leather coat that almost skimmed the ground, its collar standing up. Leather boots showed beneath it, and dark trousers. He seemed taller than I remembered, but maybe that was the fear.

I made my first mistake, right then.

Stephen moved away from Aegyir and came to stand between me and the rock face. I should have moved. I should have taken two paces closer to Aegyir but I was scared and I stayed where I was. Things could have been so different if I hadn't.

I shifted my balance, aware of Stephen's position. Finn moved so that he could protect me from either of them, but that took him closer to Aegyir than I wanted him to be and further from the sword. I wondered if Aegyir knew it was there somehow and instead of moving closer to Aegyir, I moved towards the gorse bush. When might I have to use the sword? To retrieve it too soon might be as big a disaster as retrieving it too late.

Aegyir faced me, the large boulder on his left, me between him and the gorse bush, Finn between him and Stephen. I scanned the ground. He stood on the area where I'd scattered the soil.

"Open the portal, Aeron. Invite me into The Realm."

"I don't know where it is. And I'm not Aeron."

In the corner of my eye I saw Finn shift uneasily. Neither of us thought we could convince Aegyir that he was mistaken and the consequence of him realising I wasn't Aeron could be lethal. It was worth a shot though.

Aegyir curled his thin lips. "Open the portal. You are standing right next to it. It's four words, Aeron. I invite you in. Do it."

Stephen took a step closer to me and Finn tracked him. The four of us were making an ever tighter knot and I willed Finn to take a pace back.

"Assuming I am Aeron, assuming I do that. Why would you go into the Realm? Wouldn't the Guardians cut you to pieces?"

Aegyir laughed. "You really remember *nothing*. All those lives you have been forced to live out here must have wiped your memories. The invite doesn't expire until I'm dispersed. You invite me in. I amass my army. I can pass through the portal whenever I want and I can take whoever I want with me."

I needed Finn further away. I looked across at him and made the merest flick of my head to send him a pace further from danger. He gave me a face that asked if I was mad but eventually moved.

I made my second mistake.

I stepped backwards and grasped the hilt of the sword, the gorse thorns scratching my skin as I did so. Aegyir's red eyes followed my movements, and he laughed. Stephen took a short stride towards me, his hand out as if to grab me. Finn shot forwards and Stephen's arm dropped to his side. The four of us were no further apart from each other than a metre. Aegyir very deliberately took a step to the side. Off the area where the bag of soil had been scattered. My heart sank and my breathing juddered. I needed him back on the soil. I turned to Stephen.

"Back off. Don't think I would hesitate for a *moment* over hacking you to bits with this." I raised the sword towards him, half an eye on where Aegyir was. I really needed Finn further away.

"Enough!"

All of us turned to Aegyir who was pointing at Finn.

"I have given you a choice, Aeron. Open the portal or I kill Finn. Do you love him so little that you would let him die rather than betray The Realm? Are you going to choose to sacrifice him to protect the world that banished you all those lifetimes ago? Will you stand there and watch me rip the life out of him, rather than say four words?"

I launched myself at him, the sword whirling, but Stephen grabbed the back of my neck and yanked me almost off my feet. The sword cut no more than air. Aegyir turned, his face contorting with rage, his bony hand reaching towards Finn. I screamed, my heart stopping. Aegyir grasped Finn by the chin, his claw-like hands bunching the skin of Finn's cheeks into ridges. Finn drove his fists into Aegyir's midriff but he merely twisted Finn's face in response.

"I would not do that if I were you, *boy*. Aeron is currently being held by Stephen, and Stephen is under my control."

Aegyir straightened his arm, pushing Finn back so that his fists could no longer reach him, however hard he tried.

Aegyir looked over to Stephen, who reached around and held a knife to my throat, the metal cold against my skin.

"Finn, stop," I gasped.

He stilled immediately, though his eyes blazed with fury. Aegyir released his grip on him.

Immediately, I drove my elbow back into Stephen's midriff as hard as I could, knocking the air out of him and making him release me. I followed this up with an uppercut that split his lip and a left-hook that made blood pour from his nose. Aegyir swivelled on the spot and marched towards me, hand outstretched. Back on to Realm soil.

My third mistake was to believe that Aegyir would attack me. I should have known that he wouldn't. I should have stood my ground instead of stepping backwards. I should have let his hand touch my chest and prove the point that he wouldn't harm me. But I didn't. I recoiled and Finn… Finn who would protect me against anything, even the demons of hell, stepped forwards to put himself between me and Aegyir.

Time moved slowly, but things happened fast.

Aegyir reached into Finn's chest as if the Kevlar didn't exist. My chest constricted, my heart shattering as I watched a ball of light coalesce around his fist and Finn begin to crumple. Panicked, I smashed backwards, stamping on Stephen, and lashed out with the sword. It cut cleanly through Aegyir's outstretched arm, severing it from his body. The ball of light swirled and split, some tendrils entering Aegyir, some flowing back into Finn.

I howled as Finn's legs buckled under him and he collapsed to the ground. The arm I'd cut off disintegrated into smoke and more smoke poured out of Aegyir's shoulder. I launched myself at Aegyir, aiming the blade at his neck but he grabbed at it with his remaining hand, twisting it out of my grasp and tossing it away. Behind me,

Stephen was getting to his feet. Aegyir held his hand out to Stephen, palm out and he froze.

"Perhaps now you will open the portal."

"Never!" I scrambled for the sword, shoulder-barging Aegyir out of the way to get it. He was no longer on the scattered soil but I was beyond reason. The sword was beautifully balanced in my hand and I whirled it, slashing into Aegyir's body. Smoke gushed forth.

Aegyir stumbled backwards, eyes burning. I scanned him. Vitality flowed from his wounds, thin streams of light dissipating into the air. What could he do to me now? Nothing.

"Kill her?" said Stephen, still standing a few feet away from me.

I turned, gripping the sword firmly. "Bring it on. I'm more than happy to show you *both* what I can do." I would happily have slaughtered both of them.

Aegyir straightened. "No. Let her realise what she has done. We all knew he would protect you at any cost. I could not have taken your vitality, even if I had no further use for you, Aeron. You are a *Guardian*, even if you do not remember it. I hope The Realm is grateful."

"I will *never* open the portal for you. *Never*!"

He smiled beatifically. "Oh. I think you will."

I ran to Finn and held him against me. "Finn! Finn?"

He was unresponsive.

Aegyir beckoned Stephen to him. "Come. Let us leave Aeron to contemplate the consequences of her decision."

The two of them strode back down the hill, while the man I loved lay cradled in my arms. Dying.

I had failed.

19

"Finn?"

He was crumpled in a heap, unconscious, his eyes open but unseeing. I slapped his cheek lightly. "Finn? Finn?"

He came round and blinked groggily. "What the hell?" He passed a hand over his brow.

"Are you okay?" I searched his face frantically. He was the colour of a snowdrift.

"Yeah... No... I feel like shit. It felt so weird. Like it was sucking strength out of me."

Tears poured down my face. His eyes fluttered shut, and my heart almost stopped.

"Finn?" Panic rippled through my voice.

He felt around until his hand found me and he patted at me. "Hey! It's okay. He didn't kill me. You stopped him."

I swallowed down sobs. "Come on. Let's get you home." My voice mangled in my throat.

Finn started to get to his feet. Almost immediately, his legs gave way underneath him and he hit the turf again with a thud.

"Finn? You okay?"

He breathed deeply, scowling. "You're gonna need to help me. My legs are rubbish."

I squatted next to him, draped his arm around my shoulders and wrapped my arm around his waist. We stood slowly, Finn needing a moment to steady himself. Thank

God I was as tall as I was. Anyone smaller than me would struggle to hold him up.

"Okay?" My heart was breaking into a thousand pieces.

"Yeah. I'll be fine, Rea. He didn't kill me. You chopped his arm off." He kissed me. "Thank you."

There was nothing I could say. I picked the sword up, though what exactly I thought I was going to do with it, I don't know.

Finn shuffled towards the path. "We're not gonna be breaking any speed records. Sorry."

"Sh. It's okay. Take your time."

It felt like forever before we made it back to the cottage, Finn apologising all the way. I was grateful for the lights from the cottages to guide us, as it was long after sundown by the time we were crossing the farmer's field. When we got home, Finn sank down on the sofa.

"Jaysus, I feel shit." He clasped his head in his hands, his colour shifting from snow-white to a grubbier grey colour. "Can you get me some water?"

As soon as I entered the kitchen, my temper flared. Sitting on the table were a flat leather pouch, and a ceramic vessel about the size of a biscuit barrel. I flipped open the pouch, even though I knew exactly what would be in it. Three daggers.

Frustration billowed out of me in a primal scream. I hurled the daggers and the pot across the room with as much force as I could muster. The pot landed with a hollow ringing sound and the lid came off, but neither part broke. The daggers spilled from the pouch and clattered across the floor.

"Rea? You okay?" called Finn, alarm in his voice.

I took a glass of water through, unable to contain all the emotions that were battering me. "Oh, yeah. I'm just fine. The love of my life has been attacked by a demon I *spectacularly* failed to kill and in the kitchen are three fucking daggers and a pot!"

I sank down next to him.

"He didn't kill me," said Finn, soothingly.

My breathing juddered in my chest.

He had. He just hadn't died yet. Should I tell him? Would it be better to know? Or to believe it was all okay, when it wasn't?

"I'm calling an ambulance," I said. He opened his mouth to protest but I held my hand up. "No. No arguments."

Half an hour later, the paramedics had been and gone. They'd checked Finn over, measured his blood pressure (low), taken an ECG (normal) and asked repeatedly if he'd been on the bike when he collapsed. I told them he was only in his motorbike clothes because they were warm.

"Keep an eye on him. Call us out again if he gets worse. Call the doctor in the morning. I suspect he's got flu. There's a lot of it about," said the paramedic as he finished and peeled off his gloves. "There's nothing we can do for him and he's not ill enough to take up a hospital bed. Rest, fluids and paracetamol."

"Okay."

I don't know what I'd hoped they would be able to do. Give him a vitality transfusion? I thanked them and showed them out.

Back in the lounge, I sat next to Finn on the sofa, brushing back his hair and peering at him. "Will you manage any dinner?"

"No. I just want to grab a shower and go to bed I think."

He stood up and swayed, putting his hand out to steady himself.

"Are you going to manage a shower?"

"You gonna come and help?" he said, shooting me a raunchy glance.

"Yeah, if you need me to."

He straightened, his skin ashen, and reached out to catch hold of my shoulder for support. I ducked under his arm to walk him up the stairs to the bathroom. It took all my acting skills not to look devastated. I shepherded him into the bathroom and helped him to perch on the edge of the bath.

The paramedics had already got him out of his Kevlar jacket and leather trousers, leaving him in socks, shorts and a long-sleeved t-shirt.

"I'm going to run you a bath," I said. "You're not going to manage to stand."

I ran a hot bath for him with a good squirt of shower gel in it and then helped him until he was lying in it, his knees poking out but the rest of him up to his neck in foamy water. I let him soak for a bit before offering to wash his back. He leaned forwards on to his knees and I soaped his shoulders, tracing out his dragon.

"Can you just do all of me? I can't even lift the soap," he said, scrunching his face up at me.

"That's a really rubbish chat-up line."

He laughed. "That boat's sailed."

I pulled his towel down from the rail and held it out to him. I'd never seen him so miserable before.

Up, he wrapped the towel around him, shivering. The bedroom was chilly and Finn's flesh sprang up into goose bumps. I hustled him towards the bed and found him some clean boxer shorts and a t-shirt.

"Hot water bottle?" I asked as I tucked him under the duvet.

"Thanks."

By the time I returned with a hot water bottle, Finn was asleep. I nestled the bottle near his chest, my heart ripping apart.

I had done this to him. I had killed him. The man I loved the most in the world.

I wanted to spend every second I could with him, but I also needed to let my emotion out and I didn't want to wake him or for him to see what I knew. He thought he would be okay. Maybe he would be. Maybe I was wrong. Either way, he didn't need to see me fall apart. I went back downstairs to the lounge, poured myself a serious measure of vodka, added the smallest splash of orange juice and bawled my eyes out until I was spent.

The events replayed in my head in a non-stop loop – the shifting positions of everyone; Finn's protectiveness taking him into the firing line; Aegyir reaching into his chest; the ball of light fracturing.

Had enough flowed back into Finn? Would he survive?

20

Neither of us slept well that night. I joined Finn in bed, either curling up against him while he shivered, or sitting wrapped in a spare blanket, reading the book while he slept. His eyes darted back and forth beneath his lids, his dreams wracked with angst, and he tossed and turned and moaned or cried out all night. When I finally abandoned the book and slept, my dreams rotated through nightmare after nightmare – the two men saying it was all my fault and that I was a traitor, Stephen's attack, and what had happened on the hillside.

I'd hoped that somewhere in the book there would be something that would help, that would tell me how to save Finn. There wasn't. I scoured every tale in it, yearning to find out what happened if a connection between Aegyir and his victim was severed before all their vitality had been taken. But the stories were the same stories they'd been when I first read them and none of them offered even a crumb of comfort. Maybe there was nothing in the book because no one had chopped a demon's arm off and broken the connection mid-assault before.

Aegyir had been ripping Finn's vitality out when I cut his arm off. Did that matter? Or was it only a matter of time before the portion that had gone back into Finn was taken by Aegyir? That was what happened with the flu victims. They died. Their vitality ebbed out of them and into Aegyir.

If Aegyir had ripped Finn's spirit out of him and would have all of his vitality, what would happen to his character? The book said it would be lost to Chaos. What did that mean? I couldn't bear the thought of losing Finn, and despite having no belief in reincarnation, I certainly couldn't think about his wonderful, caring, funny, loving character being lost to some hinterland of nothing. If I could disperse Aegyir, perhaps a friendly Guide could collect Finn's vitality and reunite it with his character. If I dispersed Aegyir *before* he'd taken all of Finn's vitality, would Finn survive?

Except I wasn't a Guardian.

When Finn's watch beeped in the morning, he groaned and rolled over. I reached across him to silence the alarm, and took his watch off his wrist.

He was a weird grey colour but nonetheless, he tried to sit up.

"Where do you think you're going?" I asked.

"I have to get up. Work."

I snorted. "Don't be ridiculous. You're in no shape to go to work. I'm calling Billy."

"I'm fine," he said, swinging his legs out of bed. A moment later his legs had buckled and he was in a heap on the floor.

"I'm calling Billy," I said firmly and this time he didn't argue.

"I need the bathroom," he muttered, scowling.

I slung his arm over my shoulder and helped him across the landing. "Can you manage in there on your own? Don't lock the door."

"Mm," he said irritably.

I sat on the landing until I heard the loo flush and water run in the sink.

"Rea?"

I pushed the door open. Finn gripped the edge of the

sink, swaying slightly. I helped him back to bed and tucked him in again.

"Coffee? Breakfast?" I asked, pulling on a jumper and retrieving the hot water bottle from the bed, ready to replenish it.

"Mm."

He lay flat, his skin pale and pinched, hollows forming in his cheeks. I picked up his phone and called Billy.

"Hi, Finn." Billy sounded surprised.

"Hi, Billy. No, it's Rea but I'm on Finn's phone. Um, Finn's really ill. I think it's flu. He can barely get out of bed and he looks absolutely dreadful. I'm sorry but he's not going to make it in today. Hang on, he wants to speak to you."

I passed the phone to Finn who croaked apologetically into it. He said he'd be in the following day but I knew he wouldn't. The call over, he passed the phone back to me. I brushed his hair back and kissed his forehead.

"I'll be fine," he said. "I just need a couple of days. Get some strength back."

"Well, to get your strength back, you need to eat," I said briskly. I had to keep busy.

I fetched him a coffee and some breakfast which he forced down, his colour brightening a fraction. The only other thing he wanted was his panacea – soluble paracetamol and double vitamin C.

As he put the empty glass on the chest of drawers at the side of the bed, he met my eye. "What did you see?"

I knew exactly what he meant, but feigned ignorance, buying myself time. Did I tell him?

"You could see that Guide thing take a ball of light out of the guy who was hit by a car, just before he died. What did you see with me and Aegyir?"

I bit my lip so hard it almost bled, not trusting my voice.

"Rea? Just tell me."

"Are you sure?"

For an ill man he could still muster a filthy look.

"Okay. I saw Aegyir start to take a ball of light out of your chest. When I cut through Aegyir's arm, the light split. Some of it went into Aegyir; some of it went back into you."

Finn said nothing for a moment. Finally, he rubbed his hand through his hair. "So, he's got *some* of my energy, which is why I feel so shit. But he didn't get *all* of my energy, which is why I'm not dead?"

What could I say?

"That's about the size of it. You should rest."

"Get my strength back?"

I couldn't tell if he was being sarcastic or not. "Please, Finn. Just rest."

He shifted back under the covers and I pressed a kiss to his forehead. "I love you."

"Love you too."

I tiptoed back downstairs with no idea what to do. Should I call Alison? But say what? That her son was dying, it was all my fault and she should probably get over to see him before it was too late?

I needed him to be okay. Which meant I needed to hope that I *was* a Guardian.

***

I parked the bike up at the kerb next to Rick's place and pulled my helmet off. Rick lived in the right-hand ground-floor flat in a block of four. I stared at the windows for a moment. Was I really about to do this?

Yes.

Did a demon actually need to have a place to stay? If Aegyir *wasn't* using Rick's flat as well as his image, wouldn't Rick's neighbours wonder where he was? Probably not. He could be an antisocial bugger at times and as far as I knew, he wasn't friendly with anyone in the other flats in the block.

I swallowed. Part of me still clung to the hope that Rick was alive somewhere since no body had been found, but I knew the likelihood was slim to vanishing. The only reason Rick's body was still missing would be because Aegyir hadn't killed him at the quarry but somewhere else, and hidden the body so that he could continue to mimic it without causing confusion and suspicion.

I tugged at my jacket and hauled in a deep breath, trying to settle myself, then marched up to the communal door that led to a smart vestibule and access to the flats. Rick's door was to the right, just after all the post-boxes. My heart in my mouth, I banged on the door and cocked an ear, straining to hear if there were any sounds from within.

Nothing.

The vestibule had a sharp tang of detergent and the tiled floor looked recently mopped. I waited, letting my eyes travel over the off-white walls and up the concrete stairs leading to the flats above. I banged on the door again, harder, the sounds echoing slightly in the hallway.

Still nothing.

I wondered if any of Rick's neighbours were in and when they might last have seen him. I crossed the hallway and rapped on his neighbour's door.

Also nothing.

No huge surprise, as the flats were most likely to be owned or rented by people who were out at work. They weren't the most expensive apartments in the town, but they were far from cheap. I knocked again, then gave up. It had been a long shot.

Sighing deeply, I shoved the door to the street open and walked back to the bike, pulling my helmet back on. If I hadn't been keen on coming to Rick's, I was even less keen on my next destination.

Ten minutes later, I turned the engine off and sat on the bike, staring at the neat front garden. I'd vowed I would never come back here. Even seeing the front door made my heart rate soar and my skin prickle. It took me a good few minutes to settle myself enough but, eventually, I tugged my helmet off and swung off the bike. My hand hesitated on the wrought-iron gate, my legs wobbly at even the *thought* of being here.

"Come on," I chided myself. "You faced a demon and survived. You can do this."

I breathed steadily, trying to calm myself, then gathered my courage and pushed the gate open. In four shaky strides, I was at the front door. I pressed the doorbell, adjusting my grip on the strap of my helmet. Worst-case scenario, I could swing it at his head and break *his* nose. Return the favour.

Stephen answered the door, and I forced myself not to step back. I smiled internally at the split lip and black eyes he sported. His brows arched as he saw me and he clamped a hand on either side of the door-frame, barring my way. No need. I would *never* set foot across this threshold.

"Cuckoo!" His eyes glittered. I didn't like the look of his pupils.

"Where's Aegyir?" I said, adjusting my grip on my helmet, my hands clammy.

"Who?" Stephen's piggy little eyes narrowed further, but he was a crap actor.

"Your lord and master. The one in your head, controlling you."

"No one controls *me*, Cuckoo."

I recalled the way Aegyir had done just that, with the merest flick of a wrist. "Really. Well, perhaps he can see and hear all this from inside your tiny little mind." I leaned in and glared into Stephen's blacked eyes. "Aegyir, you piece of shit, I need to see you."

Stephen laughed lightly as I stepped back. "Once Aegyir's regains his strength, you'll be sorry."

"Thought you didn't know who he was," I mocked.

I walked backwards until I was out of reach, then turned and marched back to the bike.

Partway home, my phone vibrated in my pocket and as soon as I'd put the bike away, I checked it. It was a summary of the news headlines and I had to steady myself with one hand on the side of the shed.

Five more bodies had been found near the disused end of the quarry, none with any obvious cause of death.

***

I tiptoed back into the bedroom. Finn was sleeping fitfully and I sat on the edge of the bed and smoothed his hair back, trying not to cry. He was a dreadful colour again and felt cool to the touch.

Despite my best intentions, I managed to disturb him.

"Hey," he said sleepily. "Where'd you go?"

"To find Aegyir."

His eyes widened and I rushed to reassure him.

"I didn't find him. I found Stephen though." A wry smile tweaked my lips. "I made a bit of a mess of his face yesterday."

A brief smile crossed Finn's face but vanished almost instantly. "Why did you go to find Aegyir?"

I sighed, nibbling at my lower lip. "To find out how to help you."

He struggled to a sitting position and his fingers plucked at the covers. "I *will* get better, won't I? I'm not gonna stay this weak forever, am I? I can rebuild the strength he took. I mean, he's got *some* of it, but I can make more, right?"

I didn't know what to say so I nodded.

He glanced across at the book on the side of the bed, next to me. "Anything in that? Does it say how long it takes to recover?"

My heart splintered. "It doesn't say."

He rallied slightly over the afternoon, sitting up and chatting a bit more, giving us both a bit of hope. We reminisced about old days, recalling incidents from school like him accidentally setting his hair alight in chemistry one day, leaning over a Bunsen burner as he lit it. He'd been left with a strip missing out of his spiked up fringe. He reminded me of the time I'd been shut in the art cupboard by someone a lot bigger than me, but I'd had my revenge by drawing caricatures of him and posting them around the school.

"Do you remember how we met?" I tucked myself closer to him, knotting our legs.

"Of course I do."

It was a bittersweet memory. I was fourteen and had moved to the school after Helen and John had married. I knew no one, was gangly and rebellious and felt like it would always be me against the rest of the world. A group of boys had seen me as an easy target when I joined the school. I suppose I was at that point. I was skinny and unhappy and felt like no one was on my side, not even my adopted mother. Three boys had cornered me in a quiet part of the grounds and were harassing me. Nothing more than pushing and shoving, but there were three of them and one of me and I couldn't get away. Finn, already sick of seeing his mother getting knocked around at home and never one to hang back, had weighed in with fists flailing. He'd been my friend ever since, though it took us a while to get around to dating, only getting together when I was sixteen and Finn was almost eighteen and had left home. Within a year I'd practically moved in with him, spending more nights at the cottage than I did at home. After Stephen had almost beaten me to death, I stopped pretending I lived at home – Finn had collected everything I had from Helen and we'd been in the cottage together ever since.

Mid-afternoon, Finn called Alison. "Hey Mum. How are you?"

"I'm fine. You sound terrible! Is everything okay?"

"Oh, I've got flu and I don't think I'm gonna be able to meet you tomorrow."

"That doesn't matter! You concentrate on getting well."

"I'll be fine! I'm just washed out and I reckon I'll be struggling to get to work, never mind manage to catch up. I'm really sorry. Things are okay though?"

Code for, "Has Dad hit you?" I watched Finn's face as he listened to the answer. He seemed reassured. He promised he'd catch up with her soon and rang off. The call seemed to have taken it out of him and his colour had faded back to off-grey.

"Get some rest," I said. "I'll wake you when it's dinnertime."

He scooted down the bed and I drew the covers up to his chin. He was asleep by the time I brought a fresh hot water bottle back up and I secreted it next to his chest and kissed his brow.

While Finn slept, I pulled on my coat and boots and marched up to the rock face. My stomach lurched as I reached the place where Aegyir had attacked Finn, but I didn't have either the time or the energy for regrets. I strode over to the place where I'd heard the whispers and faced the craggy rocks, my hands planted on my hips.

"Get your fucking arses out here! Aegyir is loose. He's killing people. Do your fucking jobs and come and *help*!"

Silence.

"Get out here!" I bellowed. "I need some fucking Guardians out here!"

*"*You *are a Guardian, Aeron. Aegyir is* your *problem, not ours."*

I screamed in frustration, my voice impotently bouncing off the rock face. Spent, I sagged backwards, balling my fists.

Okay. If they wouldn't help me, I'd just have to kill the fucker on my own.

21

I took one look at Finn in the morning and called an ambulance. He was ashen and I could barely rouse him. When I did finally manage to wake him he was mumbling incoherently.

The paramedics didn't like the look of him much either, bundling him on to a stretcher and into the back of the ambulance fairly soon after arriving. I followed them on the bike without bothering to change into leathers, praying not to come off. The roads were at least drying after the downpour the night before.

At the hospital, I sat in the grey waiting room of Accident and Emergency while he was assessed in a room somewhere. Around me were people in various states of distress – a woman with a deep gash on her forehead, the blood seeping into a wad of dressing that she pressed to it; a man who hobbled painfully to and from the water-dispenser; a sobering drunk, spattered with vomit; several people looking miserable. I sat on a hard, plastic chair, my eyes glued to the doors through to the assessment area, my nose nipping from the smell of disinfectant. In front of me was a low table with a scattering of dog-eared magazines, striped with the light coming through the blinds. Despite the signs saying no mobiles, I called Alison and told her that Finn had taken a turn for the worse and was in hospital. She said she'd be there that afternoon and I promised I'd call her with an update as soon as I was allowed to see him.

He'd been transferred to the high dependency unit by the time one of the nurses came out to speak to me. She reassured me that it was merely a precaution and that they were sure it was only flu and he would be fine. I nodded rapidly and asked if I could see him.

"Of course you can. He needs to rest, but he's in a room on his own and you can sit with him if you want."

"Why is he in a room on his own?"

"Because he has flu and we don't want all the other patients getting it," she said, smiling. I must have looked panicked.

When I reached his room, I caught a sob in my throat. Finn was hooked up to a heap of monitors and there were wires and tubes everywhere. The nurse explained them gently but I didn't take any of it in. He was asleep, so I went back to the hallway and called his mum again to update her. She said she'd be there as soon as she could.

I tiptoed back into Finn's room, hoping that the nurse was right about me being allowed to stay with him. A couple of nurses came and went, measuring things on him and filling in the chart at the end of his bed and I stayed in the corner, out of their way. A doctor arrived, read the chart, looked at Finn, reassured me that he would probably be fine and asked me if I had any questions. I should have asked her about all the wires and tubes, but all I thought to ask was whether I could stay with him.

About an hour later, Finn stirred, his dark lashes fluttering. I moved my chair close to the bed and held his hand. He peered at me. "Rea? Where the hell am I?"

"Hospital. You looked pretty rubbish this morning so I called an ambulance and they brought you in. Your mum said she'd come and visit this afternoon. How are you feeling?"

"Horrible." He licked his lips, frowning. His gaze travelled around the bed, pausing on each of the tubes and wires. "Am I dying?" His voice trembled and his blue eyes were wide. His breathing rate rose, but each breath was snatched and shallow. I forced my tears down and stroked my thumb over his knuckles.

"The doctor was a bit unhappy about your blood pressure. They think you might have been dehydrated, despite my best efforts." His lips were cracked and I rummaged in my pocket for a lip balm. "Here." I rubbed it over his lips. "Better?"

"Mm. Thanks. You said Mum's coming?"

"Yeah. I called her when you were brought in."

"Thanks… Sorry, I'm shattered."

"Shh. Go back to sleep."

"Will you stay?"

"Of course. Go back to sleep. I'll be right here."

He closed his eyes again. I waited until I was sure he was asleep and retreated to my corner again, wondering if I would manage to kill Aegyir before it was too late.

Alison Cullen arrived immediately after lunch. I hadn't had anything to eat since I'd got up so I left her with him and took myself off to the cafe downstairs to grab a bite. On the telly in the corner, a TV showed the news channel, subtitles scrolling across the bottom of the screen. Our town was the main topic after another three bodies had turned up today. Not in the quarry this time – unsurprising since the police had advised people to avoid it – but in quiet areas of the town – the park, an alleyway, a lane around the back of the main church. The police were treating all deaths as suspicious and telling people not to go out alone or after dark. That wouldn't keep them safe. If Aegyir wanted your vitality, he'd just take it. My sandwich lodged in my throat as I tried to swallow. How many more people would Aegyir kill before I could try to stop him?

As I ate, I kept an eye on my wrist, half hoping it would glow blue and I could confront Aegyir right there, right then. What exactly I thought I could do, I don't know, but I wanted to do *something*. But it stayed resolutely opalescent and I finished my sandwich and returned to HDU.

Alison was still there when I arrived. Finn was awake again and more alert than he had been earlier.

"Oh Rea, there you are. I have to go and make Rory's dinner. Are you staying with Finn?"

I nodded, flexing my fingers, my nostrils flaring as I breathed. Their only son was gravely ill in hospital and she was too scared to stay with him. I assumed she wouldn't even tell Rory where she'd been.

"Yes, I'll stay. I'll call you if there's any change, but the doctors seem to think it's just flu."

"Bless you. Oh, Christ, look at the time. I have to go."

The visit from his mum seemed to have taken it out of Finn and I urged him to lie back down and rest.

"Does Billy know?" he asked, fretful.

"Yes. I called him a few minutes ago. Finn, just *rest*. Please?"

"Are you staying?"

"Of course I am."

"Sit next to me?"

The chair was still next to the bed after his mum's visit and I sat, picking up his hand.

"You look exhausted," he said.

"Yeah, you're no portrait yourself today."

He smiled weakly. "Not drawing me today then?"

"No. Not today." I lifted his hand up and kissed his knuckles, careful to avoid the needle in the back of his hand. His lips were dry again and I rubbed some more balm on them. Finn shifted slightly, his eyes on mine. "I really want to kiss you, but I don't think I can sit up again."

I leaned over and kissed him fully, taking my time.

"You should be resting," I chided as I moved back.

"Don't go!" He kept hold of my hand, his grip weak.

"I'm not going anywhere. Go back to sleep."

The doctor came in to check on him at the start of the evening shift, and evicted me to a small waiting room at the end of the corridor. A few minutes later, she found me in there.

"How is he?" I said, my hands clasped tightly in front of me.

"He's deteriorated since earlier. He seemed to be improving once we got some fluids into him, but he's a little worse now. His blood pressure is low and that's a concern, but his breathing is fine and he's a very fit young man so he has a good chance of shrugging this off."

My heart rate settled a little. "Can I stay? I won't keep him awake."

"We wouldn't normally allow that, but he's been asking for you to stay."

"I'll keep out of the way," I promised. Going back to the cottage with him still here was unimaginable.

The doctor relented. I thanked her and made my way back to Finn's room. He was on the boundary of sleep and wake but smiled feebly as I sat down.

"You're back."

"Yeah. I'm back. Go to sleep. If they think I'm tiring you out they'll make me leave."

I held his hand, playing with his fingers, watching him sleep, my heart at breaking point.

This wasn't flu. And he wasn't regenerating any of the ball of light that Aegyir had stolen.

***

Finn stirring pulled me out of my nightmares and back into his room. I don't know which was worse. He opened troubled eyes surrounded by dark circles.

"Hey, Munchkin," I said, stroking his hand.

He laughed lightly. "God, you haven't called me that in *years.*" His voice was little more than a breath.

"Yeah, well. It was barely apt when you were only six foot, never mind now!"

His smile melted. "Rea. I'm scared," he whispered. I felt my heart crack.

"What are you scared for? You just need a bit of time to get your strength back," I lied, desperate to reassure him.

"I don't think I *will* get my strength back."

"Sh. Just rest."

He wept, his tears flowing freely.

"Hey, hey. What are these for?" I said, stroking them away, using almost all my might not to look distressed.

"I'm so scared. Don't leave me?"

"Finn, it's after half ten at night. If I was going to leave, I'd have done it before now. Shh. Shh. You know I'll never leave you. Never."

I wanted to bawl but I fought my tears down and stroked his cheek.

"You need a shave." I rasped my fingertip against his stubble.

"I thought it looked sexy." His voice was still hiccupy with tears.

"Yeah. It does." I smoothed his hair back from his brow. "You're the sexiest man I've ever met."

"Rea, do you know how much I love you?"

My heart started to splinter. "Probably. But you can tell me anyway. Just in case I don't."

I ran my finger over his cheekbone, wiping away a stray tear.

"I love you to the moon and back," he said quietly. "And then all the rest."

"That's handy. That's *exactly* how much I love you."

He closed his eyes, his breathing slowing, his face relaxing.

One by one, all the monitors started screaming.

Almost instantly, the room filled with medical staff and I was bundled out of the room and into the corridor.

Oh, Christ, I was losing him.

I caught a sob in my chest, struggling to breathe. There was a window into the room and I stared through it, my heart in my mouth as someone began chest compressions on him. Another person put a mask over his face, attached to a big balloon thing.

"Clear!" called one of the medical staff and everyone stepped back a pace.

I gasped as Finn's body jerked as they tried to shock him back to life.

"Finn!" I cried, my fists clenched against the glass, tears pouring down my face. "Finn."

But however many tears I shed and however hard they worked on him, the monitors didn't change. I rested my forehead on the glass, sobbing, pleading with them to save him.

"Perhaps now you will open the portal. Or I will kill everyone."

I whirled around to see who it was who had whispered in my ear but all I saw was a pair of glowing eyes fading to nothing. I turned back to the room, just in time to see the doctors call the time of death as 22:53.

My world ended.

22

"I love you to the moon and back."

"And then all the rest."

Monitors flashing and beeping.

"We need you to leave."

"Time of death is 22:53."

I woke, sobbing, clutching the pillow. It still smelled of him, amongst all the tears and the snot.

"Finn, I miss you! Come back!"

I knew he couldn't.

I burrowed back into the pillow, not sure if I wanted to sleep and be haunted by nightmares or awake and haunted by loss. Exhaustion was going to get me, one way or another.

"You must return. You do not belong here any more. You must protect The Realm."

I shook my head. "Lilja, they will hang me if I return."

She grasped my hands so hard it hurt. "They will have no choice. They need you, or The Realm will fall."

"But..."

Tears shone in her eyes. "Come home. You are needed."

The mist we were standing in cleared. I could smell blood. Death.

All around me were the sounds of battle – clashing swords, screams of terror. Where was Orian? Everyone should have been prepared.

I turned to look at my husband. He had to believe me. He had to. I would never betray him. I would never do this. *But his face was full of hatred and his lip curled.*

"Where is your father?" I asked. We needed all three of us to be able to end this.

"Here." Lord Eredan emerged next to my shoulder, his face hard, his eyes narrowed.

"Aeron!" Aegyir roared, eyes blazing.

I flinched. Blades whirled, a head rolled and the air was filled with smoke that disappeared into the vessel. The vessel sealed, the calligraphy on its sides swirling and writhing as it did. I leaned on my sword, catching my breath before straightening.

Lord Eredan's fist cracked my cheek, whipping my head around.

"Slut! Traitor!"

I sat up, hyperventilating before flopping back, sweat clinging to me. The room was light and I tried to work out what time it was. What day it was even. I had fuzzy recollections of people coming to see me. Alison, weeping. With a shiner. Billy had been here and held me tight, almost as distraught as me. Almost. I scraped a hand through my hair, trying to remember. After Billy had gone, I'd come up here to hide from everyone and ignored the doorbell and the calls. How long had I been up here? I rolled on my side and peered at my phone. Sunday. Just after one in the afternoon.

I couldn't remember getting back from the hospital. Did Alison bring me back? Christ, she must be in hell too.

I was such a selfish cow. While I was disintegrating into a million pieces, Alison was presumably organising her only son's funeral, with no help from me and in all probability, no help from her husband either.

I stared unseeing at the ceiling, tears tracking from the corners of my eyes to dribble down my temples.

"Hey."

My head snapped to the side. Blue eyes framed with dark lashes peered at me from the other side of the bed.

"Finn?"

I reached out to touch him but he shook his head.

"How are you here?" I said, the words lumpy in my throat.

He bunched the side of his mouth. "I don't know."

"But you are here?"

"Feels like it. But it feels weird."

He couldn't really be here. I knew that. I'd watched him die in the hospital. His body must surely be in a funeral home. His vitality was obviously in Aegyir. If so, his character would be lost to Chaos.

Or lying in bed with me. Is that what ghosts were? Characters lost in Chaos until another Guide could reunite them with their vitality?

I drank in every millimetre of him. I loved him so much.

"You shouldn't have been there. If you'd stayed here, he wouldn't have killed you," I said, my voice barely above a whisper. My mind replayed the scene, frame by frame. Aegyir moving towards me; Finn stepping in to protect me.

"Maybe not then. But he would have killed me eventually. The deal was, you opened the portal or he killed me. And you don't know how to open the portal."

He was right. If he'd stayed here, Aegyir would have attacked him at work or on the street. Looked like Alison. Or Billy. Or me. Rage boiled inside me, but a thought soothed me.

I also had the daggers and the vessel now.

"I'm going to fucking *kill* him!"

Finn's eyes widened. "You're not going near him."

"I'm going to hack that bastard into a thousand pieces, stick all the daggers in and stuff him in that fucking pot! I'm going to get him back up to that rock and rip him to bits!"

"Cool it," he said softly. "He'll kill you if you try."

"Do you think I care? I don't want to keep living without you and if I can kill that monster in the process, all the better!"

"Cool it."

I stared at him for four full breaths before dipping my head. "I'm cool. But I'm still going to kill that fucking monster or die trying."

He smiled lopsidedly. "That's my kind of definition of 'I'm cool'."

I peered at him. His amusement faded and he turned serious. "Please. Don't go near him. Please?"

I wasn't about to make a promise I had no intention of keeping.

"Where's your bike?" I asked, frowning. I could remember taking it to the hospital but I was sure I hadn't ridden it back.

"It's still at the hospital. Mum brought you home."

Alison. I couldn't wallow in self-pity and grief any longer and my anger was no use to her either. I should be over there, helping her.

"I should go to her," I said.

"Yeah."

As I watched, he dissolved into nothing and I sat up sharply, searching frantically for him, breathing hard. Would he come back again? Had that been our last conversation? There was so much I hadn't said.

***

As Finn had said, the bike was at the hospital where I'd left it. I rode it over to Alison Cullen's. Technically it was hers now and anyway, my visit was long overdue.

When she answered the door she had a bruise encircling her wrist to go with the black eye. I hoped Finn wasn't looking down on us and could see. I stood awkwardly in the hallway. Alison looked even skinnier than usual, her loose-fitting shirt swamping her. Her blonde hair, normally so neatly clipped back, fell around her face. Trying to conceal the shiner?

"Alison, I am so sorry." That was all I could manage before I was in pieces.

She pulled me into a deep hug and I could feel her bones through her clothes. "Oh, Rea. Rea."

I sobbed hard on her. I knew I shouldn't – she'd lost her only child – but I couldn't stop. She propelled me through to the lounge and the two of us wept buckets over the man we loved. When I could finally speak coherently, I thanked her for bringing me back from the hospital and apologised for not having been over before now.

"You must think I'm dreadful," I said.

She had the same lopsided smile her son had. "I don't think you're dreadful at all. Just heartbroken."

Tears welled again. "Is Rory here?"

She shook her head, self-consciously touching her face. "No. It's Sunday. He's at the pub." Her answer implied it was a stupid question.

His only son was dead and he was at the pub. Bile crept into the back of my throat.

I drew in a deep breath, blew my nose and squared my shoulders. "What can I do to help? When did you want to hold the funeral?"

She squeezed my hand weakly, blue veins showing through her thin translucent skin. "It's organised for Friday."

I felt awful. While I'd been weeping and wailing and ignoring everyone's kind words yesterday, Alison had been her usual, practical self.

"Father O'Keefe came over yesterday. He helped," she said, as if she'd read my mind.

I wondered if this was before or after Rory had hurt her but said nothing.

"Would you come to the florists with me? Tomorrow? And see Father O'Keefe so we can choose the hymns?"

"Mm." I wiped a tear away and sniffed.

"It's easier if you keep busy," said Alison in a small voice and I remembered that Finn's grandfather, her father, had died the year before. "Shall I come to the cottage and help pick out some clothes?"

Her question floored me for a moment. When I realised that she meant choosing something for Finn to be buried in, I broke down.

"He's only got one suit and I don't know if it fits him any more." My voice clotted in my throat and my fingers picked at the piping on the edge of the chintzy sofa cover.

She squeezed my hand again. "Well, we'll find something. The funeral directors also wondered if you had a good picture of him for the service booklet and to show in the church?"

I had thousands of pictures of him.

"Did you want to say something? On Friday? You knew him better than anyone," she said, and I swallowed hard and stared at my lap.

"Yes… yes… Oh. I've brought his bike over. It's yours now of course," I scrambled out, desperately needing to think of something other than Friday.

Alison laughed, a light tinkling bell of a laugh, so different from the deep, rumbling belly laugh that Finn had. "What use is it to me? I can't ride the thing and I always hated him having it."

"Oh. Perhaps Rory…?"

"He doesn't even know Finn had a bike. You keep it. We can sort out the paperwork later if you need to. Finn would have wanted you to have it. He certainly wouldn't have wanted his father to have it."

I didn't really know what to say. My gaze fixed on a loose tuft in the taupe carpet in front of me.

"Will you stay on at the cottage?" Alison asked, head tilted to one side, bird-like.

I sucked in a long breath and shrugged. "I don't know. I suppose so. I don't have anywhere else. I don't know if I can afford to pay the rent and the bills on my own, even with the new job coming. I don't have anywhere else though."

"Well, maybe see what the benefits office says? I would say you could stay here but I don't think Rory would agree to it."

I didn't want to think how much Rory would batter her if she asked. Without Finn around to exact retribution, I shuddered to think how much Rory might beat her, even without that kind of provocation.

I smiled thinly. "I'm sure I'll work something out. The rent's paid for this month and I have enough for next so I'm okay for a few weeks at least."

Did it matter? I assumed I would be dead long before that.

A thought struck me. "Oh. Do you need money for the funeral?"

All of Alison's money went into a joint account that Rory controlled, and I didn't know if he would even pay to bury his son.

"No, it's fine. Rory agreed in the end."

How many more bruises did she have that weren't visible? I wished I could help her, but I knew I couldn't. If

Finn couldn't get her to leave Rory, I had no chance.

She gazed at me. "Did he ask you?"

I blinked. "Who? Ask me what?"

"Finn. Ask you to marry him?"

Tears spilled over the edges of my eyes. "No."

"He was going to. He said he would ask you on your birthday. That's what we were talking about when we went for coffee at the Farmers' Market."

"Oh. My birthday's not for a bit."

"I know. I wondered if he would wait that long. He was never very good at waiting once he'd decided to do something."

I laughed through my tears. "No, he wasn't. But he hadn't asked me."

"I think he'd chosen the ring but hadn't bought it yet."

My mind ran back to the afternoon in the pub when he'd asked me if I wanted him to make an honest woman of me. If I'd said yes, would he have proposed?

Alison reached across and held my hand. "Hang in there. It'll get better."

Maybe. But only because I intended to hack Aegyir into tiny pieces and stuff him in a pot.

***

I didn't bother trying Rick's. I had no belief Aegyir would be there. My message to the organ-grinder could go via the monkey. After leaving Alison's, I drove over to Helen and John's, parked the bike in the street and hammered on the door.

John answered. He wore what I assumed he took to be 'Sunday casual' of chinos, neatly pressed light blue rugby shirt and a navy V-necked sweater over the top. And horrible brown suede moccasin slippers. With tassels.

"You have a bloody nerve," he said, standing in the

doorway, arms tightly folded over his chest.

Even though I stood on the lower doorstep, I was still on eye-level with him and I drew myself up to my full height.

"I need to give Stephen a message. You can either pass it on from me or I can tell him in person. It's no skin off my nose which it is."

John pursed his lips, the lines around his mouth deepening. "We're going to press charges for what you did to him."

I shrugged. "Well, the police can add the complaint to those of mine – Stephen loitering around the cottage, Stephen smashing our front door in…"

I glanced behind him at a movement from the other end of the hall that led from the front to the kitchen at the back. Helen locked eyes with me for a moment, then ducked out of view. I looked back at John.

"You've no evidence my son broke into your house. But then he comes back here with a split lip and two black eyes after seeing you and Finn. And we all know what Finn did to his father."

I pushed my bottom lip out. "Does Stephen have any witnesses?"

John sneered. "Yes, I suspect you and Finn would collude over your stories, give each other an alibi."

My breath shook. "Just get Stephen out here." I didn't want any fake tears or wringing of hands from John or Helen, and I couldn't bear to voice the news, anyway. I stamped down my sorrow, focusing on how I would cut Aegyir into chunks, glaring at John.

"He's not in. What's the message?"

"Tell Aegyir Friday. After the funeral."

John frowned and I clicked my tongue. "You need me to write it down for you? It's only six words!"

John shook his head, sneering. "No, I'll manage, thanks."

I turned on my heel and marched back down the path. "Just make sure Stephen gets the message."

***

Back at the cottage, I peered around, desperate to see Finn again, but there were empty echoes in response to my calls. Keep busy, Alison had said. Doing what? Planning how to kill a demon?

Alison had run through a list of people to tell. Most of the Cullen side had been dealt with via a single call to a cousin who would relay it on to the rest of the family, though I doubted that any of them would come to the funeral. I didn't care whether Helen and John knew. Neither of them had had much time for Finn and the feeling had been mutual. I didn't want them there on Friday. I did need to call Paul, my adopted father. A large chunk of me hoped he would come up for the funeral, but he was based on the other side of London these days and it was a long drive.

I pulled my phone out of my pocket and called him. "Hey, Paul. How are you?"

"Reagan? Hello! I'm fine thanks. How are you?"

Tears choked me. "Um. I'm not so great."

"Reagan, love, what's wrong? Oh, hell. Stephen's out, isn't he? Is everything okay? Has he done something?"

"Yeah, he's out, but that's not the problem." I juddered to a halt, took a deep breath and managed the words I still found impossible to bear. "Finn died."

"What? How? Oh, God, not on the bike?"

I swallowed hard. "Flu. There's a big flu epidemic," I lied. "He died on Friday night. I couldn't bring myself to call before now. I'm sorry."

"Oh God, that's awful. When's the funeral?"

"Friday. Friday morning."

There was a pause on the other end of the line and I could imagine Paul checking his calendar and working out how to re-jig things. "I'll be there. I can come up the night before, but I'll have to leave after work and I might not be able to stay for long after the weekend. Though you could come back here with me if you wanted? Get a break? Change of scenery?"

"It's fine. Don't worry about coming up. I know it's a long way and you're busy."

"I'll be there. Did you want to come and stay here afterwards?"

I would have loved to have gone back south with him. Unfortunately, I had a demon to kill.

"No, I'll be okay. But thank you."

"Okay. I'll book a hotel and let you know the details. Oh Reagan, love, I am so, so sorry. I know how much you love him. Are you okay?"

I fingered my hairline, staring at all of Finn's stuff everywhere – a pair of trainers kicked off in the corner of the room; his wallet on the table; a pair of sunglasses. "No. But I'll cope. Alison – Finn's mum – and I are very close. It's fine. Will I see you Thursday night?"

"Oh, I'm sorry, love. I don't think so. Even if I set off straight from work, I won't be there until midnight at the earliest."

"Okay. Paul, thanks for coming up."

"What else would I do? I love you."

"I love you too. Thank you."

I choked up again, squeaked a goodbye and finished the call. I missed Paul. He'd tried so hard to keep in good contact after he and Helen split, and until his work had taken him south, he had. I thought of his house in the suburbs with its pocket-sized garden. It might have been nice to have gone there.

Fury, sorrow and hatred began to boil inside me, but worse than all of that was guilt. It was my fault. All my fault. Just like Sarah.

I had to keep busy.

I sat at the kitchen table, a blank sheet of paper in front of me, chewing the end of a pencil. What the hell would I say on Friday? Despite telling Alison I would speak at the funeral, I wasn't at all sure I'd be able to hold it together to do anything of the sort. Absolutely nothing I tried to write came close to what I felt. I laughed hollowly. Finn had done my homework for me when we were at school to stop me getting into trouble, more times than I could count, but he couldn't help me this time.

I pushed the paper away.

The tears might be running out, but the heartbreak wasn't going anywhere. There was nothing left. Absolutely nothing. Except vengeance.

I lined up the packets of sleeping tablets and anti-anxiety pills on the table in front of me, adjusting them so that the labels all faced the same way. I would either die trying to kill Aegyir, or kill him and then come back and kill myself. All of these, washed down with a bottle of vodka should do it.

"Don't you dare miss my bloody funeral!"

I turned to see Finn gazing at me from the other end of the room, arms folded, head on one side. Then he vanished.

"Okay. See you on Friday."

Five more days. No one would miss me.

23

"I am coming for you. I will have my revenge. You will *keep your promises."*

Monitors flashing and beeping.
"We need you to leave."
"Time of death is 22:53."

Lord Eredan faced me, the assembled Council behind him, gathered in the Great Hall. "Did you invite Aegyir in?"

"Yes, but—"

He held up his hand silencing me. "Did you leave The Realm in order to find Aegyir and bring him here?"

"Yes, but—"

Dark green eyes bored into me. "Did you promise to help him to defeat The Realm?"

I stayed silent. I needed to explain. The way the questions were going would result in me being hanged. My gaze drifted over the faces of the Council sitting behind Lord Eredan. Everyone scowled at me. There was so much hatred in the hall.

"Answer the question!" snapped Lord Eredan.

I looked at my husband. His eyes were full of pain and his cheeks hollow. He turned away in disgust.

"Yes."

"And did you promise yourself to Aegyir?"

Again, I sought my husband's gaze. Slowly, he met my eye,

waiting for my answer, his face full of anger, full of devastation, full of incomprehension. My head sagged. I was under oath.

"Yes," I said, my voice tiny. His lip curled and he shook his head almost imperceptibly, his throat twitching.

Lord Eredan's voice boomed out, carrying across the hall. "Lady Aeron. You have by your own confession been found guilty of high treason. You will be hanged by the neck until you are dead."

My husband raised his head, staring at me, breathing rapidly. His eyes were bright.

"Commute it," he whispered, turning to his father, anguish etching his face. "Commute it."

The room was silent. Father and son faced each other.

"Commute it."

His father's eyes narrowed. "Lady Aeron. Your husband has pleaded for commutation of your sentence. You will be banished from The Realm. For all eternity. Immediately."

My heart fluttered. Why had Faran done this? I only knew The Realm. I only wanted to be with him.

Two guards stepped forward and wrenched my arms behind my back. I yearned for Faran to look at me, but he turned his back. I was dragged from the Great Hall, past throngs of Guardians, all snarling their hatred of me. Several of them struck me with sticks as I passed.

At the end of the narrow passageway leading to the portal to Outside, my father-in-law turned to me. "Lady Aeron, I banish you." His face was full of glee, hatred, relief. "If you return, you will be hanged."

I was shoved through the portal, the rocks dissolving around me then reforming as a barrier behind me.

I woke, my breath gasping in my throat. It was Monday morning and I had to meet Alison in an hour to choose flowers. I couldn't do this. I just couldn't.

"You're bleeding."

I turned. Azure eyes peered at me from beneath tousled blond hair. "You're bleeding."

I touched my head, bringing scarlet-coated fingers away from the places I'd been struck.

"Don't be late for Mum."

I sucked the blood off my fingers. "I won't. What flowers do you want?"

"Sunflowers. They make me think of you."

I smiled. "The first flowers you ever gave me. I remember."

His rumbly laugh filled the bed before fading away.

I was going mad. My dreams were getting so real I was getting hurt and I was talking to a dead man.

***

By late afternoon I was exhausted. It had taken all of my energy to hold it together in front of Alison, the florist, and Father O'Keefe. I slumped at the table in the kitchen, my head on my folded arms. The doorbell buzzed and I scraped myself up. "Oh, God, don't let that be Father O'Keefe."

It wasn't. It was Billy with a cardboard box in his arms.

"Rea! How are you?" Billy deposited the box on the floor and pulled me into a deep hug.

"I don't know," I answered truthfully as I drew back. "Come in. Can I make you a coffee? Get you something stronger?"

Billy picked up the box and followed me to the kitchen. There, he put the box on the table and stood next it, chewing his lip, fiddling with the flap of the box.

"Um. These are Finn's things," he said, his eyes shiny. "From his locker. I wasn't sure you would want to come in and get them."

"Thank you," I said, my voice strangled. "Tea? Coffee? Beer?"

Billy sniffed hard and tipped his head up towards the ceiling. "Er. Coffee. Thanks."

I waved at the chair and filled the kettle. Chit-chat didn't seem appropriate and neither Billy nor I could string two coherent words together so the drinks were made in near silence.

"Has Rick been over?" he asked.

I peered over my shoulder at him, belatedly checking my wrist and breathing a sigh of relief. "No. I haven't seen him. You?"

"No. I called him and got his voicemail, and went over but he wasn't in. He was Finn's best friend. I can't believe he hasn't been to see you."

I wasn't. I was glad Aegyir was leaving Billy alone, though.

"Well, maybe he came over when I was out with Alison."

Billy said nothing but he sucked his teeth, his brows flicking up.

We took the drinks through to the lounge. Billy sat on the sofa, dropping down so heavily it made the frame creak. I screwed myself into the chair.

"How's Alison?" asked Billy.

"Um, outwardly she seems better than I expected, but think she's putting on an act. Of course, Rory's neither use nor ornament, but I think keeping busy is helping her. She's a bit cut up that there won't be a proper wake."

Both Rory and Alison were Irish Catholics and although Finn had been largely raised in Cumbria, I knew that the fact his body was staying resolutely at the funeral home until Friday was because Rory wouldn't allow him in the house, even dead. In a moment of madness, I'd offered to hold a wake here but thankfully Alison had known I had no idea what was actually involved and said it would be fine.

Billy blew on his coffee. "Is the family coming over from Ireland?"

"No. Rory's side won't because of the rift and Alison's side are either already dead or too frail to travel. She was an only child."

Finn had several cousins that he hadn't spoken to in years. The last time he'd been to Ireland was for his grandfather's funeral and although the cousins were there, they'd all kept their distance. He hadn't been invited to any of their weddings. Apparently it wasn't the done thing to humiliate your father physically, even if he *was* a wife-beating alcoholic.

Billy pulled an envelope out of his pocket, fidgeting uncomfortably. "Um. We had a whip-round at the gym. For you. Anyway..."

He tailed off and thrust the envelope at me. I didn't know what to say. I was appalled that the gym thought I was a charity case but curious about how much was there. I took the envelope, mumbling something vaguely grateful.

We managed to get through bitter coffees on small talk. Billy seemed as if he would happily stay for longer but eventually, I stood up, leaving Billy no choice but to get up too. I loved Billy to bits, but I needed to be on my own.

"Thanks for coming round. And thanks for the money. You didn't have to do that," I said, showing him out.

Billy hugged me again, holding on to me tightly. "Call me anytime you need. I'm here for you."

"Thanks. I can't believe he's gone."

He blinked hard. "No. I know." He pulled me against him again, kissing the side of my head.

When he'd gone, I leaned my back against the door, exhaustion threatening to take my legs from under me. Would Billy be safe until Friday? Aegyir had killed to get vitality, then chosen his victims in order to get to me, so maybe Billy would be okay.

I felt sick at the number of people who'd died already. If I'd not gouged great chunks out of Aegyir on Friday, would so many have been killed?

"Once Aegyir's regained his strength, you'll be sorry." Stephen had been right – I was more than sorry – but not for the reasons he thought.

I collected up the dirty mugs and dumped them in the sink. I couldn't face unpacking the box they'd brought nor was I in the humour to open the envelope.

"Finn? You around? I could do with a hug."

There was no sign of him. I sucked in a deep breath. Four more days and I could be with him.

24

"You invite me in?"

My heart thudded wildly and every cell in my body screamed at me to say no.

"I invite you in," I said, forcing the words out.

I stood back on the springy turf, indicating for Aegyir to walk towards the rock face.

"It will open?" he said.

The stone shimmered and I nodded. He hesitated.

"Walk through the rock. It will open," I said.

He pushed towards the rock race and the stone dissolved around him. I followed him, into the gloomy hallway beyond, the light of the Great Hall shining at the end. Aegyir strode forwards and I matched his pace so that the two of us emerged into the Great Hall together.

I scanned the space, my heart in my mouth. Where the hell was Orian? He should be here! Where was everyone? The place should have been teeming with Guardians.

Aegyir looked at me, smiling. "I wondered if you would keep your promise, Aeron, but it seems you hate The Realm as much as I do."

This was all wrong. Where was Orian?

A guard entered.

"Sound the alarm," I said, desperate. "Now!"

I drew my sword and Aegyir turned to me, snarling, eyes burning red. Before he could speak, the clatter of boots filled the hall as Guardians streamed in, swords drawn. Behind me, other demons entered – on the back of Aegyir's invite – along with many of his slaves. In the confusion, Aegyir grabbed me, holding me in front of him as a shield.

"You might wonder how I am here," he said, his voice silky, facing the gathered throng. "Well, I was invited.*"*

He hurled me away from him and lashed out at the Guardians closest to him. I turned and saw my family running to me.

Aegyir killed them all before they reached me, his hand outstretched, reaching into them and ripping their light out. Mother. Father. My sister Cia. And my little brother Torfan.

I stared at the ceiling, half expecting to be bleeding again. I felt around the top of my head and found a lump like an egg there.

"Morning, Finn."

"Morning. When are you gonna get that lazy arse of yours out for a run?"

I laughed. "You coming?"

"Wish I could, my love. Wish I could. Go hit the hills."

I rolled on to my side and gazed at him. "Are you in Chaos?"

His brow creased. "I'm here. Go for a run. Clear your head. Get some fresh air."

I couldn't face going up the path past the rock face and the boulder, so I ran the long route to the quarry – out on the main road and then up the hill to reach the track that led to the disused end of the quarry – the end loved by dog-walkers and runners. Near the end where the first bodies had been found and where the police had told people to avoid. Finn and I had run this route hundreds of times. The paths gave multiple routes through the grass and scrubby bushes and trees that covered the worked-out area. I had no intention of going to the bit where Aegyir had been so prolific in his hunting; I meant to skirt the edge of that and cut down to the road.

As I reached a long, winding path that descended steadily back towards the main road, I could see blue and white tape fluttering in the breeze, barring the route, a few metres on from where I was and after the turn I would be taking. A solitary policeman was standing guard and I jogged up to him.

"Hi. What's happened?"

"There's been another incident. I'm sorry, I can't tell you about it."

"Oh. Okay."

I wondered if Rick's body had finally been found, but he never came up here. All the bodies found near here had been of people out walking or running. I peered down the path but was none the wiser. There was no one down there, but a large area was taped off and a square white tent covered the side of the path. The policeman cleared his throat to chivvy me away and I took the hint.

Back at the cottage, I stretched, showered and changed, before booting up the laptop and searching the internet. After the recent spate of bodies found anywhere *but* the quarry, the body of a middle-aged man and of his dog had been found just off the long path I'd been on. The dog had been torn apart but the man had no visible injuries. The police were treating the death as suspicious and linked to the earlier deaths, but beyond that, there were few details. No name had been released. The bodies had been found on Monday evening by another dog-walker and the reports seemed to imply that the victim had died either some time on Sunday afternoon or Monday morning. The police repeated their advice to stay away from the area.

I rubbed the back of my neck. Yet another 'meal' for

Aegyir? Yet another death I was responsible for?

I closed the laptop down and checked the time. Alison was coming soon to help choose Finn's outfit. I glanced across to the sofa. Finn sat in his usual corner, his feet tucked up, wearing thick sports socks with a hole in the left toe.

"What do you want to wear?" I asked. "Does your suit even fit you?"

"Don't know. Doubt it. It's not very me either. I mean, what image do you have of me? Jeans and a sweatshirt?"

I laughed. That was exactly what he was wearing now. "Yeah. But I think your mum will cavil at the thought!"

"Mm… But there's no wake so who will see?"

"When did you last wear your suit?"

"Grandpa's funeral."

"I don't think you'll get your shoulders in the jacket."

"Nah, I won't. Jaysus, that would be embarrassing, Mr What's His Face the funeral guy struggling to jam me into it."

My throat thickened. "Finn, don't."

"Sorry. The trousers will fit. What about them plus a shirt and tie?"

"Still not very you."

"With my Superman boxers on underneath?"

There was a knock on the door before I could reply. I scrubbed my hands over my face and went to answer it.

Alison had thick foundation on the side of her face. It was probably convincing no one but her.

"Has Rory hit you again?" I asked bluntly.

"Oh, no. No. I, um…"

She stared at me with china-blue eyes like her son's and said nothing. This wasn't the time to talk to her about leaving Rory. It wasn't only me who had lost their protector, and I had neither money nor security to offer her.

We went up to the bedroom which looked like a bomb had exploded in it. I picked up my running kit and clothes and stuffed them into the laundry basket. I hadn't yet done any laundry since Finn had died. I couldn't bear to wash the smell of Finn out of anything.

I pulled his suit trousers out of the wardrobe, trying not to cry. "What about these, with a white shirt and a tie?"

"Does he *have* a tie?" said Alison, surprised.

"Er, he has two. A black one and one with a pattern on."

"Perhaps the black one?"

Again, not very Finn, but considering it was a funeral, maybe more appropriate. I found it and we packed the trousers, a shirt and the tie into a bag. I sneaked the Superman boxers in and a pair of novelty socks while Alison's back was turned.

"I can drop it around tomorrow if you want?" It was about time I began shouldering a bit more of the burden.

"Have you seen him yet?"

I caught my breath, then realised she meant at the funeral home and shook my head. I wasn't sure I would. I wanted different memories.

"Have you found a picture for the funeral?" Alison asked, her eyes picking over the mess in the room.

"Not yet. I'll find one tonight and take it in on a stick with the clothes."

"Thank you." Her brow creased. "Do you know where Finn's rosary is?"

"He doesn't have one. Well, not here. Not as far as I know."

Finn hadn't been to Mass since before he'd left home and he sure as hell didn't say his rosary with me. I wasn't a hundred per cent sure that he would want to be buried with one but said nothing.

Alison seemed to be mentally checking things off a list

and I waited. She looked up at last. "Well, I'd better run. Thanks for taking the clothes in."

"Did you want a tea? Coffee?"

She hesitated before agreeing. We pattered back downstairs and I filled the kettle to make coffees. We'd just sat down in the lounge to drink them when there was a sharp rapping at the front door. I frowned, not expecting anyone.

"Sorry. Let me go and see who that is."

When I opened the door, my breath shuddered in my chest. "Rick. What do you want?"

I wanted to rip his head off.

"You know what I want, Aeron. And you did ask to see me."

He smiled eerily and I stepped out of the house, pulling the door shut behind me. He leaned back so that he could see in the window.

"Who will you sacrifice next?" he said. "Her? Billy?"

I glowered at him, my fingers itching to punch him.

"Perhaps I will start with Billy. And then the woman in your house. A wave of death, rippling out from you."

I thought quickly. My plan was to try to kill Aegyir after Finn's funeral, but how did I hold him off until then?

"You forgot my second message," I said. "I'll open the portal on Friday. Once I've buried Finn. If you go near anyone before then, the deal's off."

His eyes narrowed. "Why should I wait? I could drag you there now."

"And achieve what? Why should I open it under duress when I've said I'll open it on Friday? You can't kill me and you need a Guardian to open the portal. Good luck with finding another one. The deal is Friday. You touch anyone before then, the deal is off. You threaten me again, the deal is off."

Aegyir scrutinised me and I forced myself to stand firm. "I do not need a Guardian if I am strong enough. Perhaps if you will not open it for me now, I will build enough strength to force my way in. Beginning with her."

"And the Realm will see. Do you think the Scouts won't notice the flood of deaths? There are no plagues any more. People don't tend to die in their hundreds or thousands any longer. Did you want to call out all of the Guardians?"

Aegyir averted his gaze, a scowl settling. "Why have you changed your mind, Aeron? Why will you open the portal on Friday for me?"

"Because I know you'll kill everyone if I don't. You killed Finn. I don't want anyone else close to me to die if I can prevent it. And the Realm owes me nothing. My loyalties are with this world and I have no desire to see it slaughtered merely to delay an inevitable attack on the Realm."

I turned back to the door. As my fingers touched the doorknob, Aegyir grabbed my shoulder and spun me round, slamming my back against the wall.

"You will not betray me a second time," he hissed, his face close, his eyes red.

I glanced down the lane. Lena had just arrived home and was staring at us from her doorway.

"Everything okay, Reagan?" she called, one hand pausing as she unlocked the door, her phone in her other hand.

"Everything's fine. Rick's just leaving."

I pushed Aegyir away from me and glared at him until he bowed his head a fraction and strode towards the gate in the field at the end of the lane. Lena still watched me. "You sure everything's okay? Was he hassling you?"

I smiled, my heart rate beginning to settle. "It's fine. He was being a jerk. Thanks for asking."

I pushed the door open and returned to the lounge.

"Was that Rick?" asked Alison, moving back from the window, her mug of coffee still in her hand. She must have been watching everything.

"Yeah. He was just coming to say he was sorry about Finn." I hoped she hadn't seen the red eyes and the cold body-language.

"You should have invited him in. I like Rick."

My mouth turned to sandpaper at her words and my eyes shot to my charm. Not glowing.

"He couldn't stay."

"He'll be there on Friday, won't he? He's Finn's best friend."

"Yes, I think so."

But if 'Rick' went within ten feet of Alison, I would kill him.

She drained her mug. "I need to get back. Thank you for taking Finn's clothes in."

She hugged me tightly at the door, until I thought I would crack. When I took the mugs back to the kitchen, I saw Finn, still in jeans and a sweatshirt, leaning against the kitchen sink. He bit his lips. He'd seen his mum's face.

"You think Aegyir will wait until Friday?"

I stuck my bottom lip out. "I don't know. I said that if he killed anyone before then or if he threatened me again, I wouldn't open the portal. He said the other night that he can't kill me." I ground to a halt for a moment before being able to continue. "He needs me."

"Are you really sure about Friday?"

I sighed. "No. But I'm sure that I don't have anything left in this world."

We lapsed into silence.

"I don't know," he said, casting around him. "I'm gone a few days and this place is like a bomb site."

I smiled ruefully. Finn was the tidiest person I knew and

the place was normally spotless. It only had four rooms and keeping on top of it shouldn't have been a major operation but as I looked around, I acknowledged he had a point and got to work. I blitzed my way round the cottage, vacuuming the carpets in the lounge, hall and bedroom, and washing the floors in the kitchen and bathroom. I cleaned the sinks, scrubbed the shower and loo and put some laundry on. Just my stuff. Finn was conspicuous by his absence during this rare flurry of domesticity from me.

Finished, I settled down in the now pristine lounge with a coffee and my laptop to choose a picture of Finn for the funeral.

"Do you have *any* where I've got all my clothes on?" he asked, reappearing and settling next to me to peer over my shoulder.

"Yes! Plenty." Though in fairness, I did have quite a lot of him half-naked.

"Good. I'm not sure Father O'Keefe would cope otherwise."

We sifted through folder upon folder of pictures, focusing on reasonably recent ones. If I'd thought that choosing clothes for him for Friday was heart-breaking, this was unimaginably worse.

After a lot of crying, I had a shortlist of five.

"Not that one. I've got a goofy look on my face," said Finn, as I scrolled through them. I deleted it from the list.

"What about this one?"

"Hm. Maybe."

Eventually we settled on one where he had his lopsided smile and was wearing a blue top which emphasised his eyes. I saved it to a memory-stick and closed the laptop down, tears sliding down my face.

Three more days.

25

The door closed behind me, the bell jangling as it did; overly cheerful, considering. The air outside was cold and fresh in comparison with the stuffy interior of the funeral directors. Perhaps the breeze would blow the sickly-sweet smell of lilies out of my clothes. I'd taken the bag of clothes and the picture in but hadn't been able to bear it in there for long. I certainly hadn't been able to see Finn or his coffin. I also hadn't expected to be given a bag containing the clothes that Finn had been wearing to hospital and I wasn't sure what to do with them.

My tasks for the day done, I was at a loose end. I should be practising self-defence ready for Friday, but who with? I couldn't face going to the gym and didn't know who to ask even if I did. I could go for another run, but it was going to get dark soon, and anyway, I wasn't as big a fan of it as Finn had been.

Two days to prepare. Should I write a will? Didn't they need to be done officially and cost money? Who would witness my signature on it? The neighbours? I barely had anything worth leaving and I had official next of kin, even if I hated some of them. I huffed out my breath. Helen and John might as well have everything. They'd throw it away in all likelihood. The only thing that concerned me was Finn's bike. I didn't want anyone to have it. It was Finn's.

"Good afternoon, Aeron."

Aegyir, wearing Rick's image again, had fallen into step with me.

I scowled at him. "I told you Friday. Let me bury my dead."

He said nothing. We walked on together and I scanned the buildings ahead for CCTV cameras. When we reached the corner, I checked sight-lines and stopped abruptly.

"Where's Rick's body? Why are you still looking like him?"

Aegyir faced me. The only hints that he wasn't Rick were the red glint in his eyes and the fact that my charm was burning blue.

"His body will never be found. It consumes too much vitality to wear someone's form whom I have not killed."

That figured. He'd killed and then mimicked the others until their bodies had been found, then moved to a new victim and a new form. If Rick's body was found, Aegyir could no longer walk the streets looking like him. A lump formed in my throat. If Aegyir gave up looking like Rick and moved on again, Rick's family would never know he was dead. People would report him missing. They could have *years* wondering what had happened to him.

A thought almost felled me. I had more than enough rage in me to slaughter Aegyir, but anyone else? What if he rocked up looking like Finn?

"Leave me alone, Aegyir. You've waited this long for your revenge. Another two days won't matter. Leave me alone, or I'll start screaming and draw a *lot* of attention."

My eyes indicated the CCTV camera above us, before dropping back to glare at him.

"I *said*, leave me alone!" I yelled, causing several passers-by to stop and turn.

Aegyir glanced around. A middle-aged man hurried towards us, eyes darting from me to Aegyir.

"Is everything okay?"

Aegyir glowered at the man and then at me. "Friday." He stalked away, heading away from the more populated area of town.

"Thank you," I said, gratefully, turning to the man. "He keeps pestering me. He won't get the message that I'm not interested."

The man stared at Aegyir's disappearing back. "Be careful. He looks dodgy."

My stomach clenched. I hoped I hadn't just signed *his* death warrant too, just for having come to help me.

***

Almost as soon as I got back to the cottage, there was a knock at the door. I sighed. Who now?

When I swung the door open, I found Ösk and Lena, with Mike and Polly from next door almost hiding behind them.

"Hi," I said.

"Oh, Rea, we've been meaning to come over for a couple of days. We're so sorry about Finn," said Lena, stepping in and pulling me into a hug, her necklaces clinking. She was in her on-duty clothes – smart skirt with fine knitwear on top and a neat gold watch wrapping her wrist rather than a leather cuff.

Ösk waved at me over her shoulder, looking like he'd just been starring in an Icelandic TV drama. A thick patterned sweater sat atop cord trousers and chunky boots. He jammed his hands back in his pockets. Mike and Polly looked as if they didn't want to be there, lurking at the back and fidgeting. I stood back to let them all in and they trooped after me to the lounge.

"Let me grab some chairs from the kitchen," I said.

Mike beat me to it. I suspect he didn't want to be there

at all but felt as if he should come. Lena and Ösk sat on the sofa, Polly took the chair and Mike and I ended up on the two wooden chairs from the kitchen.

"I am so sorry about Finn," said Ösk, his dark blue eyes clouding. "I knew him from the gym. He was always so much fun."

Tears stabbed at my eyes and my throat felt tight. "Yeah. He was."

"Oh, he was such a beautiful man," said Lena. "So beautiful. And such a wonderful person."

Her words confirmed what I'd suspected for a while. So she *had* fancied him. I looked at Polly and Mike, waiting to see what they might say. They'd barely given either me or Finn the time of day, apart from the one time Mike's car wouldn't start and he'd asked Finn for help.

"Yes, we were both sorry to hear about Finn," said Mike. "I heard it was flu."

"Mm."

"It was so quick!" he added, sounding incredulous.

And tactless.

"Mm."

"I've never seen you without your make-up before." Polly obviously felt as if she ought to contribute *something* to the conversation. "You look so different! So *normal*."

I stifled a smile, imagining what Finn would have made of that. Lena shot Polly a filthy look. I suspected that Polly and Mike had been forced to come by Lena.

"Er, when's the funeral?" asked Ösk.

"Friday morning. The Catholic church. No flowers."

They all nodded. Ösk and Lena would probably come to it, but I doubted that Mike or Polly would.

I shifted on my seat, my knees aching. I'd got my feet tucked back under my seat to leave leg-room for everyone else. The room was barely big enough for me and Finn, never mind five adults in here. Granted, Lena and Polly were smaller than me, but Mike was almost as tall as me and Ösk a little bigger.

"Who was that who was hassling you yesterday?" asked Lena, her brow creasing.

"Rick. Um, the guy who runs the tattoo place. He's a friend."

He *was* a friend. Until Aegyir killed him.

"He didn't seem that friendly yesterday."

"No. I don't know what's wrong. He's been a bit off with me for a while."

"Well, if he hassles you again, call me. Ösk or I will come over if you need us to."

I was genuinely heartened. "Thanks. That's really kind of you."

Mike and Polly were already fidgeting and I decided to help them out. "It's lovely of you all to come over, but I'm going to have to chase you out. I have a pile of things to do and it's been a difficult day today. I'm just back from the funeral director's."

"Oh! Yes, of course," said Polly, springing up as if burned. "We only came over to say how sorry we were."

"Let us know if there's anything we can do?" said Lena, getting to her feet more slowly. "We're just down the lane."

Belatedly, Mike realised he and Polly should have made the offer and he mumbled an assurance that they were there too.

"Thanks guys."

Everyone was standing and Lena pulled me into a deep hug. "Oh, Rea. He was so wonderful. I'm so sorry!"

I extricated myself from her, only to be instantly swept into a hug from Ösk. "Take care. And call us if we can do *anything*."

"Thanks. I will."

We all knew I wouldn't.

As soon as they'd gone, the silence crowded in on me. It was a different silence from when I'd been home without Finn in the past. When he was alive. It was as if the cottage knew that it had lost someone. Needing noise, I filled the kettle to make a coffee, clattering the spoon in the jar and rattling it around the mug. But as soon as the coffee was made, the silence seeped back. I picked up the mug and sat in the lounge, staring at the floor, counting the swirls in the carpet.

"I've been thinking about Friday."

I turned my head to see Finn. He was wearing sweat pants and a hoodie and looked like he'd just got out of bed. Immediately, the cottage felt right again.

"Yeah? Which bit?"

"The Aegyir bit. I'm not sure you should go. You'll get hurt."

I breathed deeply. "I might. But then I'm getting dead afterwards, so what does it matter?"

"I don't want you dead." His eyes clouded.

"Why not?"

"I just don't. You're young. You're about to start your dream job. It's a waste."

"You think any of that means anything to me?"

He blinked slowly. "No. But... Mum will be devastated."

Alison *would* be devastated. But she would also know why I felt I couldn't keep trudging through this life without Finn. Even if I *could* find a way to live without him, I couldn't find a way to live with my guilt. He was dead because of me. The very least I could do would be to try to avenge it.

"Your mum'll understand."

He pushed his bottom lip out and I closed my eyes, tired.

"Finn, let's not talk about it?"

I clicked the television on, my usual way to indicate a conversation was over. It was some terrible programme about buying a load of junk and then trying to sell it for a profit. Neither team was making much of a fist of it, but given the dreadful bits of tat they'd bought, it wasn't a surprise. I muted the sound, waiting for the news to come on.

"Were you going to ask me to marry you?" I said, tilting my head towards him.

Finn looked startled. "Mum tell you?"

"Yeah. Were you?"

"Mm. On your birthday. I'd chosen the ring. Well, I'd seen one I thought was nice and was gonna ask you if you liked it, if you said yes."

"If? You had any doubts?" I grinned at him and he shook his head. "What was the ring like?"

"Diamond, with two emeralds – one on either side. Match your eyes."

A sob swirled in my chest before I swallowed it down. How different things could have been. I never asked for any of what had happened.

"Church or registry office?" I said, my voice hitching.

"Your choice. I suspected you wouldn't want Catholic."

I smiled. "No. Church would have been a bit hypocritical all round really. Registry would have been great. Your mum would have wanted church though."

"Yeah, but I couldn't imagine you going through the classes with Father O'Keefe."

"Oh, like you could have!"

He chuckled.

The news came on but I wasn't interested in the main headlines for the UK; I wanted to know how many more people had died at Aegyir's hands, even if they were being attributed to flu.

"Where would we have gone on honeymoon?" I asked.

"Where would you have liked?"

He bunted down the sofa towards me and I'd swear it creaked when he did.

"Somewhere quiet. Just the two of us in the middle of nowhere. Scotland maybe?"

"Sounds perfect. And cheap enough for me to have afforded!"

I laughed. "The bride's family's supposed to pay for it. Remember?"

"Yeah, like either of us would have accepted a penny from Helen and John!"

"True. But Paul would have chipped in."

"He's coming up isn't he?"

"Mm."

The picture on the TV changed to one of the town centre and I turned the volume back up. Our death toll was hitting the main UK bulletin – both because of the number of flu victims and because there appeared to be a serial killer on the loose. The toll for alleged flu victims had now passed fifty and the number of bodies found at the quarry was thirteen. Not including Rick's.

The reporter said that a local man had been helping them with their enquiries and the footage showed what could only have been Aegyir-as-Rick as he came out of the police station. Would he be able to make the police think he was innocent by having a genuine alibi for the earliest deaths, before Rick had been killed? The faces of the victims were shown. I recognised some of them as people who had either stared at me or talked to me and wondered if others were going to link them to me. At least the guy who'd helped me this afternoon wasn't one of the victims. Yet.

A health official came on to remind people to get the flu jab and to say that there would be mobile clinics set up to help with the increased numbers demanding them. Another scientist came on to talk about the fact that they hadn't yet been able to isolate the strain of flu responsible, but that taking the anti-virals he was recommending would help, regardless of which strain it turned out to be. What did *he* know? They hadn't worked yet.

"How many deaths do there need to be before the Scouts tell the Guardians?" I mused out loud.

Finn brightened fractionally. "Maybe the Guardians will come and sort out Aegyir before Friday, and then you won't have to."

Maybe. But even if they did, it wouldn't change the rest of my plans.

Two more days.

26

It was mid-morning when I awoke from a full-house of hellish dreams. Lilja, the enigmatic, timeless woman, had told me to return home so that Aegyir would be defeated; the two men who hated me had banished me for the umpteenth time; I'd watched 'my' entire family be slaughtered by Aegyir who had also insisted on standing right next to me in the room, telling me he was coming for me and that he would make me keep my promises. I was exhausted. I couldn't remember the last time I had felt so utterly devastated. The bed smelled of Finn and I wrapped the covers around me and bawled my heart out.

Spent, I scraped myself out of bed and into the shower, turning the flow up as high as it would go. The water was ice-cold as a result, shocking me into the here and now. I hurried to get dressed before the cottage chilled me to the core, and made myself a coffee, piling empty beer bottles into the recycling crate while the kettle boiled. No wonder I felt so shit.

In the lounge, I turned on the telly to tune into the local news. Another body had been found, this one on the outskirts of town.

"Shit."

Had Aegyir broken his word to me? Had he killed someone since our pact on Tuesday? Did that mean that I could call the deal off?

Did it matter? I wanted to stick those knives in Aegyir and decapitate him, regardless. Not because I wanted to save this world from his ravages, though a part of me acknowledged that should be worthy enough in its own right. No, I wanted to stab and behead that bastard because he had taken Finn from me. I would be at the rock face on Friday, whether the deal was technically off or not.

I clicked the telly off. I had too much to do to end up suckered into mindless daytime TV. Keep busy, Alison had said. Oh, I had more than enough to keep me busy today. By this time tomorrow, I would be with Finn and I had a lot of ends to tie up first. I also had less than a day to write the bloody eulogy and I was running out of excuses to avoid it.

First, I had some weapons to stash.

We'd put the vessel, sword and daggers in the cupboard in the kitchen after the fateful encounter at the boulder. I laid the pot and the daggers on the table and propped the sword against the wall, wondering what I should take up to the rock face and what I should leave here. My plan was to come back to the cottage before meeting Aegyir at the rock face, but I didn't want to leave that to chance. What if I wasn't able to retrieve things? No, I either needed to take things with me to the funeral, or to have hidden them up at the rock face before I met Aegyir. Would Aegyir be stupid enough not to check the gorse bush where we'd hidden the sword last time, before he met me? What would happen if I got up there and found that everything I needed had been disposed of?

I weighed the pot and leather pouch of knives in my hand. The daggers I could take in my bag with me; the pot and the sword were too big or heavy to be carrying around with me. They would have to be hidden up at the meeting site. Granted, having a bag full of knives in public was a criminal offence but I didn't think anyone would search me at a funeral.

The leather pouch wasn't the easiest thing to open in a hurry. I slid the daggers out and examined them. Was there a way of secreting them about me before I had to go up to the boulder, without them digging into me and slicing me to ribbons? Ideally, they would be in a belt around my middle, as depicted in the book, but that was asking for trouble. I would just have to leave them in my bag during the funeral and tuck them in my belt before I met Aegyir.

I mentally scanned the area, trying to remember what else had been close by that could act as a hiding place, but couldn't bring a clear enough image to the front of my brain. I'd have to see what was available when I took the sword and pot up there.

No time like the present.

I found a long coat that would conceal the sword well enough, though only the next door neighbours were potential witnesses and Polly and Mike already thought I was strange. As soon as I was past the gate and on to the track, no one could see me. Best to be sure though. I slipped the sword through a belt so that its hilt held it in place along my leg and fastened the coat over the top. The vessel was a lot easier to deal with – it was heavy but it fitted in a large backpack. Loaded up, I set off.

There was a light drizzle as I crunched my way up the stony track. No one saw me and I strode up the hill to the edge of the field where the track turned into the thin path leading to the rock face. It was good to be out. There was a sweet tang of damp soil in the air and the rain on my face reminded me that I was alive. At least for the moment.

I let my brain run over everything I needed to do before tomorrow. I'd spent the remains of yesterday getting the cottage and the remnants of my life in order, which was what had pushed me into clearing the house of beer last night. My head wasn't thanking me for that this morning. There were a few odds and ends that needed finishing up, but I could do them after I killed Aegyir. My main focus was making sure that I had the sword and vessel handy.

I reached the large, rounded boulder and cast around, making sure that I knew where the soil had been scattered and trying to spot potential locations for the sword and vessel. To my dismay, the best location was the exact place we'd stashed the sword before. Nowhere else was close enough to the soil for me to be able to reach out and grab the sword. If I could have someone else there it would be easier, but I'd be alone.

I poked about in the gorse, getting my hands scratched by the spikes, before finally deciding that I didn't have any choice. It was here or nowhere unless I was going to stroll about with a sword in my belt like I was an extra from a TV show. I concealed the sword, muttering a silent prayer for it not to be discovered. The vessel was slightly easier to hide as there was a small space in the gorse where a branch had broken off, leaving a void behind it. I put the vessel in, making sure it was hidden from view but easy to grab when the time came. The only issue left would be how to carry the daggers. I needed to have them in my belt when I got up here. Perhaps after the funeral I could take them out of my bag, tuck them in a belt and fasten my jacket over the top to hide them. Whatever I chose, leaving them up here wasn't a viable option. They would either be too scattered or held in the leather pouch and harder to access.

I circled the gorse bush a few times. The sword was invisible to any passer-by but would be found immediately if anyone went hunting for it. Should I leave it? Should I take it back and think of a way to conceal it on me tomorrow?

I leaned my back against the rock face, staring at the gorse bush.

"Traitor."

I caught my breath and snatched myself away from the rock. There had been so much venom in the voice. I turned to face the rock.

"Send some fucking Scouts out here! See what's going on! We need some Guardians!"

My voice ricocheted off the rock and I glared at the stone. I don't know what I expected to happen. A troop of soldiers to come marching out of the cliff? There was nothing. I turned away, ready to make my way back down the hill.

"You are not welcome, Aeron."

Pissed off, I turned on the spot. "Will I be more welcome after I do your dirty work for you? Anyway, don't worry about it. I have *no* intention of coming in! I owe you *nothing*!"

With that, I stomped back towards the cottage.

One more day.

27

Pearly grey light crept into the bedroom and my eyes were gritty from a lack of sleep. As I lay in the gloaming, the margins between reality and the world of my dreams were so blurred they barely existed. It was probably exhaustion, coupled with the stress of what was coming, but I felt as if I was two people, superimposed upon each other. Part of me was Reagan – grieving, hopeless, shattered Reagan who wanted to die. Part of me felt fierce and angry and maligned and desperate to put some stories straight. They met in the middle. Furious, devastated Reagan who wanted to destroy the monster that had killed Finn.

My dreams had been full of emotion-wrenching horror. In one, Lilja had been sobbing. In another, she was begging me to come home, telling me that Aegyir was too strong and that I would never defeat him Outside. Aegyir had popped up in the rest of my dreams, laughing, claiming he would have his revenge and that the time was soon. The only dream that hadn't been full of the Realm had been of Finn's death.

It was almost seven. The funeral would be at ten. I still hadn't written the eulogy and I was due to meet Paul at nine. Scraping my hair back, I crawled out of bed.

"Finn?"

Nothing.

"Hey. Finn. I need you. Get your sorry ass in here."

Still nothing.

I stripped off and stood under the shower, keeping the flow on maximum, needing to be drenched. The water cascading over me was significantly colder than blood temperature but I didn't care. In the grand scheme of things, that was nothing. Not compared to burying Finn. My hope that the water would wash away all the nightmares of the night before wasn't fulfilled. Whenever I closed my eyes, the backs of my eyelids were covered with images of slaughter and blood, of trials and banishment, of hatred and betrayal.

I switched the water off, chilled to my core and wrapped a scratchy towel around me. I rubbed myself dry so hard that my skin shone pink. I had no shortage of black clothes so I chose comfort over style and my favourite black boots rather than anything delicate. Finn would be laughing at the ensemble. I slung a leather belt around my waist. It didn't match the rest of the outfit, but I was going to need it later.

Should I wear what Finn had called my 'sod off and leave me alone' make-up or go bare-faced? Finn knew me bare-faced, but I really, *really* needed everyone to sod off and leave me alone, so I stained my lips dark purple and lined my eyes heavily with black, filled my ears with studs and put my nose-ring in. I could be bare-faced when I joined him and anyway, he'd always seen through the war-paint and would understand why I needed it today of all days.

I tipped my wallet, keys, lip-balm and all the other junk I carried around with me into the only bag I had that I could also stash a dagger in. My phone was almost dead and I tossed it to one side. There was no one I wanted to call and no one I wanted to hear from. Lastly, I took two of the daggers out of the pouch and slid one into each of my boots so that at least two of them were to hand. I put the other in my bag and prayed I would have a chance to retrieve it and secrete it about me before I had to face Aegyir.

I was due to meet Paul at a cafe about quarter of an hour's walk away. It was now almost eight. I made myself a strong black coffee and some toast. All the Pop Tarts had been binned when I'd come back from the hospital and I both craved them and was glad they were gone. The bread had green flecks in it but I picked them out. There was no other food in the house.

What should I do with my sketchbooks? Would anyone look at them? Should I give them to Paul? He was the only one who would want them. I packed them into a bag and stuck a note on the front. Eleven words. *Dear Paul, These are for you. I'm sorry. I love you*. It barely covered what I wanted to say but it would have to do. I could write a better one if I made it back from meeting Aegyir.

I could put off leaving no longer and took a last look around the house before shrugging my leather jacket on and slinging my bag over my shoulder.

"Chin up," said Finn as I passed him in the hall. "I'll be right with you."

***

Paul was already there when I arrived, sitting towards the back of the room with a pot of tea and a plate of bacon and eggs in front of him. I waited for him to look up, my tongue poked into my cheek. A grin crept across his face the moment he saw me and he scrambled up to hug me hard.

"Reagan! My darling Reagan."

"Hey, Dad."

"Dad? Not Paul? Progress?"

I smiled shyly. He was as close to a father figure as I would ever have, but I'd called him Paul since I found out I was adopted. Stupid, pointless rebellion.

I squeezed him and pulled free. The cafe was bright and cheerful, with red and white gingham checked tablecloths and real flowers in small vases on the tables. The early morning sun streamed in through large, plate-glass windows. I craved black and darkness. As I sat, I caught the eye of the waitress and ordered a glass of water. Paul's face was full of concern. He reached across the table and held my hand.

"I am so, so sorry about Finn."

I swatted his words away with my hand. "Yeah. Everyone is. Don't make me cry. I'll smudge my mascara. Tell me about you."

As he filled me in on what had been happening since we last saw each other, I felt a lead weight forming in my chest. Was I wrong to be planning my exit? Was it horribly selfish? People might understand, but that didn't mean I wouldn't hurt them or that they would forgive me.

Paul ground to a halt. "You still with me?"

"Yeah. Sorry. Difficult day ahead."

"I know. Sure you don't want to come back with me? Get a break?"

"Maybe. Ask me again after the funeral."

"Sure."

I finished my water and glanced at the clock. "We have to go."

It was the last place on earth I had ever wanted to be.

***

It was unbearable. Alison asked me to sit in the front pew with her, and Paul slid in next to me and held my hand. In the middle of the nave, only a few feet away was the coffin. I couldn't look at it. Finn was inside. I couldn't let my brain even start to think that.

Rory Cullen wasn't there. He wouldn't even come to his

son's funeral.

I squeezed Alison's hand, but actually, it was me who was the wreck. She seemed stoic and past the grief in some ways, though I knew she couldn't be. She squeezed my hand back and smiled wanly. I stole a glance around the church, my eyes skipping past the coffin and avoiding the picture of Finn projected on to a screen at the front. Seeing that would have finished me off. The church was packed and there was a low, steady murmur filling the space. Billy and all the staff from the gym were a few pews back and I nodded to them. There were old school friends, clients of the gym, people from the pub. Helen.

I turned away, furious. She'd hated Finn. How *dare* she come?

My hands shook, making the order of service tremble in my hands. Paul dipped his head.

"You okay?"

"Helen's here."

Paul swivelled around to look and then turned back. "Maybe she came to support you."

"Maybe she should have tried that when I lived at home."

Paul slid his arm around me. "Ignore her. Don't let her rile you."

I nodded, staring at the order of service. On the front was the picture of Finn we'd chosen and my heart lurched and tears burned my eyes. I blinked hard, tipping my chin up and breathing deeply.

I still can't remember much of the service. I stumbled over the first verse of the first hymn, but after that I was crying too much to sing. Alison indicated when I was supposed to go up and read my eulogy, but I'd never written it and was empty-handed. I inched past Paul and up to the lectern, where tears streamed down my face and splashed on to the wood. I swallowed hard and looked up.

"Finn Cullen was my best friend," I managed before breaking down again. "He was from the moment we met, nine years ago." I took another breath. "I told him the other day that he was perfect. He was. I loved him with all my heart. And I miss him so much."

I scuttled back to the pew and buried my head in my hands. Alison drew me against her and Paul slid his arm around me from the other side.

Most of the rest of the service was a bit of a blur. There were more hymns and some readings from the bible but I couldn't remember what any of them were. After what felt like eternity, but yet nowhere near enough time, Finn's coffin was being carried out of the church, ready to be buried, and Alison and I stood at the door while a never-ending ribbon of people shook our hands and murmured words that couldn't bring him back and gave no comfort. Eventually, we were in the churchyard, clustered around a hole while the man I loved was lowered into the ground in a wooden box and Father O'Keefe said more prayers. The freshly dug earth smelled of leaf mould and dirt. It was a scent I will never forget.

Finally, the service was over, but I couldn't leave. Everyone else was going to a nearby hotel where refreshments were being served but my feet were rooted to the turf. Paul and Alison urged me but I shook my head and told them I'd see them in there in a bit. I needed some time with Finn. Helen came over.

"You couldn't *stand* Finn," I hissed. "Why are you here? Hypocrite!"

"I'm here for you," she said softly and I glared at her.

"Too little, too late."

Tears welled up and she blinked, spilling them down her cheeks. A client from the gym stood next to us and put her arm around her shoulders. Like *Helen* needed any comfort over Finn's death.

"Come on. Come away," she murmured quietly to Helen. "Let Reagan have a few minutes."

She led her away and I was left staring at handfuls of dirt on a wooden box with some loose flowers scattered over the top, my world in tatters.

I sat down, my arms wrapped around my knees, my toes pointing towards the edge of his grave.

"Dad's asked me to go back with him. I said to ask me again after..." I stopped and wiped my face. "When he asked, I thought I could, but... I can't. I can't go on Finn. There's nothing. *Nothing.* I don't want to be here without you."

If ever there was a time when I needed him there with me, comforting me, this was it, but I was all alone. I talked and talked as if he was with me, reliving all the great times we'd had as well as some of the fights. Then I put my head on my knees and wanted the earth to eat me.

I became aware of someone crouching next to me.

"Oh, *now* you come, Finn. Great timing."

"Aeron? We have a deal."

My head snapped up. Not Finn. Aegyir, still looking like Rick. I clenched my teeth, furious.

"How *dare* you come here."

He smiled. "We have a deal."

I wanted to punch him.

He offered me a hand up. I eschewed it. It was everything I could do not to spit at him.

"I have to go to the hotel. People will expect me. Then I'll go to the rock face."

"You said you needed to bury your dead. He is buried. We have a deal."

I cast around me. I'd been out here so long that

everyone else had gone to the hotel ages ago. The thought of all the tea and sympathy that would be there decided me. No one who mattered would be offended.

"Okay."

The route up to the rock face from the church meant we would walk right past the cottage. I prayed that I'd be able to go in and get the final dagger in place around my waist; I had no chance before then or once we were on the farm track.

I turned to the grave. "See you soon, Munchkin." I blew a kiss at him, before striding away towards the cottage.

Aegyir kept pace with me. No one from the funeral saw me leave and I wondered briefly what Alison and Paul would be thinking about my absence. I hoped I would see them again to apologise for worrying them.

As we crossed the town, I mentally rehearsed what needed to happen at the rock face. Would I get to the swords and the vessel okay? What was the best place to hide the daggers so that Aegyir wouldn't see them?

We turned on to the lane up to the cottage, Aegyir still resembling Rick as we passed my neighbours' houses. I stopped as we reached mine and Finn's.

"I need to go inside for a moment."

"No."

Shit! I scrambled for a reason to go in, but in my stress, nothing helpful sprang to mind.

"I need the bathroom," I said eventually. "You can come in and wait if you need to. I'll only be a moment."

"No."

I felt panic flutter in my chest. I *had* to get the dagger out of my bag and somewhere handy. I put my hand out to the door, ready to open it and Aegyir wrenched my arm back. I yelled out in pain.

"I said, no."

He twisted my arm up my back and I bellowed for help. Aegyir's response was to grip me tighter and try to force me to the gate at the end of the track.

Polly shot out of her cottage. "Reagan?"

"Call the police! He's going to kill me! Don't come any closer. Call the police!"

She gawped for a second and then yanked her phone out of her back pocket. I didn't see any more than that. Aegyir frog-marched me through the gate, my arm twisted so far up my back that I was bent over.

Daggers handy or not, I was going to kill this fucking bastard.

28

"You killed him!" I wrenched myself free from his grip, staggering from the effort. "You fucking bastard! You killed him!"

Aegyir felled me with a punch and I sprawled to the ground, seeing stars. Peering behind him I could see Polly still on the phone, her eyes wide as she watched us.

"Indeed I did, Aeron." Aegyir grabbed me by the back of my neck and hauled me to my feet.

I squirmed to get free, only to be battered to the ground again and kicked so hard I was sure my ribs were broken. Breathing was excruciating. Memories of Stephen's attack came flooding back to me. I was *not* going to let that happen to me again.

"Now," he said, bending down and speaking into my ear. "We have some unfinished business."

He dragged me up again and marched me towards the path that led to the rock face. I squirmed round to look back, in time to see Polly disappearing back into her cottage, still on the phone. Her door slammed. I hoped she was still calling the police and not just hiding.

As soon as we were out of sight of the cottages, Aegyir stopped bothering to be Rick and morphed into Aegyir. I didn't care. I was going to kill him, whatever he looked like.

However much I kicked and wriggled, I was inexorably being dragged to the place where he had connected with

Finn. I hoped the sword was still there and I could incapacitate Aegyir enough to use it and get to the daggers. To do any of that, I needed to get free though.

Before long we were at the side of the large, rounded boulder and I was staring at the rock face, breathing like a landed fish. Aegyir moved so that his arm was around my neck, the crook of his elbow jamming into my throat, half suffocating me. My left arm was still wrenched up my back by his other arm. The two daggers in my boot were terrifyingly out of reach.

"Here we are again, Aeron." His voice was harsh and nasal. "Invite me in."

My vision was blacking, my brain filling with images of fighting and chaos. Something screamed at me to deny him. His hold on me tightened. "Invite me in."

"Where?" I croaked. "It's just a rock!"

He laughed unpleasantly. "We both know that is not true... Invite me in!"

"Never."

His breathing rasped in my ear. "Would you rather die? Because believe me, Aeron, I would have great pleasure in killing you after what you did to me."

I didn't answer. I might have had no desire to live beyond that day, but I was determined to kill him in revenge for Finn before then. My legs felt as if they would give way beneath me but I forced myself to stand firm and spot any weak points in his hold on me. I ran several manoeuvres in my head, trying to figure out a way to get myself free. I needed time.

"I'm a Guardian, Aegyir. You have neither the strength nor the authority to kill me."

I had no idea if that was true. I was cobbling it together from the bits I could remember from the book and what he'd said before. It caused Aegyir to pause though.

"That is true. But that does not make you immortal."

I managed to turn so that I could see down the track. Stephen was lumbering his way up it. Aegyir might not be able to kill me, but Stephen would have no hesitation. If I was to stand any chance of ridding the world of Aegyir, I needed to get free and soon.

I let all my weight drop as if I'd fainted. This increased the pressure on my windpipe as my body sagged against Aegyir's arm but it also did the trick of taking him off balance, which was my main aim. Despite my height, once I was a dead weight, my centre of gravity was significantly lower, forcing Aegyir into a hunched position. I planted my feet, ready to drive upwards when I was ready. My right hand was now close enough to my boot for me to slip out the dagger I'd secreted there and I gripped the handle of it while I assessed the area.

Stephen was about twenty metres away; the gorse bush with the sword and vessel about two big strides away.

It was now or never.

I drove my body upwards, smashing the back of my head into Aegyir's face. He staggered and released his grip just enough for me to wrench myself free. I whirled on the spot and slammed the dagger into his right shoulder. A thin trickle of smoke began to emerge from the site. I sprinted to the gorse bush and reached in.

The sword had gone.

My breath stalled in my chest and I turned, panicked. Aegyir smiled cruelly at me.

"Is this what you seek?" He pointed towards the track.

My heart plummeted as I saw Stephen brandishing the sword, a smug smile on his lips.

While I stared at Stephen, my plans collapsing, Aegyir was on me, his arm snaking around my throat again, pinning me against his torso. I bent my left leg, bringing my ankle up, and grabbed the dagger in my boot, turning it in my hand so that the blade pointed backwards before driving it back and into Aegyir's middle. He stumbled, another stream of smoke emerging from him, but his face still mocked me.

"Two is not enough, Aeron. I will just replenish this lost vitality with someone else's."

He stood before me, weakening. But not defeated. And not decapitated.

My back was a couple of metres from the rock face; the gorse bush protected my left-hand side. The boulder lay to my right but there was an easy path around the back of it that Stephen was now taking and he had the sword.

My brain rattled over the instructions in the book. I had thrust the two daggers into Aegyir in approximately the right places. The knife sticking out of his right shoulder was close enough. The one in his abdomen was in exactly the right place. However, I needed all three in before I could lop his head off.

As fast as I could, I jammed my hand into my bag. I felt the dagger and grabbed the hilt.

Stephen was advancing along the path behind the boulder and was about five metres away now. Aegyir had a sneer on his face, standing just clear of the area where I'd sprinkled the soil with Finn. This wasn't going as I'd planned. I took a step back, moving closer to the rock face.

"Traitor. You are not welcome."

The voices filled my head, snarling and full of venom.

"You cannot defeat me on your own," mocked Aegyir. "And I see no signs of any Guardians coming to help you. They will never accept you again. You do *know* that?"

He stepped back on to the area where Finn and I had scattered the soil, almost as if taunting me. The voices from behind me grew louder. I moved forwards, hoping they would fade.

They did. But I'd been forced closer to Stephen. He was now less than two metres away, waving the sword around – *my* sword – as if it were a plastic toy. Aegyir advanced. The gorse bush that had been my protection was now trapping me.

I needed Aegyir close enough that I could stick another dagger in him and I needed my fucking sword back. I sucked in a breath. Aegyir wasn't the threat; Stephen was. If I could just punch him hard enough, he would drop the sword.

Old memories and fears made me hesitate too long. Stephen closed the gap faster than I thought he could move given his shape, and he yanked me backwards by my hair. I drove my elbow backwards, to little avail, then grabbed his thumb, wrenching it back until I almost dislocated it. The sword dropped from his grip to lie tantalisingly close on the turf. Before I could grab it, Stephen pinned both of my arms back, gripping them at the elbows and wrenching them until my wrists were at the small of my back. I tried to stab him with the dagger in my hand but he twisted me, making pain shoot through my whole arm and shoulder. A thin, cruel smile settled on Aegyir's lips and he stepped forwards and plucked the dagger from my hand, dropping it on to the short grass alongside the sword.

"Open the portal, Aeron. Invite me in."

"Never."

He took a long look at me as if weighing up options, and punched me in the face, forcing me back against Stephen. He might not be able to kill me, but he could certainly inflict considerable damage on me.

"Perhaps I should get your brother to kill you. I know he wants to."

"He is *not* my brother." I turned my head and spat blood.

"Hit me all you like. I am *not* inviting you anywhere."

Aegyir shrugged. "Regardless. He would happily kill you even without instruction from me, but I think you would choose death."

"And I'm no use to you dead, am I? A dead Guardian can't open the portal. And as you say, I don't see any other Guardians around here."

"You surprise me, Aeron. Betrayal has been one of your defining characteristics. Yet now, after all these years of banishment and all the hatred The Realm has shown you, you still will not say four simple words."

"No. I will not."

In the corner of my eye I could see hi-vis jackets on the track across the field. Polly *had* called the police. They weren't going to get here for a good few minutes. I needed to kill this fucker before then. All those years of Finn teaching me self-defence were not going to be for nothing.

As I looked back at Aegyir, he made a small motion with his head towards Stephen. Stephen hurled me down on to the boulder as if I weighed nothing and splayed my right arm and hand across its smooth surface.

"Aeron the Guardian. How well do Guardians function with only one hand?"

Aegyir crouched and picked the sword up. My breath shuddered as he positioned the sword. If he leaned on the hilt, the blade would slice down through my wrist, like a butcher jointing a carcass.

"Invite me in," he snarled. "Or lose your hand."

My eyes darted to the police. How long could I hold out? Aegyir tilted his head to one side.

"You think I would not?" he said, his voice silky.

A scarlet line was already beading along the edge of the blade. Still my head was screaming at me not to meet his request. In the corner of my eye, the rock face shimmered.

Stephen shifted his weight fractionally and I sensed a chance.

Before I could act, pain ripped through my right hand and I howled. The little finger from my right hand lay on the grass next to the rock and blood poured from my hand.

"Do not make me wait, Aeron. Next time it will be your hand. Invite me in."

"No," I sobbed, watching the stream of scarlet coat the boulder.

My scream had galvanised the police and the hi-vis jackets were now bobbing up and down at the edge of my sight-line as they ran up the path towards us. It was now or never to dispose of Aegyir. And if Stephen took the blame for my finger? Good.

I reached down with my left hand, my palm sneaking between the boulder and my stomach, and then on between my legs. Stephen was pinning me down with his weight, too focused on keeping my right arm stretched out across the boulder to concentrate on my other hand. I grasped at the soft tissue at his crotch and twisted as hard as I could. Stephen bellowed with pain and yanked me upright. I wrenched his scrotum harder and he released me. Clutching my right hand, I dodged backwards, twisting to the side to avoid a bone-crunching blow.

I grabbed the dagger from the grass, spun on the spot, and buried it to the hilt in the left side of Aegyir's chest. Close enough. Black smoke began to pour from him and his face distorted into a twisted snarl. With Stephen still clutching his balls, I snatched the sword up. Pain screamed from my mutilated hand, but sweet revenge dulled it. I whirled the sword with an agility I didn't know I possessed, the blade aimed perfectly. It sliced cleanly through Aegyir's neck, with the softest of hisses.

"That's for Finn, you fucker!"

Aegyir's body was dissolving into smoke.

I turned to grab the jar from the gorse bush, just in time to see Stephen aiming a punch at my head. I ducked, but not nimbly enough. With a roar, he grabbed me by my jacket with his left fist while his right slammed into my face, his knuckles crunching into my cheekbone.

Stars danced and I reeled from the blow. Before I could recover, Stephen picked me up and hurled me head-first at the rock face behind us. Fleetingly, I wondered what it would feel like when my neck snapped. I closed my eyes, waiting for the impact, dimly aware of the column of smoke that was all that remained of Aegyir, dissipating into the air.

29

Pain ripped through me as if I was being sliced in half, and I fell to the floor, gasping, curled into the foetal position, my hand pouring with blood, my head ringing. My vision pulsed and I rested my forehead on my knees. The pain ebbed away, and I breathed more easily. I peered around. I wasn't in the sunshine on the grass and I didn't think I'd smacked my face into the rock and broken my neck. Where the hell was I? Fuck me gently, was this the Realm?

The floor beneath me was smooth stone: cold, hard, unforgiving. I heaved myself up until I was sitting, remnants of pain searing channels in my body. I was in a dark, narrow passageway with smooth walls on either side of me. In the gloom ahead I could see a faint green-gold light. The silence was oppressive, crushing me to the floor. My teeth began to chatter and not just from the cold.

I shouldn't be here.

I clapped my palm around my right hand and let my forehead sink back on to my knees, sticky blood beginning to congeal against my fingers, pain screaming from the stump.

"You shouldn't be here."

Who had whispered that? It had sounded right in my ear. My heart hammered against my ribs and I stared wildly into the murk.

"You shouldn't be here. Aeron."

The voice was insistent; the final word snarled. I tried

to focus on my breathing the way Finn had taught me. Slow... Slow down. There's nothing there. There's nothing there. It's a dream. You're unconscious and this is a dream.

I scraped my feet under me, my legs threatening to go from under me. Finn's voice murmured to me: check your three-sixty. I took two long, shaky breaths and turned on the spot. The rock face behind me had disappeared, replaced by the same smooth walls that lined the long hallway. The roof of the place could have been two metres above me, it could have been two miles. The light, such as there was, showed nothing. How had I got here? Stephen had hurled me against the rock face. Was that the portal? How had I passed through a block of rock? Was it one-way? Could I go back? The police would be there by now. I'd be safe. I peered at the wall but it was featureless and I turned back to the hall.

Where the hell had *they* come from?

I froze. Standing in front of me were two tall, dark-haired men. They glared at me. If the place had felt unwelcoming before, it had suddenly become malevolent. They were dressed in brown leather trousers with medieval-style leather jackets on the top. One pointed a sword at my chest; the other wielded a knife. They were identical to the guys who cuffed me in my dreams.

"Er, hi," I said, hearing the squeak in my voice with shame. "I'm—"

The guy on the left said something utterly unintelligible. He reached forward to take my arm, but I snatched it from him, whirling on my back foot and landing a kick to his ribs. I might as well have kicked a boulder. I heard the swish of a blade, ducked sharply and brought my elbow up under the guy on the right's chin, before slamming the heel of my hand into the base of his nose. He staggered back, and I turned to deal with the guy from the left again. His fist drove into my face, sending me sprawling. I tried to get up, my head hanging, my vision swimming, only to fall back to my knees. The man I'd kicked grabbed my arm and there was a soft click as he cuffed my right wrist. He hauled me to my feet by the cuff, the metal biting into my skin. He growled another string of words I didn't understand, though in the midst of it, I heard "Aeron."

"Uh. My name is Reagan. Reagan Bennett."

The other man brushed his hands over his body, looking at me as if he would happily murder me. His nose seeped blood, and he wiped at it brusquely.

My captor clicked the cuffs around my left wrist then grabbed my hair, forcing my head back. The cold of a metal blade rested against my neck.

His cheek rasped against mine and another string of gibberish spewed forth.

"I have no idea what you're saying!"

He didn't respond, propelling me along the narrow hall towards the greenish light at the end.

Christ, I was sunk. They thought I was Aeron, the traitor.

Who would be hanged if she ever returned to The Realm.

If you enjoyed reading this, I would be enormously grateful if you would leave a review – on Amazon or Goodreads or wherever! Also, most authors get their sales via word-of-mouth, so if you *did* enjoy it, please tell people about it? Talk about it on social media? Or perhaps have it as your next book-group book?

Thank you!

Aeron Returns

Guardians of The Realm: Book 2

Thrown through a portal into a world she thought only existed in her dreams, Reagan Bennett finds herself in The Realm: a place where everyone thinks she is the warrior Aeron. Unfortunately, Aeron was a traitor who was banished, and forbidden from ever returning to The Realm. No one is pleased to see her. Not even her husband, Faran, a man Reagan has dreamed about, but never met.

With no choice but to stay, Reagan has to fight not only the demon Aegyir, but all those in The Realm who are determined to be rid of her forever. Can she survive long enough to protect not only The Realm, but the world she once knew – Earth – from Aegyir's murderous intentions?

About the Author

Amanda Fleet is a physiologist by training and a writer at heart. She spent 18 years teaching science and medicine undergraduates at St Andrews University, but now uses her knowledge to work out how to kill people (in her books). During her time at St Andrews, she was involved with two Scottish Government funded projects, working with the College of Medicine in Blantyre, Malawi. While in Malawi, she learned about the plight of the many street children there and helped to set up a Community Based Organisation that works with homeless Malawian children to support them through education and training—Chimwemwe Children's Centre.

Amanda lives in Scotland with her husband, where she can be found writing, walking and running.

Acknowledgements

The Guardians of The Realm Trilogy has been a labour of love since 2014, one way or another. There are a lot of people who helped me cope with all the blood, sweat and tears along the way and I apologise profusely to anyone I miss out here. First and foremost, I need to thank my amazing editor, Fiona McLaren for all her advice, encouragement and work on all three of the books. Thank you. For telling me when things needed work (and how to fix it!), but also for telling me all the bits you loved. I also need to thank the fantastic circle of writing friends I have, who have held me together and supported me when things have been difficult, and who have been there to celebrate the successes. There are too many of you to list individually, but I do need to thank Jackie McLean and Tana Collins in particular. I also need to thank my writing buddy, Stuart Lennon, for all his advice and help (and for keeping me supplied with notebooks!). My wonderful beta-readers, Lisa Davies, Gerard McCabe, Jackie McLean, and Stuart Lennon helped both with early and late drafts. My thanks also to MiblArt, who did such a great job with the covers. And last but most certainly not least, my love and thanks to my husband, Colin, without whom none of these books would have happened.

www.ingramcontent.com/pod-product-compliance
Ingram Content Group UK Ltd.
Pitfield, Milton Keynes, MK11 3LW, UK
UKHW020224250726
13967UKWH00001B/178